ARIEL TACHNA
Contemporary M/M Romance at its Finest

Inherit the Sky

"...a well-crafted, beautiful book that I would recommend to anyone looking for a love story that takes courage." —Guilty Indulgence

"I enjoyed this excellently researched and written book very much and hope there will be additional stories about all of the characters on and near the Lang Down sheep station." —Mrs. Condit

"This story is beautifully, realistically handled." —Joyfully Jay

Her Two Dads

"...one of the most emotionally rewarding and uplifting love stories that I have read in a long time." —Dark Diva Reviews

"This is one of the best books I have ever read."
—Judging the Book by Its Pages

"...a sweet and stirring novel about the power of love and family."
—Romance Junkies

Seducing C.C.

"...a great comfort read." —Blackraven Reviews

"...a seductively sexy and romantic story." —Night Owl Reviews

Once in a Lifetime

"... a coming-of-age story that introduces heart-pounding firsts and nostalgic lasts." —¡Miraculous!

http://www.dreamspinnerpress.com

CHASE THE STARS

ARIEL TACHNA

Dreamspinner Press

Published by
Dreamspinner Press
382 NE 191st Street #88329
Miami, FL 33179-3899, USA
http://www.dreamspinnerpress.com/

Chase the Stars

Cover Art by Anne Cain
annecain.art@gmail.com

ISBN: 978-1-62380-080-2

Printed in the United States of America
First Edition
September 2012

eBook edition available
eBook ISBN: 978-1-62380-081-9

To Nicki, Emmet, Amy, Mary, and Andrew,
who refused to let me give up on this one.

ONE

"HELP me, please. Oh God, somebody help me!"

The shouts of the kid who half ran, half fell into the Yass Hotel drew Caine's attention away from what should have been a quiet lunch with his lover and partner of three months.

"They're going to kill him. Please, he's all I have."

"Who?" Macklin asked, rising from the table.

"These thugs." The boy was crying now. "They said he was a poofter and they'd kill him for it."

Macklin's expression, never soft to begin with, hardened to stone. Caine swore Macklin's shoulders grew broader as he approached the boy.

"Where are they?"

The boy had barely finished his answer before Macklin was out the door.

"Neil—"

"Yes, boss," the jackaroo at the next table replied, already on his feet and following Macklin out the door before Caine finished speaking. Ian and Kyle, the other two hands who had come to Yass to help him hire new blood for Lang Downs, followed Neil without being prompted, bringing a smile to Caine's face despite the seriousness of the situation. He still had trouble believing he had won their loyalty.

"I'm C-c-caine Neiheisel," Caine said, approaching the boy slowly. His heart pounded in his chest so hard it felt like someone was squeezing his ribs tight, making it hard to breathe. He couldn't go with Macklin. He was useless in a fight, but that didn't stop his body's fight-or-flight response. He took a deep breath, shaking his hands slightly to clear the tingling from the rush of adrenaline. "You w-want to have a s-seat?"

"Shouldn't we go help them?"

Caine shook his head. "Macklin and the others will t-t-take care of it, don't worry. Wh-what's your name?"

"Seth. Are you sure?"

"I'm sure. Macklin won't stand for that kind of nonsense," Caine promised, his confidence so profound that he got that sentence out without a stutter, even as upset as he was at the thought of that kind of homophobia in what constituted his own backyard and the danger it presented to Macklin and himself. "Where are you from?"

"Nowhere anymore," Seth replied, his voice so bitter Caine wanted to pull the kid into his arms and comfort him. He remembered what it had been like to be a teenager, though, and refrained, figuring the embrace wouldn't be welcome from a total stranger.

"What about your parents?"

"Mum died six months ago, and the no-good bastard she married kicked us out the day after the funeral," Seth said. "It's just Chris and me now, if that scary dude can save him."

"That 'scary dude' is Macklin," Caine said, "or Mr. Armstrong to you since you can't be more than fourteen."

"I'm sixteen," Seth retorted quickly.

He was way too small and skinny to be sixteen. Not that Caine thought he was lying. It was just proof of how hard his life had been.

Caine had already decided that was going to change. His great-uncle, Michael Lang, had made a habit of taking in strays at his station, much to Caine's good fortune. He wouldn't have Macklin now if Uncle Michael hadn't taken the foreman in when he was the same age as this kid. Now Caine just had to convince Seth that coming to Lang Downs would be the right choice for him and his brother. "So where are you staying?"

"We've got a room," Seth said defensively.

Probably some flop in a drug house so cheap they could afford it.

"Are you using?"

"What? No!"

"Pushing?"

"Fuck no!"

That was good. Caine was all for lending a helping hand, but he would not have drugs on his land. He had too much to lose. "Good. Your brother's clean too?"

"What's it to you?"

"I don't hire men with drug problems."

"What?"

"If all you've got is 'a room' and no parents and no one but your brother, that pretty much means no future, at least from where I'm sitting. I run a sheep station north of Boorowa. I thought you might like a job."

"You're a Yank!"

"And you're a brat who is about to lose the best chance to come his way," Caine retorted. "Ask around if you don't believe me. I've been here all week signing on jackaroos. I've got space for two more."

They didn't really. They'd hired the last of their crew this morning and planned to head back to Boorowa after lunch to pick up supplies and then drive back to Lang Downs tomorrow morning. Seth didn't need to know that, though. Caine had already seen enough of the boy's pride to know he wouldn't take charity.

It wouldn't be charity. Seth would work harder on Lang Downs than he had in his life. He'd earn every cent they paid him and his brother. He wouldn't have many expenses, though, so he could put almost every penny away toward college, if he wanted, or into a savings account against the day he left Lang Downs and pursued a different path in life, and if he chose to stay, he'd have a family to replace the one he'd lost with his mother's death.

CHRIS SIMMS grunted as another hard kick landed on his kidneys, directly below his ribs. He'd tried to fight his attackers, but they were too numerous. He'd rolled into a ball instead, trying to protect tender places in the hope that someone would interrupt and scare off his attackers before they killed him. His whole body hurt, sharp lances of agony each time they landed a blow blending with the sea of pain from the injuries they'd already inflicted, but he clung to consciousness and hope. He couldn't die because he couldn't abandon Seth the way everyone else in their lives had done. He just couldn't.

A shout from the street slowed the blows raining down on him. He lifted his head as an avenging angel bore down on his attackers. His vision blurred when he tried to focus on his savior's face, but then another blow to his head rattled him. His last thought as consciousness deserted him was that the man looked like he was carved out of stone.

MACKLIN stood over the body of the unconscious kid, rubbing absently at his sore knuckles. He was too old to be brawling in the streets, but that hadn't mattered when he'd seen the kid on the ground being pummeled by five attackers. He supposed this young man was a little older than the one at the hotel, but not by much. The five hoodlums who'd jumped him had changed their minds when faced with real men who knew how to handle themselves in a fight. Macklin spared a quick nod of thanks for Neil, Ian, and Kyle. Neil had a bloody nose where someone had landed a blow, but other than that, they all seemed in good shape. He'd have a bruise on his jaw in the morning, for that matter. "He needs a doctor, but it doesn't look like anything's too broken. Get the ute, Ian. We'll take him to the hospital and see what's wrong with him."

"You don't want to call an ambulance?" Ian asked.

"He's unconscious, but he's breathing. He isn't bleeding. We can get him to the hospital probably as fast as an ambo can get here, and that way we don't have to pay for it. I can guarantee he isn't an ambulance member."

Ian nodded and ran toward the truck.

"You should call Caine, boss," Neil said, staunching the blood flow with his sleeve. "He'll be worried."

"Once we get this bloke in the ute and we're on the way," Macklin said. "He can take the car and meet us there."

Macklin looked down at the kid, trying to figure out the best way to move him without hurting him worse. "Neil, get his feet. Kyle, help me with his shoulders."

The kid moaned softly as they moved him, reassuring Macklin more. He might be unconscious, but he wasn't in a coma or anything. As they carried him out of the alley and lifted him into the back of the ute, one thought stuck firmly in Macklin's head.

But for the grace of God in the form of Michael Lang, this could have been him.

THE emergency room in Yass was about as crowded and busy as the rest of the town, which was to say not at all. The doctor looked surprised to see anyone, much less someone in the young man's condition.

"What happened?"

"We found five guys trying to kick the shite out of him," Macklin said. "His brother's on his way here with our boss. The brother can give you medical background, I hope, but we didn't want to wait to bring him in."

"No, of course not," the doctor said. "Put him on the gurney. I'll need to do an X-ray and...."

Macklin tuned out the mumbling as the doctor rolled the gurney deeper into the emergency room. The man would do what he could and they'd go from there. He was more concerned with Caine. He didn't really think the thugs he'd run off would stumble across Caine and realize he was the grazier from Lang Downs, much less that they'd do anything after Macklin had kicked their arses once, but he would still be happier once he could see Caine again to be sure. More than that, though, he knew his lover's tender heart and could easily guess how this entire situation would bother Caine. Macklin didn't know the whole story, although he'd bet Caine had gotten it out of the kid's brother by now, but he knew it couldn't be good, and that would tear at Caine. As far as Macklin was concerned, nothing was allowed to upset his lover, which meant finding a solution.

Now.

Caine arrived a few minutes later, the younger brother in tow. Macklin saw the way Caine's eyes raked over him checking for scuffs or injuries. He squeezed Caine's shoulder as the younger brother rushed past him into the hospital. It was a subtle gesture, all Macklin would let pass between them in public, especially here in Yass, but it would reassure Caine for the moment. His lover could strip him bare and check every centimeter of him later.

"Where's Chris?"

"The doctor took him for an X-ray," Macklin said, turning to face the boy who had skidded to a halt in the middle of the lobby when he didn't see the object of his search, "and I don't know what else. He was unconscious but alive when we brought him in. He'll be sore for a while, but he didn't look hurt bad enough to worry about him getting well."

"Macklin, this is Seth," Caine said. "Seth, this is Mr. Armstrong."

"Thank you for saving my brother, Mr. Armstrong," the kid said. "You didn't have to get involved."

The kid might see it that way, but Macklin hadn't had a choice, not from the moment he'd understood that homophobia had motivated the attack.

The doctor came back out before Macklin could reply.

"Has the brother got here yet? I need some medical background."

"I'm Chris's brother," Seth said.

Macklin caught Caine's arm when he would have followed Seth and the doctor. "Let him do this. I need to talk to you."

"They're coming to Lang Downs," Caine said immediately, "as soon as Chris can travel safely."

"Of course they are," Macklin said. "What did the kid tell you?"

"They're orphans; their stepfather kicked them out after their mom died. They have a room here in Yass, but I'm guessing it's temporary. They need a chance."

"And we'll give them one," Macklin agreed. "Michael would approve."

Caine beamed the way he did any time Macklin brought up his great-uncle, making Macklin resolve, once again, to mention the old man more often.

"HE'S still unconscious," the doctor told Seth, "but we expect him to come to any minute. He has three cracked ribs, bruised kidneys, multiple lacerations and contusions, and a broken arm. None of that is good, but it'll all heal in time."

"How much time?"

"The bruises and scrapes will heal in a few days. His arm, which will take the longest, will need to be in a cast for six to eight weeks," the doctor said.

"Which arm is it?"

"His right."

Seth cursed silently. If it had been his left arm, Chris might have been able to keep working, but he was worthless with his left hand. He'd lose his job, they'd lose their room, and they'd be back to living in the car, trying to stay presentable enough that someone would give them a chance at another job and another room.

Unless they took the offer to go to the station....

"Can I see him? I want to be there when he wakes up."

"Of course."

The doctor led Seth into a small hospital room where Chris lay on the bed, various machines monitoring his vitals. "Don't let the wires bother you," the doctor said. "They're keeping tabs on his systems, but he's doing everything himself. As soon as he's awake, we'll start taking them off, and once we know he doesn't have a concussion, we can send him home. Do you have somewhere to go?"

"Yes, of course," Seth lied. He had no idea where they'd go. Their landlord let them pay by the week since that's how Chris got paid, but they'd owe rent again in three days, and Seth didn't know if they'd have enough to cover it. Even if they did, that would only delay the inevitable by a week, because Chris wouldn't be able to work for some time, based on what the doctor said. "Wake up, Chris," Seth begged. "We have to figure this out, and I can't do it by myself."

They had the offer from the grazier, but Seth didn't trust it. He didn't trust anyone but Chris these days. Too many people had betrayed their trust for Seth to believe that anyone but Chris cared about what happened to them. Looking around the room to make sure he was alone, not that he expected anyone to come in, he put his hand on Chris's. "Come on, Chris. Don't do this to me."

He could feel the tears threatening, but he had too much pride to snivel like a little kid. Chris needed him to be strong. He wondered what would happen if he showed up at the restaurant where Chris worked tomorrow to take Chris's shift. It wasn't like he'd be doing anything but washing dishes anyway. Surely he could do that well enough to keep a roof over their heads for a couple of weeks until Chris could work again.

The fingers beneath his twitched slightly, drawing Seth's attention from his spiraling thoughts back to his brother. Chris's eyes were still closed, but Seth thought he saw more movement beneath the lids, like maybe Chris was waking up. "Can you hear me, Chris? Come on. Help me get this sorted here, okay? You've got to wake up and tell me how to fix all of this because I can't do it on my own."

Chris's fingers twitched again, but his eyes didn't open. "What are we going to do?" Seth asked, hoping the sound of his voice would help rouse his brother. "Even if they let me work your job, they're going to bitch about school and the number of hours I can work. I'm not sure I can make enough in the hours they're likely to give me to make the rent. I need you to wake up and give me the solution. You always have the answers, Chris. Now would be a good time."

Noise in the hallway interrupted him. He jerked his hand back, as if whoever was out there would think him unmanly for holding his brother's hand. He watched the door for several seconds, but no one came in so he turned back to Chris again. "The men who helped you offered us a job, but I don't know if they really meant it, or if they'll still mean it when they realize you broke your arm. The doc says you'll be in a cast for six to eight weeks. I don't know much about sheep, but I don't think there's much you could do with your arm busted up like that. I guess we tell them thanks but no thanks and hope Mr. Harrell will let us miss a rent payment or two until you're back on your feet. Just when I thought we were getting ahead a little bit, this had to go and happen."

"WE HAVE to do something."

"We will," Macklin said, his hand back on Caine's arm again, keeping him from going into the hospital room, "but that kid in there doesn't know us and doesn't trust us, and as much as you'd like him to, there's no reason why he should. We have to be patient and let his brother wake up first. Then you're going to stay out here with Neil and I'm going to talk to Chris man to man."

"And I'm not a man?" Caine asked.

"You're an amazing man, but right now your mother hen instincts have kicked in, and those kids have no idea how to deal with that," Macklin said. "You want to comfort them. That might make you feel better, but it isn't going to help them."

"How do you know?"

"Because I was those two kids when I ended up on Lang Downs," Macklin said. "I'd run away from home because I was tired of taking blows meant for my mother, going down, and watching her take them anyway. I was tired of homophobic rants and living in fear. I figured even the streets were better than that. I was wrong, of course, until Michael kicked me in the arse and set me straight. He didn't do it by comforting me, pup. He did it by telling me if this was my choice, then I had to grow up and act like a man, and then he taught me how to do it. That's what those boys in there are going to respond to, and because I've been where they are, I can do for them what Michael did for me. You can comfort them later, when they know us well enough to trust it."

Caine's heart ached hearing those words. He'd guessed some of it from things Macklin had and hadn't said, but hearing it laid out that bluntly made him want to pull Macklin into his arms and heal all the old hurts. He chuckled. Macklin was right about his protective side. "Okay, fine. We'll do it your way."

TWO

NEEDLES. Someone was driving needles into his arm. Chris struggled against the pain, aware only of the need to escape it. Then memory returned with a flash and he bolted upright in bed. "Seth!"

"You're awake!"

Chris slumped back against the hard mattress, the flat pillows doing nothing to cushion his back, and he gasped as pain lanced outward from his ribs. "Where am I?"

"In hospital," Seth said, looking small and scared under the fluorescent lights. "I got help. This big guy named Macklin and his boss, I guess, a Yank named Caine something unpronounceable. The Yank owns a sheep station, he said, and he said we should come work for him."

"Back up," Chris said. "You aren't making sense. What happened when you ran?"

"I went to the hotel. It was close and I figured there would be people there. I was right. I begged for help, and almost before I'd finished, Macklin asked me where you were. I told him, and he and three others went to help."

Macklin must be the man Chris saw before he lost consciousness. "How'd you get from asking for help to a job?"

"Caine, the Yank, wouldn't let me go back with Macklin and the others. He asked a bunch of questions about where we lived and stuff, and when I was done, he said we should come work at Lang Downs, the station he owns."

"You didn't tell him the truth, did you?" They'd been over this. If people knew where they were living and why, they could end up with the Department of Community Services and separated, and that was Chris's greatest fear. He didn't have much in his life, but he wouldn't let anyone take the one thing he did have: his brother.

"I know I wasn't supposed to, but I couldn't remember what I was supposed to say. I was too upset and…."

"No worries, Seth," Chris said with a sigh. "He offered us a job, not to call the cops. Not that I can do much work at the moment."

"I could probably work your shifts at the restaurant," Seth offered.

"You need to be in school."

"I'm not going to be in school on a sheep station either," Seth pointed out. "At least here we'll be in town."

In town where people now knew he was gay. Seth talked about doing Chris's job, but he wasn't sure he'd have a job after the confrontation that had led to him being bashed. Even if he didn't lose his job and Seth worked the shifts until he was well, he could run into those guys again at any time, and Seth might not be around next time to find help.

"Let's think about it before we make a decision," Chris said. "I'm too tired to sort it out now."

A cough in the doorway drew Chris's attention.

"Oh, Mr. Armstrong," Seth said, jumping to his feet. "I didn't see you come in."

Chris might have chuckled at the awe in Seth's voice, usually reserved for visiting heads of state or local demigods, but the situation was too serious for laughter.

"Good to see you awake," the man said, addressing Chris. "Seth, could you maybe find some tea for me while I talk with your brother?"

Seth scampered out of the room like an eager puppy.

"You've certainly impressed my brother."

"He's just grateful I took him seriously when he asked for help."

"You saved my life."

"Probably. Macklin Armstrong."

"Chris Simms." Chris held out his left hand. The gesture was awkward, but it was the best he could manage with his right arm in a cast. "Thank you."

"Glad I could help. So Caine tells me you've had a bit of a rough time recently."

"Nothing we can't handle," Chris said defensively. "I've got a job."

"You can cut the bullshit, Chris," Macklin said. "You have a dead-end job, a flat you can barely afford to keep, and no way to get anything better because you're trying to take care of your brother. You're not eating well, even if you're eating regularly, because you're both way too skinny. You're doing your best, and you should be proud of that, but it's not enough."

"Why are you telling me this?" Chris demanded. "You think I don't know how bad our lives are?"

"No, I'm pretty sure you know exactly how bad it is," Macklin said, "but I wanted you to understand that *I* know it too."

"Why? So you can lord it over me?"

"Bloody hell, kid. If you weren't already in that bed, I'd put you there," Macklin roared. "I hope I wasn't as stupidly stubborn as you when Michael Lang found me squatting in one of his drover's huts. I've been where you are. I wasn't bashed, but I was on my own at sixteen because my father beat my mother and me and spent the rest of his time ranting about pillow biters and queers. The words hurt worse than his fists ever did."

"You're...." Chris didn't finish the sentence because he didn't know how to do it without offending the other man.

"Yes, and?"

Chris blinked a couple of times, looking the older man over carefully. He was tall, although not obnoxiously so, maybe six feet, with broad shoulders and muscled arms where they were visible beneath the short sleeves of his shirt. His hair was shaggy and his boots were dusty. He was the picture of a masculine stockman. And he was gay.

"And nothing. I was just surprised, that's all."

"Surprised that I'd admit it or surprised that I'm gay in the first place?"

"A little of both," Chris said. "Not a lot of people out here will say it even if it's true."

Macklin snorted softly in amusement. "Truer words, but I'm not most people and Lang Downs isn't most stations. I imagine your brother told you my partner offered him a job."

"He's only sixteen," Chris said. "He needs to be in school."

"He'll get his lessons done," Macklin said. "We've got a number of kids on the station, and we make sure they all get their HSC. What they do after they finish high school is up to them. Finishing high school isn't optional, but we use School of the Air so the schedule is a bit flexible. He can work and go to school at the same time, and you can work in the kitchen until you get rid of that plaster on your arm. Then we'll see what you're made of."

"Why should we trust you?"

"You shouldn't," Macklin replied. "You shouldn't trust anyone but your brother until you know us a little better, but we're offering you a chance, the same as Caine's great-uncle offered me when I was sixteen and too stupid to know better. You won't get a better offer, and if you decide at the end of the season that the station isn't for you, you can leave when the other jackaroos do in May. What do you have to lose?"

A flop of a flat, a shit job in a dingy restaurant....

"Will the others care that I'm gay? I always heard the stations weren't, well, kind to people like me."

"You weren't listening, were you?" Macklin asked. "Caine Neiheisel, the owner at Lang Downs, is my partner."

"Oh, that kind of partner," Chris said as the coin dropped. "I thought.... It doesn't matter what I thought. I was obviously wrong. So everyone knows about you?"

"It's hard to hide it when I sleep in the station house at night despite there being a perfectly good foreman's house down the road," Macklin said. "I don't talk about it because it's nobody's business, but I don't hide it."

"You did save my life. I suppose this could be a way to say thank you."

"You don't owe me anything," Macklin said. "But you do owe your brother the best chance in life he can get, and while I know you're doing the best you can for him right now, I also know it isn't enough. He'd have a real chance on Lang Downs, and so would you. Think about it while you're here. You can tell us what you decide when they let you out."

"That's it?"

Chris had no idea why he was arguing, but it seemed too simple.

"What else would there be?"

"I don't know. Threats to call DoCS, something to try to make me do things your way?"

"You're not a child to be bullied," Macklin said with a shrug. "You're a man. A young one to be sure, but a man. You can make your own decisions without any pressure from me, and you'll live with the consequences of your choices, good or bad, without any pressure from me. You proved you were a man when you kept your brother with you and worked to support him. Keep doing what's best for him and you'll be fine. We're going back to the hotel for dinner, but we'll be by in the morning to see what you decide."

Seth came running back into the room. "I'm sorry, Mr. Armstrong. I couldn't find any tea."

"That's all right, kid," Macklin said, ruffling Seth's hair as he walked toward the door. "I'll get some at the hotel. Take care of your brother. We'll come by in the morning to see what you've decided."

"What we've decided?" Seth asked, turning to Chris. "What are we deciding?"

"What we're going to do now," Chris replied. "Armstrong thinks we should go to the station. He makes a pretty compelling argument."

"What arguments?"

Seth's distrust was palpable, but Chris was less certain of that necessity than he had been an hour ago. It would be a relief not to be the only person looking out for Seth. Not that he expected the men at the station to take responsibility for Seth's education, or really even for his well-being, but they had to work together, and Armstrong had seemed to offer an avuncular relationship. Then there was the allure of not being the only gay person in the room for the first time in his life. Even if he chose not to share that fact openly, a few people already knew, so he didn't really expect to keep it a complete secret. If Armstrong was right, on Lang Downs, he wouldn't have to.

"That we're barely keeping our heads above water right now, and that with my arm, we aren't even going to manage that for much longer," Chris explained. "Room and board is included at the station."

"We don't know anything about sheep," Seth pointed out.

"So we'll learn," Chris said with an approximation of a shrug, the best he could manage in a sling and with the bandages around his chest. "We're both smart. We can follow directions. We can figure out the rest once we get there."

"You really want to do this?"

Chris tried to shrug again to cover how badly he suddenly wanted to be in a place where he had a chance of belonging. If nothing else, he wanted the chance to study Macklin and Caine, to see how they interacted and how they negotiated a life together. He wanted to believe two men could have a healthy relationship, but since he had little enough idea of what a healthy relationship looked like to begin with, he'd had trouble imagining it up until now. "Yeah, I really kinda do."

"Then I guess I'd better see what kind of gear we need so we can get that sorted."

"Check the pocket of the jeans I was wearing if you can find them," Chris said. "I got paid today and since we aren't going back to living in the flat, we don't have to worry about making rent."

"I'll see if I can find them when I go to ask Mr. Armstrong about our gear," Seth said.

The nurse came in before Seth could say anything more, so Chris waved him off with his good hand and lay back to let the woman poke and prod at him. By the time she was done, he was grateful for the dose of painkillers she gave him because he was hurting badly before the medicine took him under.

WHEN he woke up the next time, he found a new face next to his bed. The man had short brown hair, much more neatly cropped than Armstrong's had been, a paler complexion, though by no means untouched by the sun, and softer eyes. When he realized Chris was awake, he smiled, the expression so kind Chris wasn't sure how to react.

"Hello," the man said, his accent immediately giving him away as a Yank. "I'm Caine Neiheisel. I hear you're going to c-come to Lang Downs with us."

"Seth told you?" Chris asked, his voice rough from his dry throat. So this was Macklin Armstrong's partner. It seemed too intimate to think of them as lovers, though he knew that's what they were.

Caine poured a glass of water and handed it to him without being asked. "Yes, he told us. He's gone looking for your gear, although we'll stop in Boorowa on the way back to the station and you can find anything there that he c-can't find here."

"I don't know how to thank you and Mr. Armstrong," Chris said after he took a sip of water. "I'd be dead without him and would wish I were without you."

"It's nothing," Caine said. "My uncle had a habit of t-taking in strays. I try to emulate him whenever I can, and this seemed like as g-good a chance as any. Believe me, you'll earn your supper."

"With this on my arm?" Chris scoffed, lifting his broken arm.

"You'll be out of that cast before long, and I'm sure we can find things for you to do between now and then," Caine assured him. "They put me to work when I didn't know the first thing about sheep. Macklin will find a way to keep you busy as well."

"I'm glad I won't be the first blow-in at the station."

"Not the first, and probably not the last," Caine agreed. "We seem to have become a magnet for people who don't fit in anywhere else."

"People like me," Chris said slowly.

"People like us," Caine replied. "Seems there's a lot more poofters working the stations than the bigots want to believe, and more than one of them's made his way to Lang Downs this spring. Since it would be hypocritical of me to care about their orientation, I'm fine with that as long as they do their jobs. The same goes for you and Seth. Do your jobs to the best of your ability, and everything else will take care of itself."

"We'll do our best, I promise," Chris said. "Have the doctors said how soon I can leave?"

"When they aren't worried about your concussion leading to a coma," Caine replied. "Probably tomorrow morning, which suits us fine. We'll leave as early as we can, get to Boorowa for supplies, and then decide if we're ready to drive on or if we'll spend the night and head to the station the following morning. It's only about an hour to get to Boorowa, but it's five hours beyond that, and the last four hours are hard driving. You'll be better off with another day to heal too. The bumps in the roads as we cross through Taylor Peak won't feel very good on your ribs."

THREE

CAINE'S words proved more than a little prophetic, even after another night in the hospital and a night in Boorowa. Chris had felt better that morning as the other jackaroos loaded up utes with supplies and headed north, but by the time Chris and Seth had climbed into the car with Caine and Macklin and followed suit, he was already starting to hurt a little from standing around, and when they left the main road for the dirt tracks that crossed Taylor Peak, the station between Lang Downs and the main road, Chris thought he'd entered a new circle of hell. On top of everything else, they hadn't even let him drive his own car. One of the other jackaroos was driving it. Caine had insisted that between the pain meds, the broken arm, and the bad roads, Chris was in no shape to drive. Chris refused to admit the grazier might have been right.

The roads got better once they left Taylor Peak and started across Lang Downs property, but better was such a relative term when every jolt jarred his broken ribs. Long before they reached the main part of the station with its well-tended lawns and neatly maintained buildings, Chris was ready to throw in the towel and head back to Yass. Even sleeping in the car until they could find a new flop had to be better than this.

Then the car stopped, and Caine and Macklin climbed out. Watching them standing there, not touching but together, and simply breathing as if the air were fresher here than anywhere else, drew Chris up short. Yass had brought him a bashing. Lang Downs brought these men peace. Maybe, if he gave it a chance, it would bring him peace and safety as well.

"So where should we toss our kits?" Chris asked, moving stiffly.

"In the main house," Caine replied. "You'll be helping Kami in the kitchen, so it makes sense to have you close." He took Chris's good arm and led him in one direction while Macklin took Seth in the opposite direction.

"You don't really want your little brother in with the other jackaroos," Caine added when they were out of Seth's earshot. "They're not a bad bunch, but they aren't exactly kid-safe either. I know Seth has probably seen and heard more than a lot of kids his age, but that doesn't mean he needs to keep seeing and hearing it."

The logic of Caine's argument hit Chris hard. He'd tried to do his best by his brother, but living in cheap rooms, working odd hours, not staying in one place for very long had taken their toll. Seth was doing badly in school. He'd developed a dirty mouth and a bad attitude, becoming far too much like the hoodlums on the streets for Chris's peace of mind. "I can see why he should stay there, but I can stay in the bunkhouse. I'm not sixteen."

"Do you really think he'll stay anywhere you aren't?" Caine asked. "He adores you. Idolizes you, even. If you're in the bunkhouse, he will be too."

"I suppose," Chris said, feeling a little like he'd been bulldozed, but he couldn't find the fallacy in the argument. He could always insist on moving out later if necessary.

"Good," Caine said, leading Chris toward the station house. "Let's get your stuff and get you settled. There are a couple of guest rooms so you can each have your own space if you want. I'm not sure who Uncle Michael thought they were for since he never married or had kids, but I'm glad they're there."

The house itself wasn't new. Chris could tell that much from looking at it, although he couldn't have guessed when it was built. The inside had obviously been updated, though. The furniture, while comfortable and homey, was clearly new, done in warm, dark tones that complemented the stone fireplace and light wood floors.

"The kitchen is back that way," Caine said, pointing down a long hallway to an addition to the main house. "I'll introduce you to Kami after you pick your room. He's our cook. While your arm is healing, you can help him. The doctor said you could use your hand, right? So you can cut vegetables and stuff while he does the heavy lifting."

"I don't have any experience working in a kitchen," Chris warned. "All I did at the restaurant was wash dishes."

"Don't worry about that," Caine said. "Kami will get you all fixed up."

As they climbed the stairs to the bedrooms, Chris wondered about the sudden absence of Caine's stutter. It hadn't been heavy at the hospital yesterday, but now it was completely gone. He shrugged, deciding it didn't matter. He had to stop halfway up the stairs to catch his breath, even with Caine carrying his bag, because he couldn't breathe deeply with the bandages around his ribs. "Bloody hell," he muttered.

"Broken ribs hurt, don't they?" Macklin said from the bottom of the stairs. "I broke two falling off a horse when I first got here. Michael wasn't sympathetic at all, telling me I shouldn't have gotten on a horse I didn't know how to handle, but he taped my ribs every night for a month until I could move without it hurting again."

Chris's ribs slowed him down enough in turning to look at Macklin that he saw the expression on Caine's face change as he looked down at the foreman. His eyes seemed brighter, and his smile grew wider. *Is that what love looks like?* Chris wondered.

"Where's Seth?"

"I set him up with School of the Air," Macklin explained. "We'll see where he is and what he needs to do to finish school. He'll be there for at least a couple of hours if you want to unpack or lie down for a bit."

"I'm not an invalid," Chris snapped, conveniently forgetting he hadn't even been able to walk up the stairs without having to stop.

"No, you're not," Macklin agreed, "but you are recovering from a beating, and you're on pretty strong pain medication if what I saw on the prescription label is any indication. You're entitled to a little time to recover from the trip. Seth isn't starting work until tomorrow. You aren't either. And before you argue, I'm the foreman. I'm the one who makes those decisions."

"He doesn't let anyone work when they're hurt or sick," Caine added. "Even me."

"Especially you," Macklin said, his voice a low growl.

There it was again, Chris realized. They might not proclaim their relationship from the hilltops, but that didn't make it less powerful or real. "Can I at least walk around and get my bearings a little?"

"Just don't overdo it," Macklin said. "Kami starts fixing breakfast at four thirty. You'll have to be up early tomorrow."

"I'll just take a quick walk then," Chris said. He needed the rest, but now that he'd insisted on his right not to rest, his pride wouldn't let him give in.

"After I show you your room," Caine interrupted. "I may not be around when you come back from your walk, and you'll want to know where it is."

Chris nodded and followed Caine the rest of the way up the stairs. The bedroom Caine showed him wasn't large, but it was neat, with large windows, a wide bed, and a big chest of drawers. "The bathroom's down the hall for you and Seth to use. Make yourselves at home."

Caine left before Chris could thank him again. Bending gingerly, Chris opened the suitcase and took a couple of minutes to unpack, the one picture of his mother he'd managed to steal from his stepfather going center stage on the chest. He tossed his clothes haphazardly into drawers and headed back toward the stairs.

Going down was easier than going up, fortunately, and he made it outside without too much trouble, although he took a moment to sit in one of the wooden chairs on the veranda before continuing.

The station was bustling with activity, twenty or more new men settling in at the bunkhouse and elsewhere, not to mention the people who lived on the station year-round. He could hear the sheep baaing in the pens. Shearing would be the first order of business, he'd heard some of the men say during dinner in Boorowa, but he'd miss that because of his arm. He had no idea how long that would take or what would come next, but a part of him was eager to learn. He didn't know how long it would last since nothing in his life seemed to last long these days, but he would give it his all and hope for the best.

Standing up slowly, he walked toward the bunkhouse. Macklin hadn't been alone in saving him, and Chris wanted to thank the others as well if he could find them. He crossed the yard and the road and had just stepped onto the veranda of the bunkhouse when he heard a voice inside.

"Some of you may have heard rumors about the boss."

Chris slipped inside to listen.

"You might have heard people say he's a poofter," the man went on. Chris thought he'd heard Caine and Macklin call him Neil, but he wasn't sure. "You might have even heard less polite things about him."

Chris hoped Neil wasn't getting ready to deny it. Macklin had said they didn't talk about it but they didn't hide it either.

"Let me make this very clear," Neil continued, all but bristling as he spoke. "Caine Neiheisel and Macklin Armstrong are the backbone of this station. If you can't deal with working for a poofter, leave now, because there's not a man on this station who will tolerate any kind of slur against either of them."

"Wait," one of the men said. "Either of them? Armstrong is gay too?"

"Do you have a problem with that?" Neil demanded.

"No," the man said, raising his hands in pacification. "I'm just… surprised. And, well, a little surprised everyone is so open about it."

"Caine saved Neil's life," another of the hands explained. "He now feels the need to defend the boss against any threat, real or otherwise."

"Like Macklin would let Caine get so much as a bruise," another hand joked.

"Caine works his arse off just like the rest of us," Neil insisted.

"And then works Macklin's arse at night."

"No way in hell Macklin lets anyone fuck him."

"Caine's the boss."

"On the station. No way he's the boss in the bedroom."

"Enough!" Neil roared. "Get your sorry arses out of here and get to work!"

The men filed out dutifully, leaving Chris alone in the bunkhouse with Neil. "What are you looking at?" Neil demanded.

"I wanted to say thank you," Chris said quietly. "You were with Macklin, weren't you? When he ran off the guys who were trying to kill me?"

"Yes," Neil said with a shrug. "It was no big deal."

"Just like Caine saving your life was no big deal?" Chris said. "I'm not going to start following you around like a puppy or anything. I just wanted to say thank you. You didn't have to help me."

"Caine asked me to," Neil said. "I told him then I was his man for life. I keep my promises."

"Well, whatever the reason, thank you," Chris said. "And thank you for what you said to the others today. I know it doesn't apply to me since you don't know me really, but if they can accept Caine and Macklin, maybe they can accept me too."

"Macklin earned our respect long before we knew what he was," Neil warned, "and Caine is… well, he's Caine. There's no way not to like him. Even when I thought I hated him, I liked him. You'll have to earn our respect the same way, but being gay won't make that an uphill battle here."

"I can't ask for more than that, can I?" Chris agreed. "I'm supposed to help Kami in the kitchens. Caine was going to introduce me, but then Macklin sidetracked us."

"Macklin has that effect on people," Neil said with a chuckle. "He comes in with a plan, and everyone else just falls in line, even the boss. We're lucky to have him. He's one hell of a foreman. Come on, I'll introduce you to Kami."

Kami, as his name suggested, was aborigine, his skin dark as midnight, with crinkles around his eyes that suggested he smiled frequently, but he wasn't smiling when Neil led Chris into the kitchen.

"What?" he snapped. "If you want dinner on time, you have to leave me alone to cook it."

"Kami doesn't like people," Neil told Chris in a whisper far too loud not to be overheard.

"I like people, just not when they're in my kitchen," Kami replied. "Go away."

Chris's stomach sank. He was supposed to help this guy?

"Stop it, Kami," Neil said. "You'll scare off your new help."

"What, so I'm too old to manage the kitchen now?"

Chris wished the floor would open up and swallow him. "It's just temporary," he said softly. "Until I get rid of my cast and can do other stuff. I think Caine and Macklin felt sorry for me."

"Who are you?"

"Your new help," Neil repeated. "Chris, but I didn't catch your last name."

"Simms. I'd offer to shake hands, but that's a little hard at the moment with this on my arm."

"What happened?" Kami asked, some of his grouchiness fading.

"Some guys took exception to me being gay," Chris said. "They thought they'd beat it out of me. Macklin and Neil and a couple of others dissuaded them."

"Well, why didn't you say so?" Kami demanded, turning on Neil. "Get out. Leave him here."

"Good luck," Neil said with a laugh as he left Chris in the kitchen with Kami.

Chris had a feeling he'd need it.

"I don't know how much help I'll be, honestly," Chris said. "I can move my shoulder and my wrist, but not my elbow."

"You let me worry about that," Kami said. "Right now you have a seat. Do you want a cup of tea?"

"That would be wonderful," Chris said. "I didn't want to impose, but the trip was rough."

"Sit," Kami said again, bustling toward the stove and the electric kettle next to it. "They didn't just break your arm, did they?"

They'd come damn close to breaking his spirit.

"No, they cracked my ribs too."

"We'll set you to rights in no time," Kami promised. "Dinner's mostly done for tonight so you can start tomorrow. Did Macklin tell you what time I start cooking?"

"Caine said you usually start at four thirty."

"Unless they're going out to the back paddocks, at which point I serve breakfast at four thirty," Kami said, "but that's not very often. Early to bed, early to rise, and all that. Where are you sleeping?"

"Upstairs in the main house," Chris said. "Caine was worried about my brother if we moved into the bunkhouse."

"That's better anyway," Kami agreed. "In the bunkhouse you'd have to listen to the jackaroos complain about your alarm going off earlier than theirs. That won't be a problem in the main house. Even if Caine and Macklin aren't awake, you won't wake them coming downstairs."

The kettle whistled so Kami poured the water over the tea bag, added milk, and handed the cup to Chris. "Here you go. Drink that and tell me about your brother while I finish making dinner. Tomorrow morning we won't have time to talk."

Chris sipped his tea and pondered what he wanted to say. Seth had become two people in his mind: the brother he was fighting to protect and the little shit he'd become to protect himself. Hoping those days were over, Chris focused on Seth as he'd been before their mother's death. "He's a clown," Chris said, "always looking for a way to crack a joke or make people laugh. Unlike a lot of clowns, though, he never does it by tearing people down. If anything, he makes himself the butt of the joke because he knows he can handle it."

"He sounds like a good kid."

"He is," Chris said.

"But?"

"But what?" Chris asked, feeling all the defensive walls go up.

"You tell me," Kami said, moving around the kitchen so his back was to Chris, making it easier for Chris to contemplate the truth. "There was a 'but' in your voice."

"But the past six months have been hard," Chris admitted. "We've been living one step away from the streets, and we've been around some people we never would have been around before."

"Your folks kicked you out because you were gay?" Kami asked.

"No, Mum died. We never knew our real father. He disappeared soon after Seth was born. The drongo Mum married kicked us out after the funeral. He said he didn't have time for her bastard kids."

"Not very charitable of him," Kami observed.

Chris snorted, nearly choking on his tea. "Not a word I'd use to describe him, and I've come up with a few over the past six months."

"I'm sure you have, but that's in the past now," Kami said. "Lang Downs is a good place to start over, whether you stay for a season or a lifetime."

"Is that what happened to you?" Chris asked curiously.

"The old man happened to me," Kami replied. "I'd say Caine's uncle was one of a kind except Caine seems determined to follow in his footsteps."

"Macklin said the same thing," Chris commented.

"Macklin told you about the old man?"

"About Michael Lang? Yes. Why?"

"Because as far as I know, Macklin's never told anyone that story, except maybe Caine," Kami said. "I wonder why he told you now."

To get me to trust him.

"I don't know. I was in the hospital trying to figure out what to do next, and he told me he'd been where I was and that Michael Lang made him see sense. He said he wanted to do the same for me," Chris explained.

Kami hummed an acknowledgment softly as he bustled around the kitchen, putting the final touches on what Chris thought might be pad thai of some variety, although he wasn't completely sure. "He must have thought it was really important to have you here if he told you about himself. I know none of the other jackaroos have the slightest idea he was ever a kid with nowhere to go."

"You know."

"I was already here when he arrived. The old man took me in the year before he took Macklin in."

"Why don't you say his name?"

"It hasn't been a year since he died," Kami replied. "It's not respectful to say his name."

"I'm sorry," Chris said. "I didn't know."

Kami smiled. "It's not your culture to avoid the names of the dead. It doesn't grieve me to hear it spoken, but I'll pay him the respect he was due in my own way, the same way he always paid me respect when he was alive."

"He must have been an amazing man," Chris marveled. "I wish I could have met him."

"You know Caine, and that's close enough," Kami said. "They don't look all that much alike, but Caine has his uncle's spirit. There's no doubt about that."

"How long has Caine been here?"

"Since March," Kami replied. "He came a few months after his uncle passed."

"He seems so… settled, but that's only six months ago."

"He belongs here," Kami said. "Give yourself six months and see how you feel. I think you'll be surprised."

FOUR

CHRIS finished his tea, thanked Kami, and used his injuries as an excuse to retreat to his room for an hour or two before dinner. The bed was surprisingly comfortable despite his sore ribs, far more comfortable than the hospital bed had been. Chris lay down and closed his eyes, consciously relaxing his muscles starting with his feet and working his way up. It was a game he'd played with his mother when he was younger and had trouble sleeping. They'd put each part of his body to sleep until they reached his head, although most nights they didn't get that far before he fell asleep. He smiled at the memory of the days before she'd married Tony, when everything had been simple, or so it had seemed to him at the time.

He was nearly asleep when the door to his room burst open. "Chris! Guess what?"

The jolt of adrenaline from waking so quickly left Chris's hands tingling and his heart pounding. It took a moment to realize what he heard in Seth's voice was excitement, not anger or fear or worry. He had gotten so used to a shout being cause for concern that he'd forgotten what joy sounded like. "What?" he said, opening his eyes and smiling at his brother without trying to sit up.

"I met the awesomest kid today. His name's Jason. He's fourteen, but he's been here forever. Since he was two. He has his own sheepdog and everything! He lives here on the station all year and goes to school on the Internet, which means he can do his schoolwork on his own schedule and help around the station when he's needed. He said he'd teach me all the commands for the dogs and show me everything I need to know around the station and maybe even help me with my schoolwork. Oh, and his dad's one of the mechanics here. Do you think he'd let me help him a bit too? I could learn so much from him. You know how much I love engines."

"It sounds like you had a good afternoon," Chris said, the spate of words widening his smile. It had been too long since he last saw this kind of enthusiasm from Seth. He might not trust Caine's offer completely, but anything that gave Seth this kind of joy was worth it, no matter what the price was down the road. "Maybe this was the right decision after all?"

"Maybe it was," Seth said with a shy smile.

"Just remember they don't know us yet, so if you get up to your tricks, tread carefully until you know people better," Chris warned. "We don't want anyone to get hacked off and have to leave because of it."

"I'll be good," Seth promised. "If we stay, I can maybe get a dog of my own."

Chris's smile faded. For as long as he could remember, Seth had wanted a dog, but when they were little, there hadn't been space in their flat, and later, after their mother married Tony, they had space, but Tony didn't like dogs. Seth had learned not to ask, but the desire clearly hadn't gone away. "Maybe you can. You can ask Jason where he got his dog and maybe we can save up enough money for you to get one of your own. If we decide to stay, that is."

Seth's face grew serious as he sat down on the floor next to Chris's bed so they were close to eye level. "I want to stay."

Chris ruffled Seth's hair affectionately. "Then we'll have to do our best to fit in. I learned two things today."

"What's that?" Seth asked.

"That pretty much everyone here thinks Caine is a saint and that everyone except Caine and maybe Kami the cook lives in awe and fear of Macklin. Keep that in mind when you're talking to people."

"They saved your life," Seth reminded Chris. "I'm not going to repay that by doing stupid shite."

Chris cuffed the side of Seth's head lightly. "Watch your language. You're not one of the jackaroos yet and I don't want to hear it."

"You swear sometimes too."

"I know. It's a bad habit I need to break," Chris said. "More than that, though, you said Jason was only fourteen. Do you want Jason's dad to decide you shouldn't come around because you're a bad influence on him?"

"No."

"Then watch your mouth so he doesn't have a reason to question you being there."

"I will," Seth promised. "I really want to stay. I won't do anything to mess that up. I promise."

Chris pulled Seth into a tight hug. It hurt his ribs, but he held on anyway. He didn't know how badly Seth needed the embrace, but he knew how much he needed it. It would just have to hurt.

Finally Seth squirmed a little in his arms so Chris let him go. "So who else did you meet today? Anyone?"

"One other jackaroo," Seth said. "His name's Jesse. He's also a mechanic, although I don't think he was hired for that. I think he hired on just as a jackaroo."

"It sounds like you'll have plenty of people to teach you then," Chris said. "That's good."

The bell tolled signaling mealtime. "Help me up so we can go eat dinner. I'm starving."

Seth helped Chris get out of bed and stayed at his side as they negotiated the steps. By the time they made it to the canteen, it was full of men waiting for their dinner. Chris looked around for any familiar faces, but he really only knew Caine, Macklin, and Neil, and he didn't want to impose on the boss. Seth solved the problem by dragging Chris over to meet Jason and his father. Chris smiled politely and let the rest of the conversation drift past him as they discussed the various kinds of machinery on the farm.

"You look bored."

Startled, Chris looked up into the greenest eyes he'd ever seen. "N-no," he stammered, fighting not to let his eyes linger inappropriately on the other jackaroo. He'd learned how to look without being caught, but it was hard not to stare since they were actually talking. "Lost, but not bored. I'm not much of a mechanic, so their conversation is completely over my head."

The other man laughed, the smile softening his face. He wasn't weathered enough to have the whole carved-from-granite thing going on like Macklin did, but Chris figured he only needed another year or two to get there. Until he smiled. "I'm sure it is. I'm Jesse Harris. Nice to meet you."

"Chris Simms. I'd offer to shake hands, but, well…." He lifted his cast to show Jesse his injury. "Not exactly in top form at the moment."

"You're Seth's brother. He mentioned you'd been hurt, but I didn't realize it was quite that dramatic. You've got a beautiful bruise on your cheek there."

Chris lifted his hand self-consciously to his cheek. He hated looking less than his best at any time, but especially sitting next to someone as… potent as Jesse. He didn't hold out any hope the other man was gay, but that didn't mean he couldn't look. "Does it look awful?"

"Not awful," Jesse replied. "Painful, but it'll heal. I'm sure the other guy looks worse."

If only, Christ thought with a grimace. "There were five of them. If it weren't for Macklin and the others, I'd be dead."

"I heard Ian and Kyle bragging, but I figured they were talking shite. You were really bashed like that?"

"That's what they said before they attacked me," Chris said, "but I think we'll be safe here."

"Yeah, it would take quite a drongo to hassle someone for being gay when the boss and foreman are both gay too," Jesse agreed. "Have you worked on a station before?"

Chris shook his head. "We're city kids through and through, but we won't let Caine and Macklin down."

"They do seem to inspire that determination in people," Jesse said. "I haven't figured out what it is about them, but the year-rounders and the ones who've been here before all agree this is the best station around to work at. I figure that's about the best recommendation you can get."

"This is your first year too?" Chris asked.

"My first year at Lang Downs," Jesse replied. "I've been working other stations since I was eighteen."

"So not quite as much of a blow-in as I am," Chris said.

"Stick with me, kid," Jesse said with a grin, the expression making Chris's stomach turn over with desire. He wondered how hard it would be to jerk off left-handed. "Well, when your arm gets better anyway. I'll show you the ropes."

"Thanks," Chris said. "I'd really appreciate it. I'm feeling a little lost at the moment. I'm supposed to help in the kitchen starting tomorrow, but I don't know much about cooking, and with my arm in a cast, I can't even do the heavy lifting and leave the rest to Kami."

"I'm sure Kami will teach you," Jesse said. "He'll be the one listening to the complaints if he doesn't. I've eaten in a lot of canteens in the past ten years, and this is one of the best. He's not going to let that suffer because his jackaroos are used to this quality. From what I heard in the bunkhouse, nobody's shy about expressing their opinions."

"I couldn't believe they talked about Caine and Macklin like that," Chris said, lowering his voice. "Can you imagine if one of them had walked in on that conversation?"

Jesse chuckled. "I wouldn't have wanted to be in their shoes if that happened, that's for sure. Macklin would hang them out by their balls for that kind of talk, but I can live with that."

"Why would it be a problem for him to do that? I mean, he has the right to defend himself."

"It's the reason why," Jesse explained. "Here, Macklin would do it because he's the foreman and Caine's the boss and it's nobody's business but theirs. Everywhere else I've worked, the foreman would've done it because someone implied he was a pillow biter. Same result, but entirely different feeling."

"Yeah, I can see that," Chris replied. "Nobody seems to care that they're gay. The conversation wasn't mean. They'd have made the same kind of comments about a man and his wife if she had him pussy-whipped."

"And that's a rare and precious thing," Jesse said. "The line's died down so I'm going to get some food. It was good talking to you."

Chris watched the other jackaroo walk across the room, admiring the way his jeans stretched over his arse, before turning his attention back to the plate in front of him. He'd known Caine and Macklin were special, but the conversation with Jesse drove home just how special this place was. Chris hadn't asked how people found out about Caine and Macklin or how they first reacted, but he could see how they reacted now. Neil had been perfectly clear that afternoon, and Jesse agreed with the assessment. Chris was safe here.

The end of the conversation made Chris wonder a little if Jesse was gay too. It would explain some of his cryptic comments, but even here, where Chris didn't worry about being bashed again because of his sexuality, he didn't want to make assumptions about other people's preferences. Jesse didn't strike Chris as gay, but then neither did Macklin, so maybe Chris wasn't as good a judge as he thought he was. He certainly wouldn't have believed Macklin was gay if anyone other than Macklin himself had told him.

With a sigh, he finished his dinner and headed slowly back to his room. He needed to sleep if he was going to help Kami in the morning.

WHEN Jesse finished eating, he wandered outside and stared up at the night sky. The stars always seemed brighter when he was on a station. Intellectually he knew it was because of the decrease in light and air pollution, but that never took away from the magic of the stars spread out above him in all their magnificence. They seemed even brighter than usual tonight. He told himself it was his imagination, but he couldn't shake the feeling of rightness.

After ten years of wandering from station to station looking for a place to fit in, he'd finally found one he thought might be a good fit. He'd heard some of the other jackaroos talking in town when he'd arrived to try his hand at New South Wales after having worked farther north. Word had gotten around that the grazier at Lang Downs was gay, not that most of the jackaroos used that kind a word for it. He'd noticed a group of men not joining in, and he'd asked them about it.

"We can't argue with them about the boss being gay," one of them replied. "It just doesn't make a difference to anyone who actually knows him."

"Why don't you say something?" Jesse asked.

"They won't care what we say, and Caine wouldn't appreciate us getting in a fight over him," another man replied. "Let them say what they want. It's less competition for us when the Lang Downs crew gets here."

"You really don't mind working for him?"

"He's a fair boss, he runs a good station, and he treats everyone well," the first man said. "What's to mind? He's not trying to sleep with us."

That didn't tell Jesse who the boss was sleeping with, but he figured it wasn't any of his business. It was enough to hear the jackaroos say it wasn't an issue. When the time came to sign on with a crew, he hadn't hesitated to approach the men from Lang Downs even if he'd kept his reasons for doing so to himself.

Then Neil had surprised him with the announcement of Caine's partner that afternoon. Jesse had met Macklin, of course, as the foreman grilled him on his experiences and references with Caine sitting right beside him, a united front for sure but without any undertones Jesse could detect. As he stood there staring at the stars, though, he saw Macklin making his rounds for the night. He nodded to Jesse as he walked by and up the path to the station house. He let himself inside with complete ease, closing the door behind him. The light in the living room went out a few minutes later.

However strange it might seem from the outside, Macklin lived in the station house and was partnered with the station owner, and everyone familiar with the station accepted that.

Jesse took a deep breath, smelling new grass over the smell of the sheep in the nearby pens. Spring was coming even here in the highlands, and he was getting a new start along with it.

Thoughts of Chris filtered through his mind as he enjoyed the cool night air. He couldn't imagine what the kid had been through. He'd always been careful not to let people find out he was gay unless he was absolutely certain of their reaction precisely because he didn't want to end up beaten or dead. Jesse didn't know whether Chris was careless or stupid or simply unlucky, but Jesse's worst nightmare had played out in Chris's life. From the little bit of conversation they'd shared and everything Seth had said about his older brother earlier in the day, Chris seemed like a good guy, far more responsible than the typical person his age, but that came with a price. Chris could probably use a friend, and Jesse saw just enough of himself at that age in Chris to want to be that friend.

It didn't hurt that Chris was cute, in a not quite pretty but definitely attractive kind of way. The summer was looking up in more ways than one, if Chris happened to be interested in a little… recreation.

"LET me see your hand."

"It's just a few scrapes on my knuckles," Macklin said.

"You're the one who lectured me on letting little cuts get infected," Caine replied, "so don't argue."

Macklin gave in gracelessly, holding out his hand so Caine could examine the bruised, scraped knuckles where Macklin's fist had connected with someone's jaw. He shook his head as he pulled Macklin toward the sink so he could clean and disinfect the cuts.

"Chris is going to need a lot of help adjusting over the next few weeks," he said as he scrubbed Macklin's skin gently.

"I'm more worried about Seth."

"Seth?" Caine asked, pouring hydrogen peroxide over the cuts. "Why?"

Macklin hissed as the cool liquid seeped into the sores. "He's sullen and angry. He's behind in school. He's gotten used to not having any structure. He's going to resent being forced to do schoolwork, probably resent having to work as hard as he will here. He's sixteen, and this isn't the life he's chosen for himself."

"Really?" Caine asked, reaching for a tube of antibiotic ointment. "Are you sure? I didn't get that impression at all." He smeared the gel on Macklin's knuckles. "I got the impression of someone so grateful not to be living on the streets again that he'd do anything we asked not to have to go back there."

"Maybe I'm misreading him," Macklin said. "I just know how I felt at the first station I worked on."

Caine wiped his hand and nudged Macklin back toward the bedroom. "You want to tell me about that now?"

"Not really."

"It wasn't a question, Macklin." Caine had let various comments from Macklin go in the past, either because Macklin had refused to talk, as he'd done the first time it came up in the early days of their acquaintance, or because it had come up at a bad time, as it had when Chris was in the hospital.

"What do you want to know?"

"Everything there is to know about you. Haven't you figured that out by now?"

Macklin scowled. "You already know everything that matters."

"If it doesn't matter, then you won't mind telling me about it," Caine retorted. He wasn't sure why he felt the need to push this, but Macklin had been pensive since they'd rescued Chris and Seth. Caine had learned to live with taciturn, but pensive didn't fit Macklin at all.

Macklin's scowl deepened. "Why is this so important to you?"

"Because it's important to you," Caine replied. "You've been out of sorts since we found them, moody and withdrawn. You haven't f-fucked me since we left to go hire the new hands."

"We can fix that," Macklin offered, pulling his shirt off and advancing on Caine.

"Oh, n-no," Caine said, backing away. "Not until you tell me about how you came to Lang Downs."

"I already told you," Macklin said. "I ran away from home and Michael took me in."

"N-not g-good enough," Caine replied.

"I think it is," Macklin said, catching Caine's arm. "You're already stuttering. You know how that turns me on."

Caine rolled his eyes even as Macklin leaned in to kiss him. He still hated to stutter, but given he only stuttered rarely these days unless Macklin was making love to him and given Macklin's clear pleasure in Caine's reaction to him, he'd stopped fighting it. He wouldn't win anyway. He returned the kiss eagerly, determined to lull Macklin into relaxing before trying again to find out what he wanted to know.

He bided his time as Macklin stripped him to the waist, giving in to his lover's dominant side because it felt too good not to. When Macklin pushed him toward the bed and started undoing his own jeans, Caine shook his head, shoving Macklin's hands out of the way so he could bare his lover himself. Macklin looked like he might protest, so Caine pulled out the big guns, dropping to his knees and nuzzling Macklin's erection through the cloth of his underwear.

"W-want t-t-to b-blow—" Caine got out with difficulty.

"Be my guest," Macklin said with a grin, settling back on the bed and spreading his legs.

Caine scowled up at him for the interruption. He hadn't finished his sentence, but he had what he wanted, Macklin sprawled on his back across their bed, waiting for Caine to make love to him, so he didn't bother complaining. He simply tugged at Macklin's pants and underwear until he had his lover completely naked. Kneeling between Macklin's feet, he kissed the inside of Macklin's knee, licking his way slowly up one hair-dusted thigh toward his ultimate goal: Macklin's cooperation.

Working his way higher, he nuzzled Macklin's balls, letting the hint of whiskers from the day add the slightest bite to the softer touch of his lips and tongue. Macklin gasped, making Caine smile as he lifted his head. "T-t-tell me the s-story."

"Bloody hell, pup," Macklin roared, his fingers pushing on Caine's head. "Finish what you started."

"Only if you t-tell me the story," Caine insisted. "After if you w-want, but you have to t-tell me."

Macklin looked so troubled that Caine almost relented, but he doubted he'd get another chance at this. The entire situation had Macklin ill at ease, and Caine needed to know why.

"After," Macklin said finally.

Caine didn't question Macklin's promise. His lover was a man of his word. Now he had to remind Macklin he wasn't telling this story to a stranger, but to his partner, the man who loved him and intended to spend the rest of his life supporting him. He lowered his head again, licking the musky skin of Macklin's perineum. Macklin might not be comfortable letting Caine top yet, but he'd taken to rimming like a duck to water, and Caine intended to use that to his advantage.

Macklin lifted his legs, making it easier for Caine to reach his target. He didn't immediately dive between the spread cheeks, though. He wanted to linger, to make Macklin so eager he'd accept not only the rimming but anything else Caine felt like doing to him. As hard as the thought of driving into Macklin's tight heat made Caine, he knew that wouldn't happen tonight, but that didn't mean he couldn't introduce his lover to other delights.

Peeking up at Macklin's face and seeing his lover's eyes closed, Caine sucked on his index finger, wetting it thoroughly before licking Macklin's entrance. Macklin gasped again and squirmed, his delight in Caine's attentions obvious in every line of his body. Caine smiled and continued what he was doing, using everything he knew about Macklin to lavish pleasure on him. When Macklin started groaning and thrashing on the bed, begging Caine to let him come, Caine decided the time was right.

Pulling back slightly, he replaced his tongue with the tip of his finger, wiggling it just inside the still tight entrance. Macklin froze but didn't pull away, so Caine took that as permission, licking around the entrance a few more times to add to the wetness already there. He pressed his finger a little deeper and left it there as he sucked Macklin's balls into his mouth, teasing them with his tongue.

By the time he'd licked his way to the tip of Macklin's cock, he had his finger inserted to the second knuckle and could press on Macklin's gland. With a grin, he sucked Macklin's erection into his mouth at the same time he flicked his finger across the little bump of flesh. The shout Macklin let out echoed off the walls of the room, making Caine grin wider. He hoped Chris and Seth were sound sleepers, because if not, they were about to get an education.

"Bloody hell," Macklin shouted when Caine continued to work his sweet spot while taking Macklin down his throat. "Stop, Caine."

Caine ignored him, doing everything he could to push Macklin into climaxing right then and there. It took a gratifyingly short time to shatter his lover's usual control, a hot gush of fluid filling his mouth as Macklin's barely loosened guardian muscle squeezed his finger mercilessly.

Licking his lips with a self-satisfied smile, Caine rocked back on his heels. "Now t-tell me the story."

"Fuck."

"Not until you tell me the story."

Macklin glared at him, but Caine didn't back down.

"Fine," Macklin huffed, sitting up and pulling the covers over his lower body. "I told you Michael took me in when I was sixteen. I ran away when I was fifteen because my father had a temper and quick fists. For as long as I can remember, he hit my mother. Eventually I got old enough to protest, and one time—I was maybe twelve—he turned on me instead of on her. I was big for my age, already bigger than she was."

That hadn't changed. Macklin's size had struck Caine from the moment they met. "So what happened next?"

"So I decided I'd do it deliberately. If he was hitting me, he wasn't hitting her."

"He shouldn't have hit anyone. Didn't someone report it?"

"I don't know if anyone did or not," Macklin said, "but nothing ever came of it if they did. I got good at pushing his buttons, at sensing when he was about to lose it with my mum and choosing that moment to draw his attention to me. I didn't manage it every time, but enough that she stopped walking around in long sleeves all the time to hide the bruises on her arms."

"It wasn't your job to protect her," Caine said softly. "She should have called the police."

"She should have," Macklin agreed. "I can say that sitting here at forty-three, but at twelve, all I knew was her begging me not to call the police and not to interfere. I couldn't stop, though."

"So how did you get from there to Lang Downs?"

"Mum found out about me," Macklin said, his hands clenched so hard around the quilt on the bed that his knuckles turned white. "I never figured out how. She told me she loved me no matter what, but that I couldn't live in the house with my father and be different. He'd kill me. I wanted to say 'Let him try,' but she was right. I'd listened to him rant for too long about poofters and pillow biters and every other foul name you could think to call someone. I begged her to come with me. We'd leave together, go somewhere he couldn't find us, but she said she'd made her choice and she'd live with it, but I shouldn't have to suffer for her weakness."

And yet he so clearly had that it tore at Caine's heart. "You listened to her eventually."

"He broke my arm," Macklin replied, his voice completely devoid of emotion. "I'd been named goalie for our footie team, and I missed a block. He went into a rage that night and broke my arm. He said I wasn't using it anyway so what did it matter?"

"Over a lost soccer match?"

"That's the worst part," Macklin said with a bleak smile. "We won. I started stocking up as soon as we got back from the doctor, making a stash to hold me through as long as I could. An extra tin of beans, a jar of Vegemite, every penny of spare change he left lying around, anything I could hide in my room. A week after the cast came off, I left, and I have regretted it every day since then."

"What?" Caine said. "Why would you regret it? You have a life because you got out of that hell!"

"I got out," Macklin said. "She didn't. I didn't have the courage to stay or the strength to take her with me."

"You were fifteen," Caine reminded him. "It wasn't your job to be the strong one."

"You weren't there," Macklin said. "She was a meter and a half at the most. He was almost two meters tall. She didn't stand a chance against him. I shouldn't have left her."

The self-loathing in Macklin's voice nearly brought Caine undone.

"So you left," Caine said, "but you didn't get here until you were sixteen, or that's the story I've always heard."

"I was almost sixteen when I left, but it took me about six months to find my way here," Macklin said. "I worked odd jobs to get across the country, never staying for more than a few weeks, until I ended up in Boorowa."

"That's where Uncle Michael found you?"

"That's where Charles Taylor found me," Macklin said. "Devlin Taylor's father."

Caine frowned at the thought of their neighbor. Taylor had been as good as his word and left the men of Lang Downs alone after firing the jackaroo who had sabotaged Caine's fences earlier in the winter, but that didn't mean Caine liked the homophobic grazier. He gestured for Macklin to continue.

"I took a job at Taylor Peaks. It was the only thing I could find in the area, and I didn't have enough money to get even to Yass. It was work for him or starve."

Macklin stopped after that, his face pensive. Caine tried to find a way to prompt him to continue, but he couldn't think of anything. Before he gave up on subtlety, Macklin shook his head and gave Caine a wan smile.

"It wasn't awful at first. Charles was a better manager than his son. He worked us hard for not a lot of pay, but he was fair," Macklin recounted.

"So what happened?" Caine asked. "I mean, why did you leave?"

"He hired a drifter who wanted room and board in exchange for a few weeks' work. The man was a bully, but Taylor never saw it. He just saw me trying to fight back and blamed the situation on me. After all, I was the punk kid. He told me to leave. I didn't know up from down in those days so I started walking and ended up going north instead of south to Boorowa. I ended up on Lang Downs. You know the rest."

Caine wasn't entirely sure he did, but he'd gotten far more out of Macklin tonight than he ever had before or than he'd really expected to get. Scooting closer to his lover, he kissed him softly. "Thank you. I know how hard it must be to talk about it."

"It's not something I think about anymore," Macklin said. Caine doubted that, but he didn't challenge it. "I've been on my own for so long that I don't dwell on it. It made me who I am, but it doesn't have the power to hurt me anymore."

Caine wondered if it could really be that easy. He wouldn't bring it up again unless Macklin gave him a reason to, but he'd keep an eye on the other man. He needed Macklin strong and steady. "I love you."

Macklin smiled and pulled Caine into a kiss.

FIVE

CHRIS stumbled down the stairs the next morning at the appointed time, quite sure he wasn't awake enough for whatever Kami would ask him to do, but he wasn't going back on his word the first day on the station. He still didn't think he'd be much help with his broken arm, but he wouldn't compound that by being late.

"There's hot water in the kettle for tea or coffee brewing for the jackaroos if you want that," Kami said as Chris walked into the kitchen. "Pour a cup and then come break these eggs."

Chris fumbled a little with holding the kettle in his left hand, but when he glanced furtively at Kami, the cook's back was turned, giving Chris the privacy to negotiate the task without scrutiny.

He managed the water, but the tea strainer was beyond him with only one hand, and his weaker one at that. He had no idea why they'd had tea bags the day before and a tea strainer and loose leaves this morning, but he didn't want to ask. "Kami," he said tentatively, "I hate to disturb you but I can't get the tea leaves into the strainer."

Kami chuckled. "We take such simple things for granted when we're well," he said, scooping tea leaves into the ball and handing it back to Chris. "You will be well again. You just have to give it time."

"Not my strong suit," Chris muttered as he carried his tea to the counter where Kami had eggs sitting out. "So I just break the eggs into the bowl?"

"Yes," Kami said. "I'm not frying eggs for that many people. They'll eat scrambled eggs or something else."

Chris nodded and picked up the first egg. The shell had an almost bluish hue. "These are an interesting color."

"That batch is from our chickens," Kami explained. "Caine's been pushing us toward organic certification for the sheep, but he's also made some other changes. We can feed the men less expensively with our own chickens than we can buying eggs elsewhere. They're fresher, healthier, and we have the added bonus of fresh meat when we want it."

"It sounds like he's made more than a few changes around here," Chris commented as he continued breaking eggs into the bowl. "I always heard stations were pretty backwards when it came to accepting change."

"You heard right," Kami said, "but that's because they're run by people whose families have been here, doing things the same way, for generations. The average jackaroo doesn't have anything to do with whether change comes. It's the graziers who make those decisions."

"Caine's great-uncle ran the station, didn't he? So it's in his family."

"It is, but not the same way," Kami said, putting a tray of scones in the oven. "Caine didn't grow up here so he isn't looking at things through the eyes of his uncle. He sees everything with fresh eyes and a business degree."

"But nobody seems to resent that," Chris said. "Sure, he's the one in charge, but that doesn't mean everyone has to like it."

"No, it doesn't," Kami agreed, continuing to bustle around the kitchen, "and there are some faces missing from the jackaroos this year, maybe because of him, but there are new faces too, and there's one face still there that might not be if it weren't for Caine."

"Neil?" Chris asked. "I heard someone say Caine saved his life."

"Damn fool boy with no more sense than any of our sheep," Kami muttered, "but yes, he saved Neil's life, and Neil won't let anyone forget that. Now finish those eggs. We have hungry jackaroos on their way for breakfast."

Chris knew the end of a conversation when he heard one, but given what he'd seen of Kami with Neil and some of the others the day before, he'd already gotten more out of the cook than most people did, and that reassured him. Working in the kitchen wouldn't be easy with his arm banged up, but Kami wouldn't make it miserable either.

FIVE hours later, he wasn't so sure about that. Kami hadn't been cruel, but he'd been grumpy and demanding, snapping orders right and left as they worked on dinner. Chris had reached a breaking point and needed out. Tossing the knife on the counter, he stomped out of the kitchen, slamming the door behind him. He made it all the way to the fence separating the house from the road when his ribs started aching and he had to stop. He leaned heavily against the rail, trying to breathe through the pain.

"You all right, mate?"

Chris looked up to see Jesse walking his way, a toolbox in his hand. "Yeah, just sore," Chris replied. "I forgot to take it easy."

"Kind of hard to do on a sheep station," Jesse said with a wave of his hand at all the industriousness going on around them. "You pull your own weight or you end up out on your arse. It's the way stations work."

Chris lifted his plaster-covered arm. "I'm not pulling much of anything at the moment."

"You're helping in the kitchen. Isn't that what Seth told me?"

"I'm trying to," Chris muttered, "but that stupid drongo won't let me finish one thing before he's told me to do ten more, and then he yells because I haven't done any of them. I've never worked in a kitchen before. I don't know what I'm doing, and I'm trying to learn with only one good arm."

"And seventy-odd people waiting for dinner tonight," Jesse finished. "I feel for you, mate. I wouldn't want Kami's job, and yours even less, even with two good arms."

"I wouldn't mind it so much if he'd let me finish one thing before asking me to do something else," Chris said. "I can learn whatever I need to learn, even one-handed, but I can't keep up with the speed of his demands."

"Try telling him that," Jesse suggested. "Maybe after dinner's over rather than now while he's busy, but let him know. Some people are born managers. Other people have to learn, and from some of the comments I heard this morning, Kami isn't one to let anyone in his kitchen, so he may never have learned."

"Great, now I'm an experiment on top of a charity case," Chris sighed.

"Don't start feeling sorry for yourself," Jesse scolded. "Take it from someone who's been around a few more times than you have. You won't win any friends or solve any problems by moping. You needed a break. Fine. You've taken a break. Now go back in there and do your job. Talk to Kami after dinner, and if it doesn't get better, talk to Caine or Macklin. They're fair men. They'll listen to you. They hired you to work at Lang Downs, not necessarily to work in the kitchen, right?"

Chris nodded.

"So then if working in the kitchen is going to cause problems, ask if you can do something else," Jesse suggested. "What's the worst they can do?"

"Kick me off the station," Chris said.

"For asking a question?" Jesse replied. "They wouldn't have the kind of loyalty they do from the year-rounders if they were like that. I've worked on enough stations to have learned that lesson. If you want to know what kind of men the foreman and the boss are, you look at the way the year-rounders think about them. The men here are so loyal to Caine and Macklin that they defend them, not just turn a blind eye to them being together, but actively defend them. I've never been on another station where something like that would happen, even the ones that were otherwise good places to work."

"Otherwise?" Chris asked, the choice of words striking him as odd.

"It's nice to be somewhere tolerant," Jesse replied with a shrug. "It makes being different easier."

"Different how?" Chris asked impulsively. He knew better than to assume Jesse's comments meant what he hoped they did. Asking outright if Jesse was gay could be as bad as letting the drongos in Yass find out. Knowing someone was gay was a far cry from having someone assume the same applied to you as far as reactions were concerned.

"How do you think?" Jesse asked in reply. "I tried to get a job here because I heard the boss was gay. I didn't expect him to be interested in me—though the rumors didn't say anything about the foreman being his partner—but I figured a station with a gay boss would be less likely to take issue with a gay jackaroo."

Chris let out the breath he hadn't realized he was holding. "You say that so easily."

"That I'm gay?" Jesse verified.

Chris nodded.

"I don't really, but you aren't going to hit me for it, and even if you decided to tell everyone, they probably wouldn't either, so I don't have much to lose," Jesse explained. "I don't say it often. I don't even think it all that often, because it's not like there's anybody to do anything with, out here in the bush. Before I got here, I'd never met another person in the outback who would admit to it. Maybe there were some people like me who were good at hiding it, but this is the first time outside the city I've ever told anyone."

Chris resolutely refused to imagine why Jesse might have told someone in the city. The other jackaroo was his only friend on the station. He was perving over Jesse enough as it was without imagining him hooking up with some guy in a bar.

"I guess I'd better be grateful Seth stumbled into the right place when he went looking for someone to help me," Chris said instead of what was really on his mind. "If he'd asked a different group of men, they might have come to help kill me instead of save me."

"Even if all they'd done was ignore his pleas, you'd still be a lot worse off than you are now," Jesse agreed. "That shiner is looking even blacker today than it did yesterday. Does it hurt?"

"Everything hurts," Chris admitted. "I don't want to take the drugs they gave me because they knock me out, but regular Nurofen isn't taking care of the pain."

"I've never been hurt as badly as you are all at once," Jesse said, "but I've taken some tumbles off a horse and some falls that have left me pretty bruised and battered. You may want to wait a few more days before trying to work anywhere, even in the kitchen. The harder you push now, the longer it will take you to get well."

"Tell that to the bosses," Chris said. "I owe them my life. I'm not going to repay them by being lazy."

"You aren't going to repay them by hurting yourself worse and making them call the flying doctor to come out here either," Jesse replied. "They'll already have to take you back to Yass to take your cast off. Making them arrange a second doctor's visit because you're too proud and stupid to tell two reasonable men that you're hurting is not a way to say thank you."

"Hi, Chris."

Chris spun around, wincing as the movement jarred his ribs. "Hi, boss."

"Taking a break?" Caine asked.

"A short one," Chris said nervously. "Kami was…."

"Being Kami?" Caine finished with a chuckle. "He's a superstitious old aborigine with an attitude the size of Ayers Rock and a heart of gold buried underneath it. I'll talk to him and remind him you aren't at full strength yet."

"About that," Jesse said. "Sorry to interrupt, boss, but Chris is hurt pretty bad and—"

"And nothing," Chris interrupted. "I'll be fine."

"You aren't fine," Jesse snapped. "You just told me everything hurt."

"I'm sorry, I don't remember your name," Caine said to Jesse.

"Jesse Harris," Jesse said. "Chris and I talked a little last night and a little more just now, and he's got a broken arm and busted ribs. He won't take the prescription because it knocks him out and he feels like he needs to be working, so he's biting his cheek and trying to deal with it, but that's going to make things worse, not better."

"Slow down," Caine said, his voice amused. "Chris, is he telling the truth?"

Chris kicked at the ground with the toe of his boot. "Yes, but he wasn't supposed to tell you," he said sullenly. "I'll be fine."

"Yes, you will be," Caine said, "but there's no reason to slow that process down. You've been working since before breakfast. You should go upstairs and take whatever the doctor gave you. If you sleep through dinner, we'll have Seth bring you a plate. You can work breakfast again tomorrow so you feel like you're contributing, but I'll check in with you after that, and you will tell me if you're in pain."

"I don't need special treatment," Chris protested.

Caine cocked an eyebrow at him. "That lump of plaster on your arm says you do for now. We aren't b-babying you, and we aren't talking d-down to you, Chris. As soon as you are healed, we will work you as hard as we do everyone else, but you have to let yourself get well or you could end up permanently disabled, and then who would take care of Seth?"

"That's a low blow."

"It wasn't intended to be one," Caine said. "It was intended to make you look at all the consequences of your choices, that's all."

"Fine, I'll go inside and take a pill, but if I don't come down to dinner, send Seth to get me," Chris insisted. "I don't want anyone waiting on me like an invalid."

He walked back toward the house, doing his best to walk like his ribs weren't broken and his whole body didn't hurt.

"WALK with me, Jesse," Caine said when Chris crossed the veranda and went inside.

"Sir?" Jesse asked, hoping he hadn't done something to upset his new boss already.

"I need to find Macklin, and he's supposed to be out in the sheds," Caine said, "but I want to t-talk to you as well, so walk with me."

Jesse fell in step beside Caine, waiting to see what the grazier wanted.

"This is your first season on Lang Downs, isn't it?" Caine asked after a moment.

"Yes," Jesse replied. "I worked out of Cowra and Grenfell the last few years, but I didn't really find a station where I fit."

"You seem to have made friends with Chris."

"He's a good kid from what I can tell," Jesse said. "Maybe caught in a bad situation, but trying to do what's right."

"That was my impression as well. He wants to impress me, to thank me for helping him, and that's fine, but he doesn't trust me yet, and he's not going to tell me if something is wrong," Caine said. "I need you to be the kind of friend he needs and keep doing what you did today. If he's pushing himself too hard and lets you see it, I need you to tell me. Macklin has driven into my head the fact that getting hurt or sick out here is bad from start to finish. I can't change Chris being hurt, but I can do my best to keep him from making it worse."

"You could just keep him in bed until his ribs have a chance to heal," Jesse suggested.

"I don't want to break his spirit while I'm helping his body heal," Caine said.

"Me spying on him isn't going to help his spirit," Jesse said. "He needs a friend, someone he really can trust to look out for him."

"Then find ways to keep him from overdoing," Caine said. "I'll tell him and Kami both that he's off duty after breakfast cleanup for the next week, but he'll find ways to fill his time if I do that and don't order him to bed."

"How am I supposed to do that? I have chores of my own to do," Jesse protested. "Macklin said the big tractor stopped running. Patrick and I have to tear the whole engine apart to figure out what's wrong with it."

"So have him hand you tools," Caine suggested.

"He isn't a mechanic," Jesse said.

"Maybe not, but I bet he knows the difference between a wrench and a screwdriver," Caine said with a chuckle. "The point isn't whether you need his help. The point is to make him rest until he's well enough to work a full day. There's Macklin. I'll leave you to your repairs."

Jesse watched Caine walk across the shed to where Macklin stood, checking the preparations for shearing which would begin in a few days. Macklin smiled briefly when Caine joined him, the expression so fleeting Jesse wasn't entirely sure he'd seen it, but it was more than anyone else got. Jesse wondered if other people saw it, the tiny little signs of a deeper relationship, or if he was the only one sensitive to it because he was a gay man in a world that wouldn't, he'd believed until now, accept him as he was.

Shaking his head at his own foolishness, he headed toward the shed where the tractor was parked. Maybe Patrick had found something while he was talking to Chris and they could get the bloody machine fixed.

BY THE time dinner rolled around, Jesse was ready to quit. They'd done everything they could think of short of taking the engine completely apart and rebuilding it, all to no avail. He tossed the wrench in the toolbox with a satisfying clang. "I don't suppose Kami has beer in the kitchen," he asked Patrick with a groan.

"I doubt Kami does, but I'll spot you one until you get into town and can pick up a supply of your own," Patrick offered. "My wife won't mind one more for dinner."

"Jason's been in the canteen at every meal. Why don't you do the same?"

Patrick chuckled. "We take advantage of every opportunity we get to spend a little time together without Jason listening in. He's a great boy, but he's not one to leave his parents much time to themselves."

"Then I shouldn't impose," Jesse said. "Someone else will spot me a beer or let me buy one off him. I don't want to put you out."

"It's not an imposition," Patrick said. "I invited you. Even if you don't stay for dinner, you can still come have a beer."

Jesse acquiesced, following Patrick back to the little house he shared with his wife and Jason. "Carley," Patrick called as they walked inside, "we have company."

Patrick's wife was a beautiful woman in her mid- to late-thirties with pitch black hair and a smile as wide as the night sky. "Come in, don't be shy," she said when she saw Jesse standing in the doorway still.

"My boots aren't exactly clean, ma'am," he said. "I wouldn't want to ruin your floor."

"You think my son is that considerate?" Carley said with a laugh. "Take them off and leave them on the veranda. I won't mind sock feet in the house. Did Patrick offer you a beer?"

"Yes, ma'am," Jesse said, undoing his boots and leaving them outside. He came into the living room, hat held awkwardly between his hands. It had been so long since he'd been invited anywhere that he had to remember how to act.

"Patrick likes to sit on the back veranda and watch the sun set if you want to join him," Carley suggested.

"Is there anything I can do to help you?"

"No, but you're sweet to offer. Your mum raised you right."

"Thank you," Jesse said, although he doubted his mother would agree with that given she hadn't spoken to him since he told her he was gay. That didn't mean he'd forgotten all her lessons in manners, though.

Before he could say anything else, Patrick stuck his head out from the kitchen. "I have Tooheys Old or Carlton Sterling."

"Tooheys, please," Jesse said, following Patrick through the house and onto the veranda again. He took a sip of the beer and settled into the seat Patrick didn't choose. "How long have you been on Lang Downs?"

"Almost thirteen years," Patrick said. "Jason was a baby. I'd lost my job in Melbourne, and I was desperate. Someone suggested I take a look at the stations up here in the tablelands. Carley and I talked about it a lot, but there wasn't anything in Melbourne, and her part-time job didn't pay the bills, so I came up here and met Michael Lang. That first year, Carley and Jason stayed in Melbourne, but that was no way to live. When Michael asked me to stay on past the summer, I mentioned my family. He asked me why I'd waited so long to say something and immediately handed me money for bus tickets. We've been here ever since."

"From what everyone has said, he sounds like he was an amazing man," Jesse said. "I'm sorry I didn't get to meet him."

"He was a special man," Patrick agreed. "We were all a little worried when we heard the station had gone to a relative in the States. Then Caine came. We worried for nothing."

"He seems pretty universally liked," Jesse said. "I would've thought, well, sheep stations aren't exactly known for being tolerant."

Patrick shrugged. "They aren't known for being organic either, but we will be in less than six months. Macklin has been here since he was a kid and foreman longer than most of us have been here. People trust him, and he trusts Caine. That counts for a lot. Then there's the fact that Caine didn't sell the place. He came and he learned and he made improvements. Sure the men were shocked when they found out he was gay, but that doesn't affect his ability to run the station."

"I'd think Macklin would be the bigger shock."

Patrick chuckled. "Yes, but would *you* want to be the one to say something to his face?"

Jesse spewed beer as he tried to swallow and cough at the same time. "Hell, no," he said when he could speak without choking. "I don't have a death wish."

"And so life goes on as it always has," Patrick said. "Only with a little more tolerance."

"Yeah, I heard Neil's speech yesterday when we got here. He was very clear about what wouldn't be allowed in his hearing."

"Neil's a hothead who had a 'come to Jesus' moment when Caine risked his life to save Neil's during a bad storm over the winter."

"I've heard a couple references to that, but everybody knows the story so no one tells it."

"Long story short, Neil got trapped on the wrong side of a flooded gulley. Caine rode across and got him and nearly drowned on the way back across," Patrick recounted. "That's when we found out about Macklin too. I've known him since we got here, and I've never seen him like he was that day."

"How was that?"

"Scared."

Jesse couldn't imagine it, but he hadn't been here, so he didn't dispute it.

"That's how we knew it was something real, not just screwing around," Patrick added. "If anyone else had done what Caine did, Macklin might have yelled, but he wouldn't have been scared."

"I wonder if they would be as tolerant of someone other than Caine and Macklin," Jesse said.

"I think that would depend on the man," Patrick replied, "but it would take quite a drongo to say something derogatory, even about someone else, on a station run by two gay men. You don't have to worry about being run off."

"I wasn't, I mean, why do you think I'm talking about myself?" Jesse stumbled.

"Because if you'd been worried about Chris, you would have said so," Patrick replied. "I'll tell you the same thing I told everyone when Caine first came out to us. I don't care what you do with another consenting adult. I just don't want to hear about it, and I don't want Jason hearing about it. And before you get upset, I say the same thing to the jackaroos who spend the summer chasing the girls."

SIX

"CHRIS, I put toothpaste on your toothbrush for you already. I'm going down because I promised Jason I'd meet him early this morning."

"Thanks," Chris called as he struggled to get his shirt buttoned. He could have called Seth back and asked for help, but he hated not being able to do even the simplest tasks for himself. Like putting toothpaste on his toothbrush.

His ribs didn't hurt as badly after two weeks of working with Kami in the morning and handing Jesse and Patrick tools in the afternoon, but that didn't help any with the chunk of plaster on his arm that kept him from bending his elbow. "Bloody hell," he muttered as the final button on the shirt came loose while he was trying to fasten it. "Now I have to find a needle and thread and fix the stupid thing."

He sighed and stuck the button in his trouser pocket. He'd worry about that later. Right now he needed to brush his teeth and get downstairs to help Kami.

He grabbed the toothbrush from the edge of the sink where Seth left it and started to brush.

The taste nearly choked him. He spit, rinsed his mouth, and spit again. "What the hell?" he shouted. "Seth!"

Not thinking about Caine and Macklin possibly still asleep in their room down the hall, Chris tore down the stairs, determined to find his little brother and thrash him within an inch of his life. Practical jokes were one thing. Shaving cream on his toothbrush was plain old disgusting.

Seth wasn't anywhere in sight when Chris hit the main road through the station, which surprised Chris. Seth usually liked to hang around at a safe distance so he could see the results of his pranks. It often meant he got caught, but he said it wasn't any fun if he couldn't see the expression on people's faces. Since most of his pranks were mischievous rather than dangerous, getting caught usually meant a bit of yelling or being grounded for a few days, but nothing to actually dissuade him from the next one. Chris could deal with the pranks, even shaving cream on his toothbrush, as long as they were directed at him. He needed to find Seth and convince him playing pranks on anyone else was a recipe for disaster. He'd get a reputation as a troublemaker and suspicion would fall on him every time something bad happened, even if he wasn't involved.

"He's over here."

Jesse's voice drew Chris's attention.

"I caught him hiding in the shadows outside the bunkhouse," Jesse said, stepping into the pool of light from the light on the veranda. "I don't know what he was up to, but I figured it couldn't be anything good."

"He thought it would be funny to put shaving cream on my toothbrush," Chris told Jesse, the lingering taste making him want to spit again even though he'd washed his mouth out twice. "Like most everything else, I can't do it myself at the moment."

Jesse gave Seth a little shake. "Not cool," he said. "It might have been funny if he weren't hurt, but you don't take advantage of someone who's down and out. That isn't a joke. That's just cruel. It's like kicking a stray dog looking for scraps. Or ganging up on a guy five to one. You didn't think it was funny when those thugs hurt Chris. Why would you do the same thing to him?"

"I'm sorry," Seth said, his eyes downcast. "It's just, I've always played tricks on him. I thought it would make him laugh and it would be like old times."

"Go tell Kami what you did and see if he has a new toothbrush Chris can have," Jesse ordered, giving Seth a little push toward the house. "If he doesn't, you're going to give Chris yours and you're going to use his."

"Gross," Seth said.

"Then you'd better hope Kami gives you a new toothbrush," Jesse said.

"He didn't really mean to hurt me," Chris said when Seth was gone.

"I'm sure he didn't," Jesse agreed, "but he's outgrowing the age where he can get away with thoughtless pranks."

"I know he is," Chris said with a sigh, "but it's been a hard few months. I'm glad he has the chance to be a kid again, even if it won't last for long."

"He hasn't really said what happened that you ended up at the wrong end of somebody's fists in Yass," Jesse said.

"It's not a pretty story," Chris replied. "He doesn't like to talk about it."

"You don't either," Jesse surmised.

"There's not a lot to tell," Chris said. "Our mum died. Her husband kicked us out. We did what we had to do to survive and stay together. Then Caine and Macklin found us and here we are."

"Somehow I doubt it's that simple," Jesse said, "but I won't push. You'll tell me when you're ready."

Chris scrubbed his hand over his face, grimacing at the scraggly beard that had grown in since he'd last been able to shave. "It's not that I don't trust you," he said. "It's just... I don't like to think of it, you know? None of us come out of it looking good."

"Unless you're going to tell me you killed somebody for his wallet, you probably aren't going to say anything that would change how I see you," Jesse replied. "You kept your brother safe when it shouldn't have been your job."

More than a little uncomfortable with the praise when he was keenly aware of all the ways he'd let Seth down, Chris tried to change the subject. "I will be so glad when this bloody cast comes off. I can't even shave."

"I noticed you were getting a little scruffy there," Jesse said. "I know you have to help with breakfast now, but I'll help you shave tonight before bed if you want."

"Really?" Chris said, the thought of getting rid of the itchy beard enough to offset the nerves at the thought of someone else near his face with a razor.

"Sure," Jesse said. "It's not all that hot yet, but I still can't imagine trying to grow a beard going into summer. I can't swear it'll be the closest shave you've ever had, but I'm sure I can do better than you can with your left hand."

"I haven't even tried," Chris admitted. "I picked up the razor and it felt so awkward I was afraid to even start."

"Tonight," Jesse said.

"It's a date," Chris replied, flushing to the roots of his blond hair when he realized what he'd said. "Um, I mean…."

"I know what you mean," Jesse said with a laugh. "Go on inside before Kami starts shouting."

CHRIS spent the morning alternating between anticipating getting rid of the itchy stubble on his face and wondering what else might come of having Jesse shave him. The date comment had slipped out without conscious thought, but it wasn't like he hadn't thought about it. Some days it felt like he hadn't thought about anything else. Not that they could actually "date" out here in the outback, but it hadn't stopped Chris from fantasizing about Jesse.

The man was gorgeous, funny, kind, confident… everything Chris could possibly want in a man, and knowing he was gay too, even if he wasn't the least bit interested in Chris, had been enough to set off more erotic dreams than Chris could ever remember having all at once. Then again, when he'd been in town, he'd figured out where to go when he needed relief. A quick blow job in the back room of a bar usually took the edge off. Until his mum died, anyway. It had gotten harder after he and Seth were on his own. Harder to leave, harder to justify the cost of even a few beers, harder to indulge his own selfish needs when Seth was shivering under a blanket that was far too thin in a drafty flat with insufficient heating.

He shook his head against the maudlin thoughts. Those days were over. For one thing, it was spring heading into summer. It wouldn't be cold for much longer, even up here in the tablelands. More importantly, though, the station house, while simple, was solidly built and comfortable. Seth would be safe here, even if Chris arranged to go into town for a weekend. Jesse could probably tell him where he could find a place to hook up. He hadn't worked out of Boorowa before, but Cowra wasn't that much farther away, and Chris did have his car. Assuming Caine and Macklin would give him a weekend off.

Or there was Jesse himself. He was gay, unattached as far as Chris knew, and just as alone out here as Chris was. He'd laughed at Chris's date comment, but he hadn't actually rejected it out of hand. Chris certainly couldn't deny his own attraction. More mornings than not since they'd met, he'd come awake hard as a rock with Jesse's face haunting him. Jerking off with his left hand was about as awkward as trying to shave with his left hand, but he'd done it anyway. He hadn't had a choice if he wanted his pants to fit right. And now, knowing that in a few hours he'd have Jesse alone in that little bathroom, Jesse's hands on his face as he shaved Chris, smearing shaving cream, running the razor over his cheeks, checking for stray whiskers….

"If you're done daydreaming over there, we have a meal to prepare," Kami said, snapping Chris out of his fantasy.

Chris blinked a couple of times and went back to awkwardly slicing potatoes for the au gratin Kami had decided to make for dinner. He could think about Jesse later.

When he'd finished his hours in the kitchen and Kami ordered him out, Chris debated what to do next. He'd gotten in the habit of hanging out with Jesse and the other mechanics because he liked Jesse and because that was usually where he could find Seth. He didn't think Seth would get up to his usual tricks with the other jackaroos, but he couldn't be entirely sure. Today, though, with his slip of the tongue that morning and the thought of Jesse shaving him that evening both in the forefront of his thoughts, Chris wasn't sure it was such a good idea. He'd end up either saying something else to embarrass himself, or he wouldn't say anything (to avoid saying something embarrassing) and Jesse would wonder what was wrong with him.

Fate took that choice from his hands when he left the kitchen and found Seth waiting for him. "Come on," Seth said. "I have to show you something."

Chris followed him dutifully toward the shed where the mechanics were still working on the tractor. He had no idea what Seth might want to show him since he didn't know one end of an engine from the other, but his brother was clearly excited. Chris would be appropriately excited for him.

"Look!" Seth said when they entered the shed to a chorus of greetings from Patrick, Jesse, and the other two mechanics. He held up a tiny piece of machinery. "I found the problem!"

Chris glanced at Jesse for confirmation. He knew Seth loved machines, but to have found something four more experienced men had missed was impressive. Jesse nodded slightly. "That's great, Seth!"

Seth started gushing about what he'd done and how he'd figured it out.

"You don't have the slightest idea what he's talking about, do you?" Jesse said at Chris's shoulder.

"Not a word," Chris replied, "but he's proud and happy, and everyone else seems impressed so he obviously did something right."

"He did. Now we can fix the broken piece and put this monster back together again. Macklin will be pleased."

That was encouraging. If Seth proved his worth as a mechanic, maybe Caine and Macklin would overlook Chris's own lack of contributions to the station to date.

"Smile," Jesse said. "Seth's going to think you aren't happy for him."

Chris hadn't realized he'd stopped smiling. "Sorry," he said, restoring a more positive expression. "I just seem to be in a down mood today."

"It's got to be hard, not being able to do stuff for yourself," Jesse said. "I think you're coping really well."

"Really?" Chris asked, tickled that Jesse thought so highly of him. "I barely feel like I'm keeping my head above water."

"But you *are* keeping it above water and that's the important thing," Jesse said. "Even when it doesn't feel that way."

"Thanks," Chris said, his smile becoming more genuine. "That makes me feel better."

"You'll feel even better when we get that rat's nest off your face this afternoon."

"It's not that bad!" Chris protested, rubbing at the scraggly beard with his left hand. "Is it?"

"No, it's not bad at all," Jesse said. "It makes you look a little rough around the edges. Some guys even find that sexy."

"Some guys?" Chris repeated, wondering if he should leave the scruff after all.

"Yeah, but not me," Jesse said. "Whisker burn is a real turn off for me. Call me a nancy boy if you want, but it's smooth skin all the way for me."

"Just on the face or smooth all over?" Chris asked, wondering if he'd have to start waxing his chest. The thought of it made him want to wince, but if he had a chance with Jesse, he wouldn't blow it over that.

"Body hair is fine," Jesse said. "It's got a different texture than a beard, not as sharp."

Chris hoped he managed to hide his relief both at not being inherently unattractive to Jesse and at not having to consider waxing in order to have a hope of catching Jesse's attention.

"Have a seat if you want," Jesse said. "Now that we know what's wrong, we should spend at least a few hours repairing it, but we'll get you fixed up before dinner too."

Chris smiled and took his habitual seat by the tool box. He still couldn't make heads or tails of the engine, but he'd learned enough to hand Jesse what he needed most of the time.

FOUR hours later, the pile of metal had started to look like an engine again, Patrick, Jesse, and the other mechanics were covered in grease and grime, and Chris was about ready to come out of his skin with anticipation. He'd focused on Jesse's hands as he worked, watching the way they moved so dexterously over the machinery. He wanted to feel those hands on him. He'd settle for having them on his face, but he'd dream of more now that he'd noticed them.

Handing the last of his tools back to Chris, Jesse wiped his hands on a greasy rag. "Shall we go get you sorted before dinner?" Jesse asked. "I'd like to have time to take a shower."

"Sure," Chris said, doing his best to hide his growing anticipation. "Or you can shower first if you want. Even if you end up helping me after dinner instead of before, that's fine with me."

"I'll help you first," Jesse said. "Let me just wash my hands."

Chris shifted from one foot to the other, trying to conceal the tension in the pit of his stomach. Jesse took his time scrubbing his hands with the industrial strength soap they kept in the machine shed to cut the grease, taking extra care with his fingernails and around his cuticles. Chris had never paid such close attention before, so he didn't know if Jesse always spent this much time cleaning up or if this was extra effort for Chris's sake. Chris couldn't decide which option he preferred. It spoke well of Jesse that he made the effort to get his hands clean at the end of the day, but at the same time, Chris wanted to be special enough in Jesse's eyes to merit extra cleaning.

Finally, Jesse turned off the water and dried his hands. "That's about as clean as they're going to get."

Chris couldn't see any trace of grease left. "Looks good to me. I, um, I guess we should go back to the station house. All my stuff is there."

"It'll be more comfortable there than trying to do it in the bunkhouse with all the other jackaroos around," Jesse agreed. "No need to give them something to talk about."

Chris remembered the way the jackaroos had speculated on Caine and Macklin's relationship. "Do they do that a lot? Talk about the bosses?"

"No," Jesse replied as they walked toward the house. "They rag on each other far more than on the bosses. Neil shuts down any discussion of Caine, even joking ones, faster than you can blink, and the others don't fight him on it. The love lives of the other jackaroos are fair game, though. Even Neil's."

Chris grinned. "Neil?"

"He's apparently gone on one of the jillaroos who came back again this summer," Jesse explained. "Since he won't let them talk about Caine and Macklin, they talk about him instead, and his authority doesn't seem to extend to keeping them from that."

"He better watch it or they'll stop listening when he says something about Caine and Macklin."

"I think that's why he doesn't shut them down when they talk about him." Jesse stopped on the veranda. "I haven't been inside the station house before."

"It's just a house," Chris said, opening the door for Jesse. "A nice one, but just a house. You're helping me out. I'm sure they won't mind."

They left their boots at the door and climbed the stairs to the bathroom. Chris handed Jesse the shaving cream and his neglected razor. "I put a new blade on it earlier today so it should be sharp."

"Good." Jesse sprayed some shaving cream into his palm. "You might want to take your shirt off so I don't get this all over your clothes by accident."

Chris frowned, not wanting Jesse to see him struggling with the buttons, but Jesse was right. He couldn't shave himself without dripping water and shaving foam everywhere. He'd be soaked through and then have to deal with the shirt after it was wet. He popped the first button one-handed, but the second one was more difficult.

"Here, let me help," Jesse offered. He rinsed the shaving cream off his hand quickly and reached for the buttons. Chris froze at the brush of hard knuckles against his sternum as Jesse worked his way down the front of Chris's shirt. He'd torn his shirt off over his head in the heat of passion before or even had a hookup pull it off, but no one had ever undressed him like this, slow and careful like he mattered. He swallowed around the constriction in his throat, hoping he wouldn't sprout wood while Jesse's hands were near his belt. That would be too embarrassing.

Chris started to pull away when Jesse finished undoing the buttons and reached for the collar of his shirt to help him pull it off, but he wanted the sensation of Jesse undressing him, even if only to shave him. By the time Jesse got his shirt off, Chris's skin tingled from the cool air and the brush of Jesse's hands, and his cock had woken up and taken notice of the proceedings.

"Okay, let's see about getting you cleaned up," Jesse said. The ease in his words relieved Chris's worry that Jesse would be as tense about the situation as Chris was. Chris turned back around to face Jesse, his heart pounding as the other man smeared shaving cream over his cheeks and around his mouth. His hands were gentle, taking care not to get the foam in Chris's nose or on his lips, which only made Chris's lips tingle more. Jesse's face was so close as he bent in to start shaving Chris, the rasp of the razor loud in the otherwise silent room.

Chris did his best to keep his breathing slow and steady so he wouldn't jostle Jesse's hand and end up with a cut on his face, but his pulse raced even faster when Jesse tilted his head to the side so he could work his way along Chris's jaw and down his neck. He couldn't stop the shiver that went through him when Jesse ran his fingers over the shaved skin, checking for stray whiskers.

"Cold?" Jesse asked sympathetically. "It is a bit cool in here, now that I think about it."

"I'm fine," Chris said, his voice hoarser than usual.

Jesse's fingers caught on a patch of stubble he'd missed. He leaned closer as he ran the razor over it again, and Chris caught a whiff of sweat, machine oil, and cologne. He couldn't place the scent exactly, but his body reacted to it. He gripped the edge of the sink behind him with his good hand as he resisted the urge to reach for Jesse. Not until he had some indication the other man wanted Chris the way Chris wanted him.

"Okay, that side's done," Jesse said, his voice sounding different enough to Chris's ears that he looked up. Jesse's green eyes were darker than usual, and his gaze seemed even more intent. Chris swallowed hard.

"Thanks."

"Turn the other way now."

Jesse's fingers felt hot on Chris's freshly shaved skin as they guided his head to the right so Jesse could start shaving the left side of Chris's face. The razor connected and scraped across Chris's cheek, but Jesse's fingers stayed where they were, not holding Chris in place, just… touching.

Chris closed his eyes. Watching Jesse shave him was too much. He'd end up doing something stupid like blurting out how much he really wanted Jesse to kiss him right now, or maybe throw him down on the bathroom floor and fuck him silly. He'd take either one and be thrilled.

The razor's movements stopped, followed again by the brush of Jesse's fingers over the newly shaved skin. He shivered again, a little gasp escaping. His eyes flew open, searching Jesse's face for any sign he'd heard it, only to find Jesse far closer than when he'd closed his eyes. Jesse's thumb brushed over Chris's chin, the nail just skirting his lower lip, and Chris lost his battle for control, another little moan sounding in his throat.

Jesse hovered at that slight distance for a moment, his eyes searching Chris's face—for what, Chris didn't know. Whatever he saw must have reassured him, because he closed the space between them, his lips covering Chris's in a tender kiss.

Chris froze, afraid to move for fear of running Jesse off, but the contact continued, Jesse's lips moving lightly over his, asking for a kiss in return but demanding nothing. It was everything a kiss was supposed to be and nothing like anything Chris had experienced in his backroom pickups. His lips parted of their own accord, offering Jesse more if he wanted it. Jesse's tongue swiped once over Chris's lower lip, but he didn't invade Chris's mouth or otherwise change the tenor of the kiss.

Needing something to steady himself, Chris reached instinctively for Jesse, drawing him closer with a hand to his hip. Jesse moved in, his body hemming Chris in, leaving him feeling surrounded. With a different man, he might have felt trapped, but he wanted to be exactly where he was far too much for that to bother him now. Jesse's shirt rasped against Chris's skin, the buttons pulling a little as they got tangled in Chris's chest hair. The little tugs only served to remind Chris that he was half-naked while Jesse was still fully clothed. Saying anything about it would have required ending the kiss, so he let his good hand speak for him, tugging at the tail of Jesse's shirt to loosen it from his waistband.

"Chris, are you upstairs?"

Caine's voice shattered the moment. Jesse pulled back enough to let Chris answer without releasing him completely. Chris struggled for something to say, but getting his voice to work at all was a challenge.

"Yes," he finally managed to call back down to Caine.

"Okay, just checking. I saw boots and weren't sure whose they were."

"I should go," Jesse said, his voice warm as he leaned forward and rubbed his stubbled cheek against Chris's smooth one. "We don't want the boss to come upstairs and find us making out. Can you wash the last of the shaving cream off by yourself?"

Chris wanted to say no so he could keep Jesse there a little longer, but that was selfish, and Caine was downstairs and could come upstairs at any time. While Chris didn't think Caine would have a problem with Jesse helping him shave, he didn't know how Caine would feel about Jesse doing other things to him, and that's what certainly would have happened if they hadn't been interrupted.

"I'm sure I can manage," Chris said. "I'll see you at dinner?"

"I'll be there," Jesse said with that warm, crooked smile that did things to Chris's insides. "And after dinner, we'll find somewhere a little more private to finish what we started. If you're interested, of course."

Interested? Hell, yes, he was interested!

"Tell me where and when," Chris said, not even caring how breathless and eager he sounded. "I, um, I don't have any condoms."

Jesse chuckled, the sound so masculine and self-assured that Chris felt his toes curl in anticipation. "We'll figure something out." He leaned back in and kissed Chris again, quickly. "See you at dinner."

SEVEN

JESSE waited until he was outside putting on his boots to start whistling, figuring he didn't need to attract Caine's attention on his way out. He hadn't done anything wrong. Chris was of age, and everything that had happened had been mutual, but Caine might not see it that way, and arguing with the boss was a sure way to kill the buzz of desire from the kiss and from the thought of meeting Chris later to see what else they could get up to.

Mentally Jesse ransacked his bag, trying to remember if he had any condoms left. He'd stocked up when he got to Melbourne last fall, but that was several months ago, and he'd burned off a little steam since then.

He thought he still had a few, but it might be wise to join the next supply run to Boorowa. He could get whatever the station needed and pick up a few extras for himself.

He adjusted his hat on his head as he left the veranda and stepped out into the sun. It wasn't late enough in the year to be hot yet, but the rays were no less bright, and Jesse had to walk due west to get to the bunkhouse. He glanced around as he walked, scouting likely locations for continuing what he and Chris had started in the bathroom. The bunkhouse would be crowded after dinner, all the jackaroos hanging out in the main room to relax a little before going to bed. The sheds where they sheared the sheep would be quiet, but Jesse figured they'd spend enough time there as the summer went on. He'd wait to deal with the smell of animals until then.

The station boasted a number of small houses, presumably for the families that lived on site. Macklin had made a comment about the foreman's house standing empty, but Jesse had no idea which one that was, and he had no desire at all to get busted sneaking in there, with or without Chris.

That left the machine shed or the canteen.

They had to eat in the canteen, which left the machine shed.

It had the advantage of being somewhat secluded from the rest of the buildings, plus no one was likely to go there after hours.

Reaching the bunkhouse, Jesse went into his room and gathered his kit for a shower. He was covered in sweat and grease and need. The shower might not do anything for the need, but his body would at least be clean.

He stripped down and wrapped a towel around his waist as he headed to the shower block the jackaroos shared. Fortunately the space was empty, the other men already finished or not yet back from the day's chores, so Jesse didn't have to worry about anyone taking exception to his presence or accusing him of staring or any of the dozen other problems he'd had on previous stations. Maybe it wouldn't happen here, with the more tolerant attitude, but Jesse saw no reason to take chances when showering at off times would avoid any problems.

He turned the water on as hot as he could stand. It helped cut the grease, but more than that, it burned away some of the tension in his neck and shoulders. Shaving someone else was not at all like shaving himself, and he'd tensed up in his effort not to cut Chris's face. Even after he'd finished, the tension hadn't faded, replaced by the effort of holding back, of going slow. Fat lot of good that had done him. He'd given in and kissed Chris anyway. He hadn't been able to help it, not with Chris's eyes closed so trustingly and his lips parted slightly.

And the little sounds he kept making.

Jesse groaned remembering them. He had no idea how he'd be able to face Chris at the dinner table without dragging him off somewhere private for another kiss. Chris had felt too good beneath his hands, his face smooth, his chest dusted with light blond hair, so light it was barely visible against his fair skin. The bandages around his ribs hid his abs and treasure trail, but they didn't hide his pecs or his nipples, a light, delicate color to match everything but Chris's eyes.

Jesse rested his forehead against the shower wall. He had to get a grip on himself—not that kind!—or he'd never be able to face Chris later. He had no idea what kind of experience Chris had, but one way or another, Jesse had to be the one in control. Even if they were just messing around, he didn't want to do anything to hurt the kid. He'd been hurt enough already, both physically and emotionally.

Grabbing the shampoo, he scrubbed at his short dark hair. He'd all but shaved it before he came to Yass, but it would be long again by the end of the summer. Done with his hair, he lathered up the soap and did his best to remove all traces of grease from his body. It was a lost cause while they still had machinery to repair, but he tried anyway, although he supposed grease was better than sheep dung. They'd start the shearing soon and then he'd really be filthy, but they had to repair the tractor first or they wouldn't have any way of hauling off the wool as they got it ready for processing. The utes could haul a small trailer, but nothing like what they'd need for the quantity of wool a spread like this one would produce. Jesse had seen the pens around the valley. Lang Downs had a lot of sheep.

He rinsed off and soaked up the water with the towel. He wrapped it around his waist and was heading back to his room when he heard someone calling his name.

"Hi, Patrick," he said. "I was just finishing my shower."

"Well, come by my place when you get dressed," Patrick said. "I fired up the barbie to celebrate fixing the bloody tractor."

"It's not fixed yet," Jesse pointed out.

"Close enough," Patrick said. "All we have to do is put the engine back together."

"Are Chris and Seth coming?"

"I hadn't invited them, but I can if you think I should."

"I don't know about Seth," Jesse said. "He might rather eat in the canteen with Jason, but I bet Chris would appreciate being included with the men."

WHEN Chris came down to the canteen for dinner, he found Jesse lounging in the doorway. "There you are," he said, his eyes raking Chris from head to toe. "Patrick invited us over to his house for a barbie. Seth wanted to stay and eat with Jason, but I thought you might enjoy it."

Chris grinned, all his nerves—all the worried ones, anyway; the anticipation ones were still on high alert—fading at the sight of Jesse's sexy grin. "I could handle a barbie," he said. "What's he cooking?"

"He didn't say, but I figure it'll be a nice change of pace from the canteen," Jesse said, stepping aside so Chris could join him outside. "Not that Kami's cooking is bad, but it's a beaut night. We can sit around, drink a few beers, watch the stars come out."

Sneak away somewhere private? Chris thought hopefully, but he kept the words to himself. He didn't want to appear too eager. Never mind that he was still half-hard from the kiss earlier.

The smell of smoke from the grill grew stronger as they crossed the station toward Patrick's house. "Dinner shouldn't be long, it smells like," Jesse said.

"Good," Chris replied. "I'm starved."

When they reached Patrick's, Jesse led Chris around to the back so they wouldn't tromp through the house in their dusty boots. The other mechanics were all there already, boots propped up on the deck rail as they sipped their beers and laughed and joked with the familiarity of men who had worked together for years. Chris was glad Jesse was there with him because he would have been the outsider for sure otherwise.

"Chris, glad you could join us," Patrick said with a wave from his place by the grill. "Grab a beer. Make yourself at home."

"Thanks, mate," Chris said. He got a beer, although Jesse had to help him open it, and settled in one of the porch chairs. Jesse sat across from him, joining the conversation with the other mechanics, but Chris didn't mind. Their relative positions gave him an excuse to stare at

Jesse without being obvious about it, and if the number of times he caught Jesse looking back at him was any indication, Jesse'd had the same thought when he sat down.

Then Jesse lifted his beer to his mouth, eyes locked on Chris's face as he closed his lips around the mouth of the bottle, sliding it in and out just the slightest bit before tipping it up and taking a drink. Chris gulped, lust curling in his gut at the sight. Jesse swallowed and winked at Chris before returning to the conversation, and Chris thought he'd go up in flames. Just spontaneously self-combust right there.

Determined not to let Jesse get the better of him—the jackaroo might be older, but Chris was no inexperienced kid—Chris lifted his own beer to his mouth, rolling the rim of the glass back and forth along his lower lip, waiting for Jesse to turn his way before licking a drop of beer off the bottle. He swore he saw sparks flare in Jesse's eyes.

He rocked onto the back legs of his chair and grinned in triumph. He might be susceptible to Jesse's flirting, but Jesse was just as susceptible to him. Oh, this was going to be fun.

"The meat's ready," Patrick called. "Grab some plates and come serve yourselves. Carley made some side dishes and there's more beer as well as soda or tea if you'd prefer that."

Chris set his beer on the table, wondering how he'd manage to hold a plate and serve himself at the same time with his bad arm when Jesse smiled at him. God, it was hard not to imagine that mouth doing things to him when Jesse winked at him again. "Get your plate and tell me what you want," Jesse said. "I'll fill you up."

Chris narrowed his eyes, but Jesse smiled at him, daring him to say anything. Chris just nodded, not trusting himself to do anything but beg Jesse to do exactly that, right now. "Later," he finally croaked.

"Later for sure," Jesse agreed, focusing in on Chris's backside. Chris swore he felt the caress like a touch, but Jesse's hands were at his side, not anywhere near the seat of Chris's jeans. He cleared his throat and tried to adjust himself discreetly. The last thing he needed was for the others to notice his hard-on. He didn't care if Jesse noticed. Hell, he hoped Jesse would do a lot more than notice before the night was over! He just didn't want the other mechanics ragging on him for it.

Fortunately no one but Jesse seemed to pay any attention to Chris's slightly awkward gait as he crossed the yard to where Patrick and Carley had the food laid out.

"What'll you have?" Jesse asked. "Steak, snags, rissoles, ooh, is that lamb?"

"You'll be tired of lamb before the summer's over," Patrick joked.

Jesse shook his head. "I never get tired of lamb. What do you want, Chris?"

"A couple of snags and a rissole," Chris said. "That salad looks good, and fresh potato salad? I haven't had that since before my mum got sick."

Jesse loaded up Chris's plate with meat and fixings, all without further comment, but Chris had no illusions the innuendo was done. He only hoped he could give as good as he got.

Back at the table, Chris nearly choked on his beer when Jesse picked up a whole sausage and put the tip in his mouth, grinning around it before biting off a mouthful.

"So, Chris," Carley said, sitting down next to Jesse, fortunately after he'd put the snag back on his plate, "where are you from?"

"Adelaide," Chris said, "but we left a while back. Mum got sick and couldn't keep her job. We ended up in Canberra because that's where her husband's family was, but after she died, there wasn't anything to keep us there."

"You didn't want to stay with your stepfather?" Carley asked.

"Carley," Patrick said, joining them. "Let the boy eat. You can give him the third degree later."

Chris shot Patrick a grateful smile. He really didn't want to talk about Tony, but maybe it would be better to get it all out in the open once and for all. Then people wouldn't always be looking for casual ways to ask about it.

"We weren't his kids," Chris said after a few bites, not looking up as he spoke. He didn't want to see their reactions. "After Mum died, he told us to get out. He hadn't ever adopted either of us or anything, so legally he didn't have to take care of us. We tried staying in Canberra, but we couldn't find a place we could afford, so we started moving inland. That's how we ended up in Yass, and now here."

"Oh, baby, I'm so sorry," Carley said, reaching across the table and squeezing his hand. "Somebody ought to take a stick to him for being so cruel."

Chris summoned a smile, trying not to let her see how close to tears he was. Jesse's foot nudged his beneath the table. Chris looked his way, and Jesse rubbed his foot against Chris's ankle. The silent support, flirting, whatever Jesse intended it to be, settled Chris again, and he was able to give Carley a real smile. "It's over. Seth is safe, and we're together. That's all that matters."

"Spoken like a real man," Patrick said approvingly. "You'll do fine here, Chris. We'll make a stockman out of you before long."

"As soon as I get rid of this," Chris said, lifting his cast. "Can't do a lot of work with this slowing me down."

"We'll keep you busy, don't you worry, mate," Jesse said.

THE look on Chris's face as he told Carley about his mother had killed Jesse's hard-on completely. He'd gone from wanting to push Chris into the nearest dark corner to wanting to stand between him and the world and demand the world stop knocking him down. Then Chris had rallied and Jesse had relaxed a little, but the desire from earlier in the day stayed on the back burner.

As everyone said their goodnights to Patrick and Carley, Jesse hovered near Chris's side. Once they'd finished with the social niceties, Jesse gestured for Chris to follow him away from the bunkhouse so they could talk without anyone else listening in.

"You okay?" Jesse asked when they were alone.

Chris shrugged. "I guess so. It's no fun talking about it, but now everyone knows, so maybe that'll be the end of it."

"I don't know if Carley will let it go at that," Jesse said, "but most of the men won't care one way or another. Jackaroos tend not to pry into other people's business because more than a few of us have pasts of our own we'd rather not discuss."

"You included?"

"Me included," Jesse said, although if Chris asked, he'd tell him. Deciding to change the subject, he pointed upward. "Look at that sky. Have you ever seen stars like that? You can see a few of them in Melbourne, but nothing like this."

Chris looked up obediently. Jesse stepped up directly behind him so he could guide Chris's gaze to the different constellations. "There's the Southern Cross," he said. "And Capricorn and Aquarius right overhead."

Chris turned his head to follow where Jesse was pointing, leaning back against Jesse so trustingly that Jesse almost told him to stop, to choose someone better to rely on that way, but Chris's body was warm against his in the cool evening air, and Jesse couldn't stop the memories of how good it had felt to kiss Chris earlier in the day.

"What else is up there?" Chris asked.

"The Milky Way, of course," Jesse said. "Pisces is just above the horizon, that way." He pointed to the east. "And the Magellanic Clouds are just a little to the left of it."

"How'd you learn so much about the stars?" Chris asked. "I remember hearing some of it in school, but not enough to remember it."

"I've spent a lot of lonely nights out with the sheep," Jesse replied. "Not much to do out there but stare at the stars. I got curious, so I started looking things up. What you can see changes from season to season, so it never gets boring. At least not to me."

Chris turned in Jesse's half embrace, his arms settling on Jesse's hips. "You'll have to show me more another time."

"Anytime you want," Jesse offered. Chris's closeness had a predictable effect, but Jesse savored the sweetness of the moment instead of rushing headlong into the heat. They had all summer. They didn't have to jump straight into bed, or a pile of hay, as the case may be.

Chris seemed to share Jesse's feelings, leaning up for a soft kiss that was an end in itself rather than the prelude to something more. Their lips met, parted, met again, and clung this time, tender and evocative without being demanding. Jesse could sense Chris's willingness to have it go farther, faster, deeper, but he held back, and Chris followed his lead, keeping the contact light and soft. Reassuring more than needy.

After a moment, Jesse pulled back slightly, resting his forehead against Chris's, but no longer kissing him. "What are we doing?"

"Enjoying each other's company," Chris replied, his voice breathy.

It was both more and less of an answer than Jesse had hoped for. Chris hadn't asked for declarations or promises that Jesse couldn't give, which should have been a relief, but a kernel of selfishness inside him wanted Chris to want more. It had been so long since anyone had wanted Jesse for himself rather than for a hot night or a casual fling. Then again, Chris wasn't pushing him against the wall or into the machine shed to demand more. He was enjoying this moment *with Jesse* exactly as it was, so maybe he did want, if not more, then at least something beyond a one-night stand.

"We should probably go inside," Jesse said. "You have to get up early in the morning. Kami will be expecting you."

"In a minute," Chris said, tipping his head for another kiss. Jesse gave it willingly, enjoying the smoothness of Chris's lips beneath his. The weight of the cast gave Chris's embrace a lopsided feel, but that only served to remind Jesse who he was with. Not some random guy he'd picked up at a bar, but Chris, his friend, maybe even his friend with benefits.

But not tonight. The mood wasn't right to bring it up, and Jesse far preferred the comfort between them to a quick tumble that would spoil this for good.

When Chris finally stepped back, Jesse let him go. "I'll see you at breakfast?"

"I'll be there," Chris promised.

EIGHT

CHRIS was all but whistling as he walked into the kitchen the next morning. Kami gave him a suspicious look, but Chris ignored it, starting the eggs for breakfast without waiting to be told. After several weeks of working in the kitchen, he knew the routine.

"Someone's in a good mood this morning," Kami said after a few minutes. "If I didn't know where you spent the night last night, I'd think you'd gotten lucky."

"Luck comes in all different forms," Chris replied. His lips were still buzzing from the kisses he and Jesse had shared. He'd resisted the urge to jerk off last night and again this morning, hoping to feel Jesse's hand sooner than later. Not before tonight, obviously, since they had to work today, but Chris had spent the night dreaming about Jesse and all the things he wanted the jackaroo to do to him.

Kami hummed in reply, and Chris went on with his work and his daydreaming, hoping he'd do enough work to satisfy Kami so the cook wouldn't ask about the daydreaming.

They got breakfast ready, and Chris even managed to flirt a bit with Jesse across the serving line. Once the jackaroos had headed out for the day and Chris went back into the kitchen to start the lunch preparations, Kami cornered him. "Sit down."

Chris swallowed nervously. "Yes, sir?"

Kami rolled his eyes. "Don't give me that 'sir' bit. I'm not your father, thank all the gods. You want to tell me what's going on?"

"Going on?" Chris asked. He didn't want to have this conversation. He didn't know what was going on with him and Jesse for one thing, but more than that, he didn't want to share it with anyone. It was too new, too precious. Even if it was nothing but harmless flirtation, it was his, and he didn't want to spoil that by sharing it.

"I'm not blind," Kami said. "I recognize infatuation when I see it. Caine walked around with the same look on his face when he and Macklin started getting together."

"I'm not infatuated," Chris protested.

"Then what would you call it?" Kami asked. "You don't know him, whoever he is, well enough to be in love with him. You've only been here a couple of weeks, and you've hardly spent any time with anyone other than your brother."

Chris didn't reply.

"It must be that new one who's been helping Patrick out," Kami said. "Dark hair, green eyes, bit of a swagger. Jesse, maybe?"

"He doesn't swagger," Chris protested.

"That is the one then," Kami said. "You defend him like Caine defended Macklin, even before anyone knew they were together. That boy's been to a few stations, I'd wager, based on the easy way he fit in here. He's going to be skittish as a sheep with a pair of dingoes on its heels. He's used to the way other stations work, not the way Lang Downs does."

"And how is that different?"

Kami laughed, the sound nearly rusty. "You think every station boss treats his employees like family? You need to go spend a few days at Taylor Peak. You don't know how lucky you were that Seth found Caine and Macklin and not some other grazier and his men. They might have saved you out of a sense of fair play, but you'd have been left in the hospital with nowhere to go and nothing to do when you lost whatever shite job you had. Instead you're living in the big house, working part of the day while your brother goes to school and learns a trade that will make him an asset on every station from here to Perth. Jesse, he's used to being an employee at best, and if they find out he's a poofter, that's the end of even that much place on a station. You can't blame him for protecting himself."

"But you said Lang Downs isn't like that."

"It isn't," Kami agreed, "but he's been here only as long as you have, not enough to trust it even if he's begun to see it. It goes against everything he's learned to expect."

"So what do I do?"

"Well, now that depends on you and on what happened between you and on what you want," Kami said.

"It would help if I knew," Chris replied honestly.

"You're young," Kami said. "No one expects you to have all the answers, but just think a little about Jesse and his experiences and what he might be feeling right now. Right or wrong, he sees a kid who's just been beaten half to death for being gay, a kid who's barely had a chance to live and then had to take on responsibility for his brother, a kid who's maybe had a sweet first love or maybe had a few one-nighters, but a kid who has a lot of living to do before he's ready to grow up and settle down."

"So what do I do?" Chris repeated. "I'm lost here."

"Forget about Jesse for a minute," Kami said. "You can't decide what to do about him until you decide what to do about yourself. He's chosen his path in life. He's a jackaroo. That doesn't mean he'll always be a drifter, but it means he'll always be on a station somewhere, isolated, living with the land, dependent on the weather and the seasons, and if he doesn't find a station to settle on, it could mean he'll never have a real home. Most jackaroos settle somewhere eventually or they get tired of the life and do something else instead. He hasn't given up yet, and he's older than most who decide to get out, so this is his life. You're younger, though. You've barely had a chance to experience life yet, much less decide what you want out of it."

"I know what I don't want," Chris said, because that much was true. "I don't want to be hungry again. I don't want to worry about having a place to live or enough money to pay the rent. I want a place I can trust, people I can trust to be there when I need them."

Kami didn't reply right away, but he leaned back a little and looked around the room. "The old man founded this station seventy-five years ago on a wish and prayer and on the belief that there was a better life ahead. He took the land no one else wanted and turned it into something good and lasting. He knew every jackaroo who came through here, even the ones who only stayed a summer. He paid every one of them a fair wage for their work and made a home for those who wanted more than just a summer's work. You have to decide if this can be your home, if this is the life you want, but Caine honors his uncle's legacy."

"It can't be that easy," Chris said.

"Why not?" Kami asked.

"Because... because they don't know me? Because I don't know anything about sheep? Because I'm just a kid they rescued from his own stupidity? Because nobody ever wants me around anyway?" The last bit was out before he could stop it. He groaned when he realized what he'd said, letting his head fall to his arms on the counter, hiding from Kami's reaction.

The hand that patted his shoulder was awkward but comforting nonetheless, giving Chris the courage to peek up at Kami. The expression on the older man's face was the exact opposite of the derision and pity he expected. Instead he saw such sympathy he nearly lost his control over the tears that threatened.

"Nobody wanted me until I got here," Kami said softly. "Nobody wanted Macklin. Neil was kicked off more stations than you can count for picking fights with other jackaroos. Even Caine thought nobody really wanted him until he got here, and you think any of us knew anything about sheep? Well, except maybe Neil since he'd worked at other stations first. Caine had never even been on a farm before, much less on a working sheep station. It's your choice, Chris, just like it was all of ours. Maybe Lang Downs isn't the right place for you. It isn't the right place for everyone—it never has been—but don't lump us in with all the people in your past who judged you for whatever reason. There's no judgment here. If you want to learn, Macklin will teach you. If you want to stay, Caine will find a place for you. You'll work harder for them than you've ever worked in your life, probably harder than you'd work at any other station because they expect more of their men, but you'll never miss a meal, you'll never be without friends, and you'll never worry about having a roof over your head, because that isn't the way we work around here. We take care of our own, and all you have to do is claim your place."

"If that's true, then this is heaven on earth," Chris murmured.

"Welcome to paradise," Kami replied, his face so serious Chris could almost believe it was real.

Almost.

"Go follow Neil around today instead of hanging out with the mechanics," Kami said. "You can't do much with the sheep, but you can learn the commands to talk to the dogs. If you're going to stay, you'll need to know how to work with all the animals, unless you're planning on being my kitchen slave for life."

JESSE told himself he wasn't looking for Chris as he walked toward the canteen for dinner, but Chris hadn't come to the machine shed that afternoon as had become his habit, and Jesse didn't know quite what to make of that. He didn't want to think he'd done something to alienate Chris already. The kissing and the potential for more aside, Jesse enjoyed Chris's company. The rest was icing on the cake. He'd missed Chris that afternoon, missed his smile as he handed Jesse tools and his conversation as he kept Jesse company and tried to pretend he understood some of what the mechanics were talking about as they worked.

Seth and Jason had been absent that afternoon as well, probably stuck at the computer doing schoolwork, leaving only Patrick and the other two mechanics, somewhat older men who knew each other from years of working side by side and didn't feel the need to fill the time with idle conversation. Fortunately they'd finished rebuilding the tractor engine that afternoon, so shearing would start in the morning. It would be at least a week of grueling, sweaty work, but it would be outside with the other jackaroos, and it would keep him too busy to think about Chris and how innocently trusting he'd been in Jesse's arms.

He shouldn't have been able to pick Chris's laughter out of the mixture of voices around him as all the jackaroos headed in for dinner, but he heard it clear as a bell, cutting through the deeper tones of the older men. Jesse couldn't stop the impulse to look around and find Chris. To his surprise, Chris was kneeling down next to Neil, playing with the old kelpie who was never far from Neil's side. Jesse had seen how protective Neil was of his dog—a mutual sentiment from what he could tell—which only added to his shock.

"Come, Max," Chris called playfully, running a few steps from where Neil watched, grinning. The dog looked up at Neil, clearly asking permission, but the moment it was given, he shot off after Chris, nipping at his heels. Chris laughed louder and kept running.

"You should go join them," Caine said, startling Jesse out of his spying.

"What?"

"Max loves to play, especially when he hasn't spent the day herding sheep. Tomorrow evening he'll be too tired to run this way, since he and Neil will spend the day driving sheep into the pen for shearing and then out to the paddocks to head out of the valley in a few days, but he'll wear Chris out in no time. Not to mention, I'm not sure Chris should be running that way with his ribs."

"He said he was feeling a lot better," Jesse replied automatically.

"That's good," Caine said, "but that wasn't what I said. You should go join them."

"You think so?" Jesse asked.

"Why wouldn't I think so?" Caine replied. "You and he have been practically inseparable since you got here. Did you have a fight?"

"No, we didn't have a fight," Jesse said, glad he could be honest about that at least. He wasn't about to tell Caine what had really happened. "He... he didn't come to the machine shed today."

Caine chuckled. "He spent the afternoon with Neil and Max, learning about sheep. I heard him and Neil while I helped Jason and Polly teach Seth the same things."

Jesse hesitated a moment longer, watching the easy laughter between Chris and Neil. He refused to label the churning in his stomach as jealousy.

"You do know Neil is so straight it's scary and that he's completely taken with Molly, right? Whatever there is between you and Chris, Neil is no threat to that."

"I was just reminding myself of that fact," Jesse admitted. "It didn't help."

"Then go over there and join them," Caine repeated. "You don't get what you want in life without fighting for it. If he's what you want, standing over here with me isn't going to help either."

"You know," Jesse said with a smile. "You're right. Thanks."

"You're welcome," Caine said, returning Jesse's smile. "Just don't be late for dinner."

Jesse had no intention of opening them up to that kind of scrutiny so soon, and certainly not without Chris's agreement, but he'd already said enough. Caine hadn't seemed disapproving. On the contrary, he seemed encouraging, but Jesse didn't want to give Caine reason to change his mind.

"Hey, mate," he said, joining Chris and Neil. "You didn't come help out with the tractor today."

"Hi, Jesse," Chris said, the smile on his face so luminous that Jesse wondered momentarily if he could drag Chris somewhere private for a kiss before dinner. "You know I'm not really any help with the engines. I thought it was time I started learning how to be a jackaroo."

"He has a way with dogs," Neil said approvingly. "Max doesn't listen to just anyone."

"He just likes me because you told him to listen to me," Chris said, reaching down to stroke Max's head.

"No," Neil insisted. "Usually the only other person he'll listen to consistently is Macklin, but he listened to you all afternoon."

Jesse almost said something flirtatious, but Neil was standing right there, smiling at Chris encouragingly. Jesse didn't think a comment directed at Chris in Neil's hearing would really have unforeseen consequences. Neil had helped save Chris's life. He'd defended Caine and Macklin to the other hands, but Jesse wasn't Caine and Macklin. He was just a new, unknown jackaroo, and if Jesse had misjudged Neil's tolerance, he had enough sway with the other jackaroos to make the summer miserable. Jesse didn't *think* it would come to that, but he wasn't quite ready to take the chance. "Caine told us not to be late to dinner," he said instead. "Maybe we should go inside."

"HI, CHRIS," Seth said, running up to his brother, Jason in tow. "Guess what I did today?"

"I don't know," Chris said, reaching out to ruffle Seth's light brown hair with his good hand. Seth had gotten their mother's coloring. Chris supposed he could attribute his own blond hair to their father, but he didn't know for sure. He nodded for Jesse and Neil to go on inside. He wanted a few minutes alone with his brother. "What did you do today?"

"I learned to herd sheep!" Seth was practically bouncing in his hand-me-down boots. "Jason taught me, and Caine pretended to be a sheep so I'd have someone to practice on!"

Chris had a hard time imagining Caine running around baaing like a sheep and trying to go the opposite direction of where the dog wanted him to go, but whatever the grazier had done, Seth was enchanted with the memory of it. "Sounds like fun."

"It was, and tomorrow Jason is going to help with the shearing, and he said I could go with him too!"

"That's great," Chris said, swallowing down his jealousy. It wasn't Seth's fault Chris had a broken arm and could only be of limited help.

"So what did you do today?" Seth asked.

"The same thing you did," Chris said, "only without Caine as the sheep. Neil taught me some commands using his training course."

"It's fun, isn't it?" Seth asked.

"It is," Chris said. "Does this mean you like it here?"

"Yes," Seth said, his voice small. "Is that all right?"

"Yes," Chris said. "I like it here too, although I think I'll like it better once I get this lead weight off my arm."

"Just a couple more weeks," Seth said.

And then physical therapy to build the muscles back up again. But Chris didn't say that to Seth. His brother was trying to make him feel better, and Chris appreciated it. It really had been a good afternoon. He'd started learning a useful skill.

"Can we go eat now?" Seth asked. "I'm hungry."

"Sure," Chris said.

Jesse was still there, sitting alone in the corner, pushing his food around his plate. Seth waved at him enthusiastically. "I can't wait to tell Jesse about Caine."

"Go do that," Chris said. "I need to talk to Kami."

Seth looked at him strangely but hurried off to grab a plate and regale Jesse with tales of his afternoon.

"What are you doing in here?" Kami asked when Chris came around to the kitchen.

"I needed to say thank you," Chris said. "I took your advice and had a good afternoon, much better than I thought I could. Neil really taught me a lot, in between talking about how wonderful Molly was and hoping she'd notice him this summer. I wouldn't have asked for his help if you hadn't made me think about what I was doing when we talked this morning."

"He's a good boy," Kami said, "now that he's starting to settle down. You could do worse when it comes to learning from someone. Now get out of here. I have work to do."

Chris chuckled and left the kitchen with a shake of his head. His reaction made him smile even more widely. A week ago, he'd have worried what he'd done to offend Kami. Now he chalked it up to the aborigine's irascibility. Lang Downs was starting to feel like home.

Out in the canteen, Chris filled his plate with Kami's extraordinary pad thai and walked over to where Seth was still recounting Caine's antics to Jesse. Chris sat down without comment, letting himself get caught up in Seth's tale. His little brother had a knack for wringing every bit of humor out of a funny story, and Jesse was grinning from ear to ear and chuckling by the time Seth was done.

"Did Caine really do that?" Jesse asked Chris.

"I don't know," Chris replied, caught up in the light-heartedness of the moment. "I didn't hear any of this until just a minute ago. I spent the afternoon with a different teacher. It was fun, but not that much fun."

"Working with the dogs takes real talent," Jesse said to Seth. "Not all the jackaroos have the patience for it. Those are the ones who end up riding fences or cleaning out barns. You should both be very proud of yourselves."

"Really?" Chris asked. "I figured everyone worked with the dogs."

"No," Jesse said, "at least not at most stations. At most stations, only a few jackaroos have dogs of their own and work with them, and they don't like to share. One more way Lang Downs is different, I suppose."

"Really!" Chris said. "I would never have guessed from the way Neil agreed to teach me that it was any big deal at all. I'll have to remember to thank him again. Did you get the tractor finished today?"

"We did," Jesse said.

"That's good. Hey, Seth, would you get me some water? I couldn't carry it and my plate."

"Sure," Seth said, jumping up from the table.

"What are you doing after dinner?" Chris said as soon as Seth was out of earshot. "I'd like some time with you, without an audience."

"We're off the clock now," Jesse said. "We can go out to the tractor shed after dinner. There shouldn't be anyone else around."

"Okay," Chris said as Seth came back with a glass of water. He tried to keep his anticipation off his face. The last thing he needed was Seth asking why he was grinning like the Cheshire cat. "Thanks, Seth."

"You're welcome," Seth said. "I have to go back over to Jason's house after dinner. We have to do some more schoolwork since we spent the afternoon with Caine and Polly."

"Makes me glad I got my HSC years ago," Jesse said. "I couldn't get out of school fast enough."

"I don't know," Chris said. "It wasn't all bad. I liked my history classes, and I loved the bio and chem stuff. I bet some of that could even be useful around here."

"Did you ever think about going to uni and getting a degree in one of the sciences?" Jesse asked. "Vets make good money around here. Some of the larger stations even have one on site full-time."

"This isn't a large station?" Seth asked, his eyes growing wide.

"It's pretty big," Jesse said, "but not like the big cattle stations in Queensland or the Northern Territory. Some of those are thousands of clicks across."

"Wow!" Seth said.

"Seth," Jason called. "Come on. I don't want to still be working on this at midnight."

"See you later," Seth said, waving at Chris and Jesse as he left.

"You ready?" Jesse asked, his smile widening.

Chris nodded. "I'll meet you there in a couple of minutes. I need to take some more medicine first."

NINE

"WHAT are you grinning at?"

Caine turned his attention to Macklin sitting across the table from him, back to the rest of the room as they ate dinner. "Chris and Jesse."

"As in Chris and Jesse or Chris *and* Jesse?"

"Oh, definitely Chris *and* Jesse," Caine said, "although I suppose either of them by himself could also be cause for a smile. Chris spent the afternoon with Neil learning to herd sheep, and Jesse didn't like it."

"Neil's not gay."

"I know that," Caine said, rolling his eyes at Macklin's lack of intuitiveness. "It's not about Neil's interest. It's about Jesse's interest."

"And why is this our business?" Macklin asked. "We can't go interfering in the lives of the men without treading very carefully. I know you like Chris—I do too, so don't get all defensive on me—but I understand him in a way you can't. He's scared, pup. He's been alone, and he didn't like it, because no one really does, no matter what they say. He's here now, and next to what he had before, Lang Downs is the land of milk and honey, but he's had good things and lost them before. It's going to take more than a week or two for him to trust in this place, to trust in us and everyone else here. If he'd been here six months or a year, it might be different, but he hasn't been. If he and Jesse start something and it goes wrong, Chris will run faster than we can blink, and he'll never get another chance like the one he has here."

"And if something goes right, wouldn't it be another reason to stay?" Caine asked.

Macklin chuckled. "You're determined to make everyone else as happy as you are, aren't you?"

"There's no harm in it," Caine said, feeling defensive.

"This time there might be. Not if it works, maybe, but Chris needs time to heal and feel safe or his fears and insecurities will sabotage his chances. I know you want to help, pup, and it's one of the many things that makes you the man you are"—Caine didn't need the words to understand the subtext, *the man I love*—"but you have to trust me this time. I've been in Chris's shoes. If I'd met you at his age, I'd have fucked things up because I wasn't ready for you then. Hell, I nearly fucked things up at twice his age."

"But you didn't," Caine said with a smile. He didn't reach over and squeeze Macklin's hand, not when they were in public. "So how do we help Chris and Jesse now?"

"We don't," Macklin said, "at least not the way you mean. We help Chris feel settled and help him gain some confidence in his place here and his value to us, and we help Jesse put down roots too, and maybe when they're both a little more certain of where they are, they'll feel comfortable thinking about who they're with or want to be with."

"Okay," Caine said. "I can do that." He leaned in closer. "I'm betting on them, though, and if I'm right, if they get it together and make it work the way I know they can, your ass is mine."

"What does my arse have to do with the success or failure of their relationship?" Macklin asked.

"Nothing," Caine said, "but it's one hell of an incentive for me to help them find their way."

"Are you suggesting I work against that?" Macklin asked.

"I should hope it would be an incentive to work for them," Caine retorted.

"You don't need an incentive to work for them. You need to let them find their own way," Macklin repeated. "We'll discuss my arse another time."

Caine frowned but let it go. He'd keep wearing Macklin down a little at a time, and eventually he'd convince his lover to let go of his control in the bedroom.

"You want to explain what you were doing with Seth and Jason this afternoon?"

Caine accepted the change of topic and smiled. "Pretending to be a sheep. Polly likes me. She played along so Seth could learn."

JESSE paced the confines of the tractor shed nervously. It wasn't dark outside yet, but without the lights on in the shed, the space was dim, closer to twilight than day, and it would only get darker as time passed. He took a deep breath, the smell of machine oil comforting him. Maybe it wasn't the most romantic smell in the world, but it represented safety for Jesse. Even at the lowest points in his life, going to a shop somewhere and working on engines had given him comfort, and usually enough income to keep a roof over his head and food in his belly.

The door creaked softly on its hinges as it opened and closed. Even in the shadows, Jesse had no problem following Chris's progress across the dusty floor. "Over here," he called when he realized Chris had not seen him as easily.

Chris turned in his direction and came over to the straw bale where Jesse was sitting. He sat down next to Jesse, staring straight ahead in silence for so long that Jesse wondered if he'd changed his mind.

"I missed you today," Jesse said finally, sliding an arm around Chris's waist, glad the cast was on Chris's other side so he could pull Chris close without the weight of the plaster between them. "I'm glad you worked with Neil and are learning about the station, but it made me realize how used I'd got to having you around."

That took care of what remained of Chris's reserve. He tipped his head up for a kiss. Jesse gave it gladly, relaxing into the contact. He'd fucked and been fucked during the winter in Melbourne, but it had been a long time since anyone had been interested in kissing him. He tugged on Chris's leg, urging him to straddle Jesse's lap so they could kiss more easily.

"Caine is onto us," Jesse said between kisses. "I don't know how much he knows, but he made some pointed comments before dinner."

"Besides telling you not to be late?"

"Yeah, about not being jealous of Neil."

"All Neil can think about is Molly."

"I know," Jesse said, "but he got to spend the afternoon with you and I didn't."

"He isn't interested in me," Chris repeated, "and I'm only interested in what he can teach me."

"Good," Jesse said, refusing to acknowledge the satisfaction he got from Chris's statement. "I couldn't decide if Caine approved or not."

"I signed on to work at the station because it was a job and a safe place for my brother," Chris said. "I didn't sign over control of my life. I'm not saying we should flaunt it. I'm not stupid, and even if I were, getting the shite beaten out of me for being gay cured me of that. It feels good to have someone else's hands on me tonight instead of my own, not that I'm getting a lot of action at the moment with my arm in this stupid cast. I haven't got laid since Tony kicked us out."

"You aren't getting laid tonight either," Jesse said with a laugh. "I don't carry condoms in my jeans when I'm at work."

"I'm sure we could think of something," Chris said, his hand moving between them to cup Jesse's cock through his jeans. "We can't let this go to waste."

"Be my guest." Jesse leaned back on his elbows, giving Chris space to decide how he wanted the rest of their encounter to go. He might say he wasn't an inexperienced kid, but Jesse would still let him set the pace.

Chris had no such hesitations, following Jesse back to kiss him far more aggressively than he'd done before. The change of mood surprised Jesse slightly, but yesterday had been romance. This was sex.

Jesse was pragmatic enough to accept the difference even if he missed the sweet tenderness of their first kisses. They'd find it again when the mood was right.

When Chris fumbled one-handed with the buckle of his belt, Jesse pushed up again to help, opening his belt and pants but leaving it up to Chris what to do next. "I could have done that," Chris said.

"I know," Jesse said, "but this was faster. Now you don't have to worry about it."

Chris grinned and slid down between Jesse's knees, pushing them apart. He buried his face against Jesse's groin and inhaled deeply. "You do want me."

"Of course I want you," Jesse groaned.

Chris didn't reply, instead slipping his hand into Jesse's pants to stroke him with more enthusiasm than finesse, adding to Jesse's sense that Chris wasn't as experienced as he claimed. He wasn't going to argue now, though, not with Chris's hand circling him eagerly, drawing him out of the open placket of his pants.

Chris's mouth more than made up for his hand's awkwardness. Maybe the problem was the left hand, not Chris's overall experience, because Chris sucked Jesse like someone who knew what to do with a hard dick and the guy it was attached to, lingering over the tip before diving deep and then backing off to tease the slit again.

Jesse groaned and collapsed back on his elbows. It felt damn good to be touched so eagerly, and not by a random stranger but by someone who knew him, someone who cared about him at least as friends. He tugged at Chris's hair, bringing him off the floor and up where Jesse could kiss him again and touch him as well. Chris's hand continued the work his mouth had begun, and Jesse didn't even mind the occasional fumble, because Chris wanted to be there with him, wanted *him*. He popped the button on Chris's jeans, getting his hand inside so he could reciprocate some of the pleasure Chris was giving him.

Chris groaned into Jesse's mouth, his hips jerking on the straw bale as Jesse stroked him urgently. "Shhh," Jesse whispered in his ear. "We don't want anyone coming to investigate any strange noises."

Chris nodded, clearly making an effort to stifle his sounds, but as soon as Jesse touched him again, the groans started back up. Jesse smiled at the thought of making Chris feel that good. Chris's hand stilled as Jesse worked him faster, but Jesse found he didn't even care. He was high on the little sounds pouring from Chris's mouth into his own. He'd get Chris off and then see to himself if Chris was too far gone to reciprocate. It just felt too good to have a hand other than his own on his body.

It didn't take long before Chris shuddered against him with a long moan, his cock spilling all over Jesse's hand. Jesse kept stroking through the aftershocks, stretching out Chris's pleasure as long as he could. Eventually Chris flinched a little, letting Jesse know he'd grown overly sensitive in the aftermath of his orgasm, so Jesse let the sated organ slip from his grasp. Chris still panted against Jesse's neck, little flutters of breath that sent shivers down Jesse's back. He waited a moment longer, but Chris's hand stayed still against his flesh. Jesse wanted to be patient, but the need for release was driving him hard. With a guy he'd picked up in a bar, he might have shoved the other man's head back down to finish what he'd started, but Chris rested too trustingly in Jesse's arms for him to do that, not this time anyway. Not when he wanted to be able to look Chris in the eye tomorrow.

Instead, he closed his hand around Chris's, moving their fists over his shaft. Chris stirred immediately. "I'm sorry, that was selfish," he said, his lips moving against Jesse's neck.

"It's fine," Jesse replied, their combined grip working him to a frenzy. "Just don't stop now."

Chris grinned at him. "Not stopping," he promised. Jesse let his hand drop to the side now that Chris was stroking him again. Chris's hand felt far better than his own ever could. His release bubbled up in his balls, trying to explode out of him. He fought it back, not wanting the moment to end since he didn't know when they'd get a chance for a repeat.

Chris wasn't having any of that, though, biting along Jesse's neck and jaw as he stroked faster.

"Don't do too much of that," Jesse moaned, "or everyone will know what we've been up to."

"Do you think they'll care?" Chris asked.

Jesse didn't know, but he didn't really want to find out when he didn't know what "this" was. If they had committed to a real relationship, he'd stick to his guns and tell everyone to fuck off if they said anything, but he couldn't risk his place at the station or the respect of the other hands for a casual fuck, and they hadn't discussed anything more. "I'd rather not take that chance."

Chris seemed to accept that, gentling the contact of his lips to soft kisses instead of the little nips from before, but it was still enough, combined with the increased rhythm of Chris's stroking, to push Jesse over the edge. He grunted as he climaxed, his release splattering his T-shirt and Chris's hand.

When the shudders eased, Jesse turned to look at Chris, only to realize darkness had fallen almost completely inside the shed and nearly as much outside. "We should probably get back," he said, his voice laced with regret. "I don't know if Macklin or Caine will look for you, but we don't want to give anyone a reason to wonder what we were doing when everyone else is hanging out in the bunkhouse unwinding or already asleep. Besides, morning comes early."

"Even earlier for me since I have to help Kami get breakfast ready," Chris said, "and with the shearing starting, it's extra early tomorrow." He fumbled with his pants, his right arm at a weird angle as he worked around the cast to get his hand to the button.

"Here, let me," Jesse said. "It's not every day I button a guy back up. I'm usually trying to get his pants undone."

"You can undo mine any time you like," Chris said. "Well, any time it's safe to do so, anyway."

"Honestly, it's probably safe here," Jesse said, finishing with Chris's pants. "Not that we want to flaunt it, necessarily, but we're both adults, and Caine and Macklin wouldn't keep people on who had a problem with them being together, so why should it be any different for us?"

"Because we aren't really together?" Chris asked. "I mean, they're the real thing. We're just...."

"Seeing what happens," Jesse finished, not willing to commit to more than he could give. He'd enjoyed the past half hour with Chris, but now they had to go their separate ways, each back to his own bunk, with no chance of a repeat during the night or even simply of a warm body to hold him close after a bad dream. He didn't have nightmares like he used to, but they still surprised him occasionally, and waking up alone with cold sweat pouring off him in rivers was no fun. Having someone there to soothe the nightmare away was a rare luxury, but one he dreamed of someday enjoying. That would have to wait for another time and another man, though. Chris was fine with sex, but he wasn't ready for the rest, and Jesse would have to respect that if he had any hope of having even the sex.

"Yeah, that," Chris said. "I'll see you at breakfast?"

"I'll be there," Jesse said, leaning in to give Chris one last kiss before they parted.

CHRIS walked slowly back to the station house. His arm hurt a little from leaning on it awkwardly, and his ribs ached a little from twisting to kiss Jesse, but the rest of his body felt incredible: loose, free, relaxed for the first time in months. Sex with Jesse was definitely an added bonus to life on Lang Downs. Happiness bubbled up inside him as he stepped onto the veranda. He could go inside, head upstairs, and hope he could get to his room in time to enjoy the moment in private, but Caine and Macklin often sat in the living room in the evenings, and Seth would want to talk about his schoolwork or about his afternoon with Jason or about whatever else popped into his head. Deciding to wait a little longer before facing them, he sat down on one of the rough-hewn wooden chairs on the veranda and rested his head against the headrest.

The afternoon had gone a long way toward easing his concerns about what life might be like long term at Lang Downs. He and Kami had developed a functioning relationship, but Chris didn't really see himself spending the rest of his life working in a kitchen. He managed under the circumstances, but it wasn't something that interested him.

He could do it well enough to help Kami out, but he wouldn't want to be the one responsible for all the meals. If Caine and Macklin had him in mind as Kami's successor for the day when the cook decided he was ready to retire, they'd need to think again.

The door opened behind him, interrupting his thoughts. He tensed a little when Macklin came out and sat down in the chair next to him. He didn't want to share the lingering afterglow with anyone.

Macklin didn't say anything beyond a simple greeting for a long time. Long enough for Chris to relax. "I like sitting out here in the evenings," Macklin said finally. "It's very relaxing."

"It is," Chris replied, not sure where the conversation was heading, but he saw no harm in agreeing.

"Sometimes Caine will join me, but tonight he's fighting with a distributor over organic seed," Macklin continued. "We're going to grow our own hay as part of the organic certification process, and that requires an initial crop of organic seed. The distributor quoted one price, but now that it's time for delivery, he's quoting something else."

"That must be frustrating."

"He'll deal with it," Macklin said. "He's amazing that way. People look at him, hear his American accent and his stutter, and they assume they know all there is to know about him. They have no idea how wrong they are."

Chris nodded, hearing the affection in Macklin's words. "He's really special to you, isn't he?"

"He's it for me," Macklin replied. "I'd given up on the idea of finding someone, anyone, out here in the outback, and then there he was, perfect and stubborn and shy and so determined to make a life here. It took me a while to believe it, to believe in him, but he's a force of nature, even if he doesn't see it."

Chris wasn't sure what to say, so he let the silence fall between them again, Macklin's words echoing in his head, or maybe not the words so much as the way he spoke of Caine, the absolute assurance that Caine was his... his everything. He wasn't sure he'd ever heard that confidence from any of the adults in his life before, even when he was younger, and to hear it now from, of all people, half of the one gay couple he knew left him reeling internally. By whatever miracle or twist of fate, Macklin had found his partner and had the courage to hold onto him. Chris could only hope he'd be so lucky someday.

"How are you settling in?" Macklin asked. "Has Kami got used to having you around yet?"

"I suppose," Chris said with a shrug that didn't hurt nearly as much as it would have a few weeks ago. "He hasn't killed me yet."

"That's a good start," Macklin said with a chuckle. "I heard you learned a bit about herding sheep today."

"Yeah," Chris said, trying not to think about why he'd spent the afternoon with Neil instead of Jesse and all that had transpired since. It was dark enough Macklin wouldn't be able to see him blush, but the foreman had a knack for knowing everything, it seemed, and Chris would rather not give Macklin any hint of his personal business.

"You aren't overdoing it, are you?"

"I'm not a kid," Chris protested automatically.

"I wasn't implying you were," Macklin said, his voice as unruffled as ever. "I'm not your father, to tell you what to do, but I am your boss, and as such, your ability to do your job is my concern. If you set back your recovery by overdoing, it affects me. If you tell me you're fine, I'm going to believe you unless you prove to me otherwise, but I expect you to tell me the truth, just like I expect all my jackaroos to tell me the truth where their jobs are concerned."

"I'm doing better," Chris replied, Macklin's frank words settling him and allowing him to reply with the honesty Macklin had demanded. "My ribs still hurt if I reach for something too far away, but I can twist some now and bend as much as the wrapping lets me. I guess my broken arm is healing, although I don't have any way to tell. It doesn't hurt, so that's something, although it itches like mad."

"Put talcum powder inside the cast as much as you can," Macklin suggested. "It won't stop the itching completely, but it's about the only thing that helps."

"I don't think I have any," Chris said. "It's not something I use very often."

"You'll want it this summer," Macklin said. "Put it in your shoes to help the smell, in the seam of your pants to keep them from chafing in the heat. There's some in the small kitchen. We can pick up more the next time we go to Boorowa for supplies."

"When is the next trip?" Chris asked, thinking about what he and Jesse hadn't done in the shed tonight. "I've thought of a few more things I should probably pick up now that I'm earning a little money again."

"We go into town about once a month," Macklin said. "If you give me a list, I can pick things up for you."

Chris blushed furiously, his cheeks burning in the cool night air. "Um, it's personal stuff. I should probably pick it up myself if I can tag along."

Macklin chuckled and stood up, opening the door before turning back. "There's nothing wrong with letting off a little steam now and then as long as both people are willing. Just make sure you both know what you're doing."

"We didn't, I mean, it's none, I mean...."

"I didn't ask for an explanation," Macklin reminded him. "You're an adult and so is Jesse, if that's who you were with, and if it's not, as long as whoever it was is also an adult, it's none of my business, as you said, but don't turn my station into a war zone because you can't keep it in your pants and aren't mature enough to handle the consequences."

"I can handle it."

"Good. Make sure you keep it that way."

"WAS that Chris you were talking to on the porch?" Caine asked.

Macklin stifled a curse. He'd hoped Caine would still be in the office. "He was sitting out there when I went out to unwind. It would have been rude not to talk to him."

"Mmhmm," Caine said, an amused smile on his face. "I thought you said we shouldn't meddle."

"Who was meddling?" Macklin retorted, refusing to let Caine discomfit him. "I asked him how his injuries were doing and if he enjoyed working with Neil and Max today."

"So you didn't say anything about Jesse?" Caine teased.

"He's an adult, Caine," Macklin said, his tone of voice telling Caine to drop it as they climbed up the stairs. "He doesn't need us telling him what to do."

Caine grinned at him and slipped his arm around Macklin's waist, his hand sliding lower to grope Macklin's arse. "You keep telling yourself that if it makes it easier for you. I'll just look forward to claiming my prize."

With a low growl, Macklin herded Caine into the bedroom, and that was the last of their coherent conversation for the night.

TEN

JESSE had no real idea what to expect when he walked into the canteen the next morning. He had gone back to his room at the bunkhouse in a daze the night before. He hadn't been surprised exactly that he and Chris had had sex in the tractor shed—they'd been dancing around each other since the kiss—but he hadn't wanted to assume it would happen so quickly either.

That had left him wondering what Chris thought about their encounter. They were two healthy, single gay men. They had no reason not to blow off a little steam now and then, but they hadn't set any ground rules, hadn't established any boundaries. Jesse was fine with a little harmless recreational sex, but he wasn't ready to settle down and start a family. He hoped Chris wouldn't make their fun and games into more than he could let it be.

They had to work at Lang Downs for the rest of the summer, if nothing else, and Jesse had seen how quickly moods could change when a jackaroo found out about him and decided to take exception to the way Jesse looked at him or talked to him. It never mattered that Jesse wouldn't have given those guys the time of day even if they were gay and available. The ones he might actually be attracted to were never the ones with the hang-ups about him. No, it was always the ones who *thought* they were God's gift to women, no matter how horrendous they really were.

He didn't think that would happen here. If nothing else, he didn't think Caine and Macklin would fire him for messing around with Chris as long as Chris was willing. He was an adult, if a young one, and had proven his maturity by taking care of his brother for the past six months, but that didn't mean the other jackaroos would be happy about it if they found out. Jesse just hoped Chris would play it cool.

Reminding himself that Chris had already been burned once for letting the wrong people find out about him, Jesse took a deep breath and walked into the canteen, looking around automatically for Chris.

Chris stood behind the serving line with Kami. He smiled and waved at Jesse when he came in, the same as he had done before their kiss and last night's sex. Jesse released the breath he didn't realize he'd been holding. Whatever else happened, at least this was back to normal. He tossed his hat on the table where he, Chris, and Seth always sat, and went to get breakfast.

"Morning, Jesse," Chris said as Jesse came through the line. "Are you helping with the shearing this morning?"

"That's the plan as far as I've heard," Jesse replied, taking the scrambled eggs Chris offered. "Are you coming out to help or are you stuck in here all day?"

"Kami said I could come help once we had lunch ready," Chris said. "Go eat while it's hot. I'll come join you as soon as I can."

Just like that. Just like nothing had changed. Then again, maybe it hadn't. Maybe this would be okay after all.

"Why are you grinning?" Seth asked, interrupting Jesse's thoughts.

"What?" Jesse asked.

"You had this look on your face like you'd just heard this great joke or this awesome secret. I want to know too."

"It's nothing," Jesse said, doing his best to school his expression.

Seth didn't look convinced, but he let it go, chattering instead about the things he and Jason had looked up online the night before while they were doing their schoolwork. "And did you know that the dot on top of the letter *i* is called a tittle?"

"No, I didn't," Jesse replied. "And why were you looking that up last night?"

"Well, we were talking about history and the printing press and copying manuscripts by hand, and it just sort of came up," Seth said with a shrug.

"Is he telling you about the tittle?" Chris asked, sitting down next to Jesse. "It was all he could talk about last night. I think he likes the way the word sounds."

"What?" Seth said defensively.

"You know, tittle, tit," Chris teased.

"Well, not all of us are gay," Seth retorted.

"No, just two of the three of us," Jesse replied, "and that's your brother you're talking about. Be nice to him."

"He's my brother. I'm supposed to give him hell," Seth said.

"Not when he takes care of you the way Chris has," Jesse insisted.

"It's fine, Jesse," Chris said, nudging Jesse's knee with his underneath the table. "I can take all the teasing he can dish out."

Jesse wanted to insist, but it wasn't his place so he let it go.

"Jesse has a secret and he won't tell me what it is," Seth announced, changing the subject. "You should see if he'll tell you, Chris."

"Really?" Chris asked turning to Jesse.

"It's nothing," Jesse said, knowing it was far more than nothing, but he didn't know what Chris had told Seth, and Jesse didn't want to let that cat out of the bag. "I like shearing. I'm looking forward to getting started for the day."

"Macklin's already come and gone, so I bet they'll be starting soon," Chris said. "I have to help Kami get the sandwiches ready for lunch, but then Neil said I could help him with Max some this afternoon. Everyone's been talking about what hard work shearing is. If you're not exhausted this evening, we'll have to go for a walk or something to help you unwind."

Translation: find someplace private where they could get each other off again. Jesse's body reacted predictably to the suggestion, and he had to smother another grin. "We'll see how the day goes."

"I promised Patrick I'd help him check the rest of the machinery they'll need for the shearing today," Seth said, bouncing up from the table. "I'd better go."

"I'll come with you," Jesse said, gulping the last of his coffee and grimacing a bit at the burn of hot liquid down his throat. "We'll see you in the pens later, okay, Chris?"

"Have a good morning," Chris said, taking their plates to save them a trip back to the kitchen. "I'll catch up with you when I can."

Jesse followed Seth out the door, glancing back over his shoulder at Chris one last time before letting the door swing shut behind him. Chris was whistling as he finished clearing the tables and grabbed a broom, holding it awkwardly because of his cast. Kami would be in the back washing dishes or possibly laying out the fixings for the platters of sandwiches he would have available for the jackaroos at lunch. Shaking his head at his own foolishness in wanting that last glimpse of Chris to get him through until lunch, Jesse turned on his heel and headed toward the tractor shed. The tractor itself was fixed, but Patrick had said he intended to check the rest of the farm machinery before releasing the mechanics to help with the shearing.

Jesse was the first one into the shed so he started opening the windows and doors, letting the fresh air in. He knew it was only in his memories that the smell of sex lingered in the air, but he saw no reason to take chances, especially since Patrick preferred to work with the doors and windows open, weather permitting.

He'd finished the preparations, setting out Patrick's tool box before opening the engine casing on the combine. Patrick came in a moment later. "You're on the ball this morning," he said.

Jesse shrugged. "I was awake. I didn't see any reason to wait."

"Let's get this done," Patrick said.

Jesse nodded and started checking the spark plugs on the combine. A few minutes later, Patrick cursed under his breath.

"What's wrong?" Jesse asked. "Is something broken?"

"No, I must have been in a real rush yesterday. My wrench wasn't in the right place," Patrick explained. "That's what I get for being so obsessive."

Jesse frowned. He didn't remember Patrick rushing at the end of the day before, and the man was definitely a creature of habit. He had that toolbox so organized he could reach in and pull out what he needed, down to the right size drill bit, without even looking.

A snicker caught Jesse's attention, but when he looked sharply at Jason and Seth cleaning up on the other side of the shed, neither of them gave any sign of paying attention to Patrick and Jesse.

A moment later, Patrick cursed again. "Now I know I didn't put the pliers back in the wrong place because I didn't even use them yesterday."

Concerned now, Jesse stopped what he was doing and walked around the combine to where Patrick stood staring into his toolbox.

"Someone's playing jokes," Patrick said with a frown. "Nothing is in the right place."

"Seth!" Jesse called, his voice sharp. "Come here."

"Yes, Jesse?" Seth asked, coming over to where Jesse and Patrick stood. He was trying to keep a straight face, but Jesse recognized the mischief in his eyes.

"Is there something you'd like to say to Patrick?" Jesse said.

"No, is there a reason I should say something to Patrick?" Seth asked, losing his battle to hold back a smile.

"You little shite," Jesse said, grabbing Seth's collar and giving him a shake. "You're going to sit down right now and put everything back the way you found it, and then you're going to spend your evenings over the next week helping Patrick at his place with anything he asks you to do."

"You aren't my boss," Seth said.

"You want me to tell Caine and Macklin about this?" Jesse asked. "I can go get them right now and see what they think a fitting punishment would be."

"It was just a harmless prank," Seth muttered.

"Sit down," Jesse said, giving Seth a push in Patrick's direction, "and get busy."

Seth glared at him but did as Jesse ordered, sitting down next to Patrick's tool box and starting to sort all the tools back out. "And apologize to Patrick while you're at it," Jesse said. "He didn't do anything to deserve your pranks."

"How did you know it was Seth?" Patrick asked.

"Besides the way he didn't play it cool? I caught him once before playing a trick on Chris," Jesse explained. "It didn't make him guilty, but it made him the prime suspect."

"And that's a lesson for you both," Patrick said to Seth and Jason. "Once you get a reputation, you're halfway to being found guilty the next time something happens, even if you aren't involved."

"You won't tell Chris, will you?" Seth asked, his voice small.

"As long as you don't play any more tricks," Patrick said. Jesse nodded his agreement.

CHRIS thought Seth looked a little subdued when he joined the others to help with the shearing. He couldn't hold the sheep and run the clipper along their skin with his arm in a cast, but Neil let him borrow Max to help drive the sheep into the outer paddocks once they were sheared. Chris chuckled every time one of the newly denuded animals came rushing out of the shearing shed, bleating madly. Max hardly needed directions, catching and herding them to the proper paddock based as much on where Neil was standing as on anything Chris said. The cavorting of the released sheep, especially the little ones, made him smile, though, and that made the dust and noise that much less annoying. Chris figured he was lucky, outside in the fresh air instead of inside the shearing shed where it was surely hot and sticky and otherwise miserable. Certainly the faces of the jackaroos who took turns manning the gate to catch a hint of breeze were red and dripping with sweat. Chris tried not to stare at the bare chests of many of the men, figuring that wouldn't go over well, even though he thought he caught a couple of the jillaroos who were also working with the dogs giving the men a thorough once over. All except Molly, Chris noticed. She seemed to have eyes only for Neil, and since it was pretty much mutual, Chris hoped Neil would get his happy ending. While he tended to think of owing Macklin his life, Neil had been there as well, helping to run off his attackers, and Chris certainly appreciated his willingness since then to teach Chris about the station.

Chris's attempts at not staring failed completely when Jesse took his turn at the gate. He'd stripped off the green work shirt he'd been wearing earlier, the one that made his eyes seem an even brighter color (not that Chris would admit to noticing, but he wasn't blind, was he?), and stood at the gate bare from the waist up. Their fumbling in the tractor shed last night hadn't prepared him for the impact that seeing Jesse, sweaty and disheveled and looking every bit the stockman in his low-hanging jeans, hat, and boots, would have on him. He couldn't tear his eyes away as Jesse opened the gate and let a few more sheep out to be sent to higher meadows. Fortunately for Chris, Max knew his job and met the sheep, keeping them from darting back toward the paddocks where they'd spent the winter. Chris certainly didn't have a working brain cell left over to tell Max what to do. They were all focused on Jesse and on planning how soon Chris could get him alone again, because now that he'd seen Jesse's chest, not quite bulky but definitely more muscular than Chris was, pale from winter but covered in a mat of dark hair to match the hair on his head, Chris wouldn't be able to keep from touching for long. Somehow he doubted molesting Jesse in the middle of the paddocks in broad daylight was a good idea. He'd have to bide his time and see if he could drag Jesse behind the bunkhouse or something when everyone took a break for lunch and headed to the canteen.

He had to do something or he'd never survive the rest of the day, thinking of Jesse working inside the shed, his muscles bunching and straining as he held the sheep in place or lifted the heavy bags of wool out of the way so other sheep could come in.

"Chris!"

Neil's voice brought Chris back to the present.

"Sorry," he called back, going after a sheep that had broken away from the others. Fortunately the system of paddocks around the shed had been designed to keep the sheep from getting far even if they did run the wrong way. Out in the higher paddocks where they could graze at will for the summer, they wouldn't be so constrained, but down in the valley, their movements were closely controlled. Chris chased the sheep back toward the others. Max met him at Neil's command and finished the job.

"What were you dreaming about, mate?" Neil asked. "You had the oddest look on your face."

"Nothing," Chris said. "How's Molly?"

It was an underhanded move but one Chris knew would work. Neil was happiest when he was talking about his dog or his girl.

Chris managed to stay sufficiently plugged into the conversation that he missed Jesse going back inside. Macklin had taken Jesse's place at the gate, and Chris couldn't stop himself from boggling a bit. He wasn't attracted to Macklin the same way he was attracted to Jesse, but that didn't stop him from appreciating a well-built man when he saw one. Chris knew Macklin had to be in his forties based on bits of conversation he'd overheard, but he didn't look it. He was leaner than Jesse, more whipcord than built, but he looked like he was chiseled out of stone, and when he pushed his hat back and wiped his forehead with the tail of the shirt he'd tucked in the back pocket of his pants, Chris couldn't help the weak-kneed feeling that swept through him. Then Caine came out of the shed, bare-chested as well, and joined his lover. He wasn't quite as solid as Macklin, but visions of the two of them together swam in front of Chris's eyes, leaving him hot and bothered and suddenly ready for a break.

"Neil, I'm going to find some more Nurofen. I'll be back in a few minutes."

Neil waved to show he'd heard Chris, and Chris hurried back to the station house. He couldn't hide in the bathroom and jerk off—it just felt too awkward with his left hand—but he could at least cool off for a minute. He wet a washcloth and wiped his face and neck. He hadn't taken his own shirt off, since the breeze off the highlands was cool. It hadn't been the weather making him hot and bothered.

"Chris?"

"Upstairs," Chris called. "In the bathroom."

Chris heard the creak of the stairs as Jesse came up to join him. "Maybe I shouldn't come in," Jesse said from the doorway. "The last time I did, we nearly got caught."

Chris grinned and reached for Jesse's belt, tugging him into the bathroom and pushing the door closed. "Maybe you should come in," he disagreed. "Everyone else is outside."

"Where we really should be," Jesse pointed out, though he made no move to pull away.

"We'll go back out," Chris said, leaning in to nibble at Jesse's lower lip. "In a minute."

"We shouldn't do this during working hours," Jesse said, even as he kissed Chris back. "Caine and Macklin won't care that we're gay and they probably won't care that we're messing around, but they'll have every reason to protest if us messing around interferes with us doing our jobs."

"You think too much," Chris said, slipping his hand beneath the shirt Jesse had put back on. "Why'd you get dressed again?"

"Because I was coming in the boss's house," Jesse replied, pulling back finally. "Is that what has you all worked up?"

"Well, that and seeing Caine and Macklin standing together," Chris admitted. "I guess I'd never really looked at them, but bloody hell they're hot."

Jesse laughed. "Should I be worried?"

"They'll never look at me," Chris said. "Why would they when they have each other?"

"That didn't answer my question," Jesse said, his voice still sounding amused, fortunately.

"No, you shouldn't be worried," Chris said firmly. "I noticed you before I noticed them, and thinking about them, it's like watching porn. It's imagining them together, not imagining me in the mix. If I'm going to do that, I'm going to think about you."

"I like the sound of that," Jesse said, "but we're not doing anything, real or imagined, until after dinner." He opened the bathroom door and pulled Chris with him. "Come on. You've been gone long enough to get something for the pain. It's time to get back to work."

Chris let Jesse lead him back downstairs, although he did stop to steal another kiss as they put their boots back on before heading back outside. "So where should I meet you after work?" Chris asked as they neared the shearing shed again.

"I don't know," Jesse said. "I'll think of something and let you know."

"Oh, Jesse, there you are," Caine said. "I was hoping you and Chris would be willing to do something for me."

"Sure, if we can," Jesse said as Chris nodded.

"You probably noticed the drover's huts as we drove in," Caine said. "We have them scattered around the station as shelter for anyone who spends a night out in the paddocks and for anyone who might need them for other reasons: a storm, a power outage, whatever. The buildings themselves are in pretty good shape, but nobody can tell me what's in any of them beyond the basics of a couple of cots. I'm hoping you two will be willing to inventory them for me and then stock them with supplies. I spent a couple of nights in the huts last fall, so I've made a list of things all the huts should have. We can load up one of the pickups with supplies. You can check each hut and add anything that's missing before you go on. That way we'll know all the huts are ready for the jackaroos before we move the sheep into the farther paddocks."

"I don't know how much I can carry, but I can certainly open drawers and see what's there," Chris said, mind racing at the thought of all that time spent alone with Jesse. "What do you say, Jesse?"

"I've spent enough nights outdoors to appreciate the possibility of a hut," Jesse said. "I'd be glad to help. When did you want us to do this?"

"In a couple of days," Caine said. "We'll have to pack the supplies and then load the pickup. I'll let you know when it's ready."

"Do you need us to help pack stuff up?" Jesse asked.

"No, I'll get Carley to put the kids to work doing that," Caine said. "They can count out batteries and flashlights and jars of Vegemite. We don't need to pull you away from the shearing for something they'll get a kick out of doing."

"Then we'll get back to work," Jesse said, starting back toward the shearing shed. Chris followed more slowly, not quite able to let go of the mental picture of Caine and Macklin together. He'd have an even harder time ignoring the occasional sounds that filtered from the other bedroom now that he'd seen them together.

ELEVEN

"HERE'S a list of everything Macklin and I decided should be in each of the drover's huts," Caine said, joining Chris and Jesse at breakfast three days later. "The younger kids have packed boxes of supplies, so all you have to do is check each hut and replenish anything that's low or missing."

Jesse took the list and scanned down it: non-perishables, flashlights, fresh batteries and bulbs, clean blankets, first aid kit, matches, water.

"Also, while you're driving around, if you notice any roads that need dragging or anything else that seems in disrepair, if you could make a note of it," Caine said. "We've had men out checking the fences, but they've been on horseback, which means they haven't necessarily been on the roads or through the same areas of the station as you'll go through in the truck. That goes for any time you're out, actually. We'd rather replace a fence post now than have to replace an entire fence later."

"Will do," Jesse said. He'd managed to avoid thinking about the hours spent alone in the ute and the drover's huts with Chris, if only to keep himself sane until the time came to head out, but that time was here now, and the anticipation was killing him. He and Chris had only managed a few stolen moments behind the tractor shed over the past few nights. Something always seemed to interrupt, either someone coming to get something or, one night, the sheep suddenly going wild. They'd found a snake trampled beneath all the hooves when they finally calmed the sheep down and could assess the situation, so then they'd had to check all the animals in the area for bites. Fortunately they hadn't found any bite marks and none of the sheep seemed sick, just scared. It had served as a reminder to Jesse that even here in the main part of the station, they had to be aware of their surroundings. He didn't know if Chris would know the difference between a harmless snake and a poisonous one, but in the dark, it would be nearly impossible to tell and the wrong choice could be a deadly one. He hadn't suggested they meet outside after dark since then, but with the days growing longer, everyone seemed to be working later hours, which meant the barns didn't provide a lot of privacy either. Jesse supposed he could invite Chris to his room in the bunkhouse, but the walls were paper thin, and he didn't really want the others overhearing anything. Chris's room in the main house was even less of an option with Seth in the next room and Caine and Macklin just down the hall. He knew they had work to do while they were out today, but at least they'd be alone, away from prying eyes, and if they spent a few minutes doing other things, well, as long as the work was done, surely no one would care.

As soon as breakfast was over, Jesse headed out to the ute. Chris followed a few minutes later, equally eager for some time alone if the expression on his face was any indication. "Shall we get started?" Jesse asked, looking down at the rough map of the drover's huts Macklin had given him as he was leaving the canteen.

"Sure," Chris said with a smile. "I've got a pad so I can take notes for Caine and Macklin."

"Good thought," Jesse said. "That way we can be as specific as possible."

"Do you have a radio?" Chris asked. "Macklin said anyone who leaves the valley is supposed to take a radio, just in case."

"It's already in the ute," Jesse said. "Come on, let's get started."

Chris climbed in and fastened his seatbelt. "Let's go."

"MEDDLING again?" Macklin asked Caine as the black ute headed out of the main station.

"It's not meddling," Caine insisted, as Macklin had known he would. "We've been saying this needed to be done, and Chris really can't help with the shearing, but he can do this."

"And you just happened to suggest Jesse go with him," Macklin replied. "Instead of Neil or Kyle or one of the others who knows his way around the station. They're as likely to get lost as they are to find the drover's huts."

"Jesse has a good head on his shoulders, and he has the map you drew with the huts marked," Caine said. "The roads might be a little overgrown from the winter, but they'll still be visible. They'll be fine."

"In other words, you were meddling again," Macklin said.

Caine grinned at him, that saucy smile that had enchanted Macklin from the moment he first saw it, even when he still worried Caine would change his mind and sell the station out from under them. Macklin didn't jump when Caine patted his arse as he walked away, but only because they were outside. He never let his control slip where the jackaroos could see.

He knew what Caine wanted, had known for some time, but knowing wasn't the same as doing. Macklin couldn't even really say what was holding him back. He'd let go of all his doubts about Caine and his commitment to the station—and to Macklin—about the same time he'd kissed Caine in front of a half-dozen jackaroos, but this wasn't about trusting Caine to stay on. It was about control of himself. He'd seen his father out of control too many times to be comfortable with the idea, and the one time he hadn't reined himself in, the results had been devastating. He'd sworn never to be out of control again.

Maybe it was time to consider loosening those reins, at least where this one thing was concerned.

THE roads crisscrossing Lang Downs weren't quite as bumpy as Chris remembered them from his arrival on the station, but they were hardly smooth either. He tried to keep track on the map of where they were going and to mark the most pitted places for repair, although he had no idea whether what he considered bad would seem that way to someone used to life on a station.

Some days he felt like he'd gone down the rabbit hole with Alice.

He could deal with that most of the time, and he knew he had the man sitting next to him to thank for that. Jesse had been his touchstone since he arrived. He glanced sideways, wishing he had the nerve to turn and drink in Jesse's appearance the way he wanted to do, but even with the intimacies they'd shared, even knowing they'd do so again the next time an opportunity presented itself, he felt strange staring openly, like that was somehow a violation of some unspoken agreement.

They weren't together like Caine and Macklin were, a couple united against the world. They were fucking around from time to time. No harm in that, but it wasn't the same kind of relationship, the kind that let Caine stand comfortably in Macklin's personal space or that let Macklin climb the stairs to sleep in Caine's bed at night. Chris didn't claim to understand the routine that left Macklin sitting on the veranda alone watching the stars before going upstairs to join his lover, but Chris had seen it happen enough nights to accept it. Those heavy, measured treads signaled the end of the day. When Macklin came upstairs, the downstairs lights were off, the doors were closed, and it was time for bed, even if not always time for sleep, to judge by the sounds that filtered down the hallway as many nights as not.

Chris didn't have that with Jesse and didn't delude himself that he would have it any time soon, certainly not living under Caine and Macklin's roof. If he stayed at Lang Downs, he could move into the bunkhouse or maybe see about moving into one of the smaller houses if there was one empty, since he'd have Seth to share it with. Or maybe Seth could stay at Caine and Macklin's while Chris moved to the bunkhouse if a separate house wasn't available. Even in the bunkhouse, though, it wouldn't be like it was for Caine and Macklin. He and Jesse might mess around. They might even sleep together sometimes, but not like that.

Someday maybe he'd have a man like that in his life, a relationship to build a lifetime on. Someday when he had his shit together and could actually make decisions for himself. It wouldn't be tomorrow, but Caine and Macklin were proof it could happen, even out here in the outback.

"You're awfully quiet," Jesse said, his voice breaking into Chris's thoughts. "You okay?"

"I'm fine," Chris said quickly. A little too quickly, to judge by the look Jesse threw him. "Just thinking about Caine and Macklin."

"You're going to give me a complex here," Jesse joked.

"Not like that," Chris said with a roll of his eyes. "The way they live together. The way they rely on each other. It's probably silly, but I look at them and…."

"And think there might be hope for guys like us," Jesse finished.

Chris nodded.

"I've worked on eight stations in the last ten years," Jesse said, "and I've never seen anything like them, not even with a grazier and his wife. They make me believe in things I'd started thinking were impossible. Maybe not anywhere else, but here, at least. I've never wanted to stay on a station for the winter. I've always gone back to Melbourne or Sydney to crash with friends. Even at the two stations I worked at for a second summer, I didn't want to stay. It's different here, though. I could stay here."

"Yeah, I get the idea this is that kind of place," Chris agreed. "Or maybe that's just who I'm spending time with. Kami, Neil, Patrick… they're all year-rounders, as dedicated to the station as Caine and Macklin are. Maybe some of the seasonal jackaroos feel differently."

"Not really," Jesse said. "I mean, there are a lot who aren't ready to settle down or who see this as something different to do for a few years as a break after uni, or before uni, but quite a few of them come back summer after summer because working here is different."

Chris pondered that as they drove on. He'd planned to go to university once upon a time, before his mum got sick and Tony turned into more and more of a bastard when she wasn't around to see him. It shouldn't have been a surprise when Tony kicked them out. He wondered about using the job at the station as a chance to get his life together, save up a little money to live on while he was at uni, maybe even go part time so he could work here from shearing to whatever event marked the end of the work year for the seasonal jackaroos. He had no idea what or when that would be, but someone could tell him. He could get his degree and "do something" with his life, as Tony had always yelled at him to do. That would mean leaving Lang Downs, though, and at least for the next couple of years, Seth would be here. Chris didn't care how hard he had to work to make sure Seth had the time he needed to get his HSC so his choices wouldn't be limited, and if staying a few more years meant Seth could go to uni, then that's what Chris would do.

He glanced over at the man sitting in the cab of the ute with him. Or he could just stay. Jesse certainly seemed to be happy with his life as it was. Kami, Neil, Patrick, Kyle, Ian, and of course Caine and Macklin had carved out lives for themselves on the station. Patrick was married, and he wasn't the only one. Neil seemed well on his way to being married before the end of the summer, and Caine and Macklin were the closest thing to it, but Kyle and Ian were both single. They weren't twenty anymore, but they made a single life on a station work year-round.

If Jesse stayed too, like his conversation suggested he might, Chris wouldn't even have to go without in the winters. He'd have company all the time for as long as their arrangement lasted.

"There's the first drover's hut," Jesse said, drawing Chris out of his thoughts. "Let's go see what it needs."

The hut was basic at best, four walls and a roof with a lean-to shed behind it, presumably for horses if the jackaroos rode in instead of driving, but the inside showed no signs of water damage, so it was that tight at least because Chris knew they'd had bad storms in the tablelands during the winter.

"It's not a lot to look at, is it?" Chris said.

"When your other choice is spending the night in the open in the pouring rain or huddling under a tree or trying to get home on horseback in the middle of a storm, this looks like paradise," Jesse replied. "You have the list Caine gave us?"

Chris pulled it out so they could inventory the cabinets and see what they needed to add from the supplies in the flatbed of the ute. They switched out the blankets for clean ones, because Caine had insisted all the blankets could use a good wash, and refilled the cabinets with tins of vegetables and fruit as well as biscuits and Vegemite. It wouldn't be fancy dining, but it would be enough to fill a man's stomach in an emergency. They changed the flashlight batteries, checked the condition of the cots, and declared the cabin ready for summer.

"Once I get rid of this lead weight, we should volunteer for a night shift out here," Chris said as they climbed back into the ute. "We might actually have some time alone and some privacy that way."

"Time alone and privacy, maybe," Jesse said, "but out here, we're working."

"Even in the middle of the night?"

"Unless we're stuck out here and are using the huts as refuge, yes," Jesse said. "From what I heard, they drive the sheep close to the drover's huts at night so the men can keep an eye on them. We'd be inside, but we'd be expected to pay attention for threats in the night. Dingoes and feral dogs like to make off with sheep when it's dark and it's harder to see them to stop them."

"Bummer," Chris said with a frown. "There goes my great idea for getting you alone."

Jesse laughed. "We'll figure it out, Chris. It's not like we have to fuck every night, you know."

"We haven't fucked yet," Chris retorted.

Jesse elbowed him lightly. "You know what I mean."

Chris did know, but hearing Jesse talk about fucking, imagining what it might be like to have Jesse inside him, did things to Chris's libido. Suddenly the air in the cab seemed charged with electricity, and Jesse's hands on the wheel steering the ute toward the next hut drew Chris's eyes constantly as he imagined those hands on his body again.

"If we can't meet behind the tractor shed, can we meet inside the tractor shed again?" Chris asked after a few minutes, his voice sounding rough to his own ears.

"Feeling horny?" Jesse joked.

Chris grabbed one of Jesse's hands and rubbed it over his crotch. "Hell, yes."

"Careful, mate," Jesse said, putting his hand back on the wheel. "If I crash the ute, we'll both be in trouble."

"You didn't answer my question," Chris said. "Can we meet in the tractor shed again?"

"I don't know," Jesse said. "There's just no guarantee we won't be interrupted, and I'm past the age where someone walking in on me having sex has any appeal."

"You make it sound like you're ancient," Chris said. "You're only, what, twenty-five, twenty-six?"

"Twenty-eight," Jesse said, "but that's not the point. The point is I'm not a fan of sex with an audience, even when it's an appreciative audience, and there's a good chance it wouldn't be an appreciative audience here."

"Everybody seems pretty tolerant to me."

"There's a difference between being tolerant in theory and having it rubbed in your face," Jesse replied. "Yes, we're both adults, but that doesn't mean anyone else wants to see us together. I'm sure you've noticed Caine and Macklin keep it pretty far under wraps in public."

"Hiding in plain sight?" Chris asked.

"I don't think they're hiding," Jesse said. "That would be kind of pointless given Neil's speech the day we all arrived. They simply choose not to act in ways that would make people around them uncomfortable. They rely on their jackaroos to do their jobs as much as the jackaroos rely on them to have a job. If people suddenly started leaving, they'd be in trouble."

"I suppose," Chris said. "Can't we do the same? Hide in plain sight?"

"We're hardly in the same situation they're in," Jesse reminded him. "We aren't the boss and foreman."

"Macklin suspects," Chris said, "and he didn't seem to care. He said what I did with my off time was my business as long as it didn't affect my work or yours."

"That's good, I suppose," Jesse said, "although I'm not sure how I feel about them knowing, honestly."

"I didn't tell them," Chris said, hoping he hadn't done something wrong. "I was sitting on the veranda and Macklin mentioned a trip into town for supplies. I said I needed to pick up a few things. He offered to pick them up for me, but I wasn't going to ask him to buy me condoms so I said I'd rather go with, and that's when he told me it was okay if we were letting off a little steam as long as we knew what we were doing. I swear I didn't tell him."

"He didn't get to be the foreman of Lang Downs by being slow or stupid," Jesse said. "If you'd needed shampoo or something, you'd have asked for it, so you either needed condoms or you had the clap and wanted medicine for it. If you had the clap, they'd have treated you at the hospital. Therefore you wanted condoms."

When Jesse put it that way.... "I guess I did sort of tell him, then."

"Don't worry about it," Jesse said. "He wasn't upset, you said, and he didn't tell you we had to stop or anything so I figure that's tacit permission."

Chris scooted closer to Jesse in the cab of the ute. "So can we spend a few extra minutes at the next hut? I've missed you."

"At lunch," Jesse relented. "Wherever we stop for lunch, we'll be on a break and I won't feel so much like we're abusing their trust."

"They won't know when we take our break as long as we get a reasonable amount of work done today," Chris cajoled.

Jesse chuckled. "You really want to take that chance? You really think you can look Macklin in the eye when he starts asking questions and not give yourself away? I know I wouldn't be able to."

Given Chris's track record, he decided not to push it. "Okay, lunch time it is."

"Think of it as foreplay," Jesse said as they pulled up to the second hut. "Another two hours of anticipation, of wondering what will happen when we stop for lunch."

"Or of planning what I'm going to do to you," Chris teased. He refused to be the only one desperately horny by lunch time. "I can think of a few things I'd like to try."

"If I let you," Jesse retorted.

Chris grinned. "Oh, you'll let me. I've got a talented mouth, or so I've been told."

TWELVE

JESSE was tempted to make a comment about Chris's experience, but he didn't want to provoke a fight, especially when his own track record for relationships was probably as spotty as Chris's. He'd had one hook-up several years ago that turned into a season of messing around, but neither he nor the other guy—Jesse couldn't even remember his name—had ever pretended it was anything more than a convenience when they didn't feel like going out on the prowl. Jesse didn't know if Chris had ever had a boyfriend, a real one with emotions involved, but since Jesse couldn't claim one in his own past, he decided not to ask. "I certainly benefited the other night," he said instead.

"Good," Chris said, his voice so smug Jesse decided right then what was going to happen when they stopped for lunch. Chris was getting his mind blown along with his dick. Chris might have a talented mouth, but he was still a kid compared to Jesse, and Jesse would bet he'd been the one doing the sucking, not the one being sucked. He knew how gay bars worked. A kid like Chris, fresh-faced and more slender than stocky, would have been the one on his knees blowing the other guy or else the one with his pants around his knees getting fucked. Unless he picked up someone even younger and skinner than him. Jesse had known a few exceptions to that dynamic, but they were few and far between, and usually in enough of a relationship to set aside some of the posturing. Chris didn't have that vibe.

"Let's get this hut stocked," Jesse said, his voice rough. "We should be able to do one more before lunch."

Chris hopped out of the ute, carrying his list inside. They checked the hut, finding this one much more depleted of supplies than the last one.

"I'm glad we're doing this," Chris said as they carried in tins of food. "I wouldn't want to be the one stuck out here with nothing more in the cupboards than what we just found."

"Me either," Jesse agreed, thinking of the nights he'd spent sleeping rough on other stations. He could see why the Lang Downs jackaroos were as loyal as they were. Accepting a gay boss had to be easier with perks like these to ease the sting. For someone like Jesse who had left jobs in the past because of discrimination, the combination seemed like a dream come true.

They switched out the blankets and closed everything back up. "Where's the next hut?"

Chris looked at the map Macklin had given him. "That way."

The roads worsened as they made their way to higher elevations, proof of the powerful storms that had hit the area over the winter. It took them nearly two hours to reach the next hut. "Lunch time," Chris declared as soon as they stopped.

"Let's check the hut first," Jesse suggested. "Then we can relax and eat."

"And fuck."

"And something," Jesse agreed. "I still don't carry condoms while I'm working."

"We'll have to do something about that," Chris insisted. "There's nowhere at the station itself, which means we have to find other places to be alone."

"We'll see," Jesse said, not entirely comfortable with that compromise unless they drove out to one of the empty huts after they finished work for the night and came back in time for breakfast. His sense of responsibility to Caine was too strong. He didn't want to lose this job, and while he didn't think he'd lose it for messing around with Chris, Caine would have every right to fire him if he messed around when he was supposed to be working.

The stench of animal dung hit them the moment they opened the door. "Damn," Jesse cursed. "Something spent the winter in there. I hope it wasn't anything nasty."

"It was nasty enough just from the smell," Chris complained, holding his nose with his good hand.

"Yeah, but there's nasty and then there's dangerous," Jesse said. "Get one of those extra flashlights and let's see if we can figure out what's in there before we go in."

Chris grabbed a flashlight out of the back of the ute, and Jesse shone it in the door, looking for the reflection of eyes or anything else to show where the animal was. He found them, finally, in the back corner of the hut. "Over there," he said to Chris. "See it?"

"I see eyes," Chris whispered, "but I can't tell what it is."

"Me either," Jesse said. "Bandicoots, bilbies, bettongs or potoroos, or if we're unlucky, a wombat."

"Why unlucky?"

"Because they're bigger and tougher than the others. If it's a wombat, we may want to talk with Macklin before we do anything else. I knew a man at another station who tangled with one and ended up in the hospital," Jesse explained, "and that one wasn't cornered and protecting its home."

"So how do we figure out what it is?" Chris asked. "If they're that tough, I'm not sure walking in and opening windows to let in light is the best idea."

"They're nocturnal," Jesse said. "I know that much. The light ought to drive it deeper into its nest if it's a wombat, and if it's not, we'll be able to see what it is. Keep the flashlight on it so we can see if it moves. I'll try to get a window open."

Chris nodded as Jesse slipped inside and edged along the wall farthest from the animal, feeling for the window rather than looking for it. He wasn't taking his eyes off the creature until he knew what it was. He found the latch and pushed it open, letting in the late morning sunlight. "It's a wombat. We'll report it to Macklin and see what he wants us to do about it."

"We'd have to come back and clean the hut out anyway," Chris said as Jesse inched back toward the door. "We don't have shovels and the like to clean out its nest, and I'm not sure how much help I'd be to you anyway. I can't hold a shovel at the moment."

"Not to mention that even if we run the wombat out, there's the question of how it got in here and keeping it from coming back. Macklin might want to send a more experienced crew out to deal with it. I'm not much of a carpenter. I mean, I could pound a couple of nails to hold a board over a hole if there is one, but that's not the real solution. I was going to suggest eating lunch in the hut, but I think we'll be better off sitting on the bed of the ute."

Chris grabbed their lunches from the cab of the ute while Jesse spread one of the clean blankets over the metal bed of the truck. It wasn't a bed, or even a cot like in the huts, but it was better than cold steel. Fortunately the sun was out, warming the day enough that the breeze off the highlands felt good, although Jesse wasn't sure about getting naked out in the open. He'd been imagining stretching Chris out on one of the cots and taking his time licking and sucking all over, not just getting him off and rushing on to the next hut. It might be a little cool for that, though. He'd see how things went.

Chris hopped up on the gate of the ute next to him. "Here's your lunch," he said, offering the bag to Jesse. Jesse waited a moment before opening his bag. Chris had been so eager earlier, but now he seemed content to sit and eat, so Jesse did the same. He wasn't eighteen and so horny he couldn't stand it. He could afford to wait until after they'd eaten or even until another time entirely.

"Seth seems to be settling in well," Jesse said as they ate. "Other than a couple of pranks, anyway. That should make you happy."

"A couple?" Chris said around his mouthful of sandwich. "I only knew about the one he played on me."

Jesse cursed under his breath. "And I told him I wouldn't tell you since he apologized and cleaned up the mess he made," Jesse said with a shake of his head.

"What did he do?"

"He messed up Patrick's toolbox," Jesse said. "It was harmless, just annoying, and he put everything back in its place. Patrick checks his box every morning now before he starts work, but other than that, he doesn't seem to be holding a grudge."

"Little shite," Chris muttered. "I *told* him not to do crap like that here on the station. He thinks it's funny, but he's past the age where he can get away with it."

"Which is what Patrick told him," Jesse said. "Even better, I really think he listened. He's been on his best behavior ever since. Just let it go."

"I guess I can do that this time since Patrick already got on him about it," Chris said slowly. "I'm trying my best to be a good role model for him, but bloody hell, I don't know what I'm doing half the time."

"Hey," Jesse said, tugging on Chris's good hand until Chris scooted into his arms. "None of that. Seth isn't a little kid you have to coach constantly. He's nearly an adult himself and old enough to make his own decisions. If he screws up, that's on him, not on you. You've done more than your part already making sure he has a place to stay and enough to eat."

Chris sighed and leaned against Jesse. "I will never, ever make a disparaging comment about a parent again. I don't know how they do it, because just six months with a mostly-grown teenager and I'm at the end of my rope."

Jesse kissed the side of Chris's neck, more in comfort than in an attempt at seduction. He had no idea how he'd handle that kind of responsibility. He only hoped he'd have half Chris's success if something like that happened to him. He hadn't seen any of his younger siblings since he left home, though, so it wasn't likely. His "baby" sister was already older than Seth.

Jesse lost track of how long they sat that way in companionable silence. It wasn't the lunch break they'd discussed, but Jesse found he didn't mind. More than anything, it seemed Chris needed a friend right now, and Jesse was happy to oblige.

"I guess we should check on the rest of the huts," Chris said eventually. "I sort of ruined our lunch break."

"You didn't ruin anything," Jesse said, catching Chris's chin and kissing him. "Sex isn't any fun if both people aren't into it, and you obviously weren't in the mood. We'll have other chances."

They finished restocking two more of the drover's huts before Jesse declared they'd done all they could do for the day. He picked up the dirty blankets, ready to head back to the ute, when Chris pushed him against the door and kissed him wildly.

Jesse started to protest out of habit, but he had just declared it the end of the work day, other than driving back to the station for dinner. Chris hadn't been in the mood earlier, but that had obviously changed, and Jesse realized he didn't mind. He let the blankets fall to the ground and pulled Chris closer, one hand on Chris's hip, the other cradling his head to take control of the kiss. The moment Chris realized Jesse was kissing him back, he relaxed, so Jesse spun them around, switching their places so Chris's back was against the door, pinned in place by Jesse's broader body. He released Chris's lips to kiss his way across his cheek, the stubble scraping against his lips.

"It'll be time to shave you again soon," he murmured when he reached the delicate shell of Chris's ear.

Chris hummed softly, a sound of assent or pleasure or both. Jesse didn't care which it was at this point. It was enough to have Chris willing in his arms again. He parted the heavy jacket Chris was wearing so he could massage his chest through the thick work shirt. It wasn't quite the same as skin on skin, but it would do for now. He'd save the rest for when they had more time, and maybe a bed. He spared a quick thought for the cots behind them, but if he started that now, they'd be late for dinner, and then there would be questions to answer. Instead he worked open the button on Chris's jeans and peeled down the zipper, slipping a hand inside to stroke Chris's burgeoning erection. Oh, yeah, Chris had sloughed off his bad mood from earlier.

Chris moaned as Jesse moved his hand up and down a few times, and Jesse reveled in the freedom to enjoy the sound rather than have to stifle it for fear of being overheard. He pulled back long enough to push Chris's jeans and boxers off his hips, letting the hard shaft pop free. He kissed Chris once more before dropping to his knees and claiming his prize.

He heard a thunk above him, presumably Chris's head hitting the door, but he didn't stop, too focused on the hard cock in his mouth, the salty flavor that leaked from the tip, the musky smell of sweat and desire that radiated from Chris's body. Of all the things Jesse loved about sex, this might be the one he loved the most, taking complete control of a man's body and senses, leaving him incapable of doing anything except moaning and shivering and coming like there was no tomorrow. He'd argued with what's-his-name about it once, the other man insisting it was better to be blown than to do the blowing, but Jesse disagreed. Oh, he'd never complain about someone sucking him off, but that was a passive pleasure. This was all about making his lover feel good, and Jesse found the little sounds and signs of Chris's desire even more arousing than simply getting his rocks off.

Chris's fingers found his scalp, rubbing through his buzzed hair. Jesse wondered for a moment if Chris would try to take control and fuck Jesse's mouth, but he didn't, seeming only to need the contact. Jesse stroked Chris's hip, offering that tenderness in return.

"Oh, fuck, close," Chris gasped above him.

Jesse pulled back, his hand taking the place of his mouth as he surged to his feet and captured Chris's lips. He stroked Chris rapidly as he plundered Chris's mouth, exploring every inch with his tongue.

Chris grunted into the kiss, his body seizing beneath Jesse's hand. Jesse slowed the movement of his palm, easing Chris back down from the high. His own need growing demanding, he rutted against Chris's thigh. If he'd been thinking ahead, he'd have moved to the other side because the angle made it hard for Chris to get his good hand between them to help Jesse along, but he realized he didn't care as Chris pushed back against him, urging him on. Jesse buried his face in Chris's neck as his climax hit him.

"Well, that's going to make for an uncomfortable ride home," Jesse muttered when he could speak again.

"Take your shorts off," Chris suggested. "Commando has to be more comfortable than sticky."

Chris was probably right, but that would mean undressing with Chris watching. He wouldn't think twice if they were rushing for bed, but it felt somehow too intimate to undress in front of him.

"I'll meet you at the ute," Jesse said.

"And deprive me of the chance to stare at your arse?" Chris joked. "I don't think so."

Swallowing down the ridiculous surge of nerves, Jesse pulled off his boots and stepped out of his pants and briefs, pulling his jeans back on as quickly as he could. Chris's appreciative stare did nothing for his composure.

"Why does this bother you?" Chris asked. "You weren't complaining a minute ago or when I had your dick in my mouth a few days ago."

"That's sex," Jesse said with a shrug. "Changing clothes in front of you is more intimate."

"How do you figure that?"

"It's not something you do when you're just fooling around," Jesse said. "You fuck, you get dressed, you go on. Changing clothes like that, it's something you do with a lover."

"Or with a friend," Chris said. "I've stayed over with friends and didn't think twice about changing with them in the room."

"Are we friends?" Jesse asked.

"What else would you call it?" Chris replied.

Jesse wasn't sure how to answer that question. They had known each other such a short time, had barely begun any kind of a relationship before the dynamic changed on them, but that was no more defined than the first days had been. "I guess we are friends," he said with a slow smile. "I don't think I've ever been friends with a guy I was sleeping with."

Chris winked at him. "You haven't slept with me yet."

Jesse resolved to remedy that at the first opportunity. Maybe he could carry a condom tomorrow after all.

THIRTEEN

"A WOMBAT?" Caine asked when Jesse and Chris reported their discovery at dinner. "I've never seen a wombat before."

Chris could practically see Macklin swallow a put-upon sigh. "You don't particularly want to see one," he said. "They can be dangerous, especially if they're cornered, which this one is. Which hut was it in?"

Jesse told him.

"I'll drive back out after dinner," Macklin decided. "When it leaves to forage for the night, we'll block whatever hole it used for an entrance so it can't get back in, and then tomorrow, I'll send someone to clean out its den."

"I'll go with you," Caine said.

Chris chuckled as Macklin rolled his eyes. "It's really a one-man job," he said. "There's no reason for both of us to stay up half the night. Someone has to be in charge of the shearing tomorrow."

"And you really think I can do that?" Caine joked. "Put Neil in charge of the shearing tomorrow if we're up too late for you to handle it."

"We'll finish the huts tomorrow unless you need us to do something different, boss," Jesse said, grabbing Chris's arm and pulling him away from the table.

Macklin didn't answer, his focus completely on Caine.

"What?" Chris said when they were outside.

"I wasn't about to stay and watch them get into it," Jesse said. "There are some things I don't need to see."

"You're no fun," Chris said.

"That's not what you thought earlier today," Jesse said with a wink.

Chris laughed, as Jesse had certainly intended, but he couldn't deny the truth of the statement either. He'd had quite a lot of fun earlier in the day. He was tempted to kiss Jesse now to show him just how much fun, but while a quick glance revealed no one within his field of vision, he knew better than to think it would stay that way for long. The canteen door would swing open and someone would come outside, or someone would step out of the bunkhouse for a smoke or to check on the sheep still in the pens. He settled for elbowing Jesse with his good arm.

"See you in the morning?" Jesse said. "We still have half the huts to finish."

"I wouldn't miss it," Chris replied.

Jesse's smile changed from that teasing grin to something more shyly pleased, making Chris's heart beat a little faster. He chided himself silently. They'd only known each other for a couple of weeks. He couldn't fall for someone that fast, especially not with everything up in the air. Keeping his smile in place so he wouldn't reveal his suddenly spinning thoughts, Chris waved good night and headed back to the station house.

He didn't go inside, taking a seat on the porch again and hoping he'd have some time with his thoughts since Caine and Macklin were going out to deal with the wombat. He wondered if Macklin had, as Jesse insisted, known what he and Jesse had gotten up to that afternoon in the drover's hut. He hoped not. He wasn't embarrassed by it; he didn't think they'd done anything wrong; it was *private*, and the thought of Macklin knowing, speculating even, rubbed him the wrong way. Maybe he and Jesse weren't in the middle of some grand love affair. Maybe they weren't meant to be together always the way Caine and Macklin were. Their time together was still special, and he didn't want to share it.

The sound of one of the utes driving by drew his attention from his thoughts momentarily. He couldn't help a smile when he saw two silhouettes in the cab as it headed out of the valley toward the hut where he and Jesse had found the wombat. He didn't envy Caine and Macklin a night spent in a truck cab, but he did feel a small twinge of jealousy at the openness that allowed them to be together.

He had to remind himself that they were the boss and the foreman and that they had paid a price for being together that way. Neil had admitted they'd never had as many new jackaroos all at once as they had this season. While quite a few of the seasonal hands had chosen to return despite Caine and Macklin's orientation, that many more had chosen not to return, a far higher turnover rate than usual. They weren't short staffed, but they could have been. For Chris, the price would be different, but he had no doubt he'd have to pay one. He'd already paid once, not for being in a relationship, but simply for being different.

One good thing had come out of it. He had a place to live for both himself and Seth, and he had Jesse.

That made two good things. Maybe Jesse wasn't "it" for Chris the way Caine was for Macklin—it was way too soon to be thinking that way, regardless of what might develop between them in the future—but Jesse was good for him. He made Chris laugh. He made Chris feel good. He listened when Chris needed to talk. Now if they could just find some time and privacy so he could fuck Chris when he needed release, everything would be damn near perfect.

The blow job in the hut had been phenomenal. Chris had gotten blow jobs before, but mostly back in school from guys who had no real idea what they were doing. They'd fumbled more than they'd sucked, and they'd always pulled off before Chris could come in their mouths.

Jesse knew what he was doing. Chris's heart beat a little faster at the memory. Jesse had kept him there pinned against the wall, and Chris had felt *taken,* like Jesse had hijacked his brain and turned his body inside out. Chris had spent enough time on his knees in this bar and that to know what it felt like to give a blow job, but he'd always felt like the control rested with the man he was blowing. Not today. He hadn't had any control over the encounter with Jesse, not from the moment Jesse's mouth had closed around him. It had been all he could do to stay vertical and not beg Jesse to take him bare and dry.

He shifted on the chair, stretching his legs out to accommodate his sudden erection. He ought to go inside and get ready for bed. Even if jerking off left-handed was awkward, he'd be more comfortable in just his boxers than in his jeans. He wasn't ready to go inside, though. The sun had set while he sat there, leaving the western horizon tinged in pink and orange while the clouds on the eastern horizon flashed with lightning. The sheep still waiting to be sheared baaed occasionally, a quiet, calming sound that carried to Chris on the light breeze. If the storm blew in overnight, the wind would undoubtedly pick up, rattling the windows of the station house, but for now it was calm.

He hoped the storm passed during the night. He didn't want the weather to keep them from going out to the rest of the huts tomorrow. He'd actually felt like he was contributing something today instead of being a drag on the station. That would change once his cast came off, he hoped, but for the time being, he was pretty much the least productive person there, and he knew it, even if everyone had the tact not to mention it.

A burst of laughter drifted across the road from the bunkhouse, making Chris wish he had an excuse to join them. Maybe he'd talk to Jesse the next day and see what the other man thought about him hanging out there some in the evenings. If he was going to make a future out of working on Lang Downs, he'd need to get to know the others as well. He couldn't always expect to work with Neil or Jesse, as much as he'd like to keep hanging out with them, Jesse especially. Expecting Neil to babysit him all the time wouldn't be reasonable and while Jesse didn't seem to mind Chris hanging around, once his arm healed up completely, Chris wouldn't have the excuse of taking it easy to spend time with Jesse when he was working on the farm machinery. Chris would have his own tasks and responsibilities, and the sooner he could learn how to carry those out, the better off he'd be.

With a resolute nod, he rose from his seat and headed upstairs to bed. He'd spend tomorrow helping Jesse with the rest of the huts, and tomorrow night, he'd start getting better acquainted with everyone else.

"THE weather report warned of storms today," Macklin said at breakfast the next morning. "If it gets bad, come back down if you can or take refuge in one of the huts if you can't. Radio in every hour and let us know where you are and what the weather is. We don't want you taking chances or getting hurt. The huts don't have to be finished today. They don't have to be finished this week if the storms blow in and stay for a while."

"Yes, sir," Jesse said. He could feel the chill and dampness on the breeze, even down in the protected valley. They'd be glad of the heater in the ute today. "Did you get rid of the wombat last night?"

"Yes, but it came back, trying to get inside. Let's give it a few days to give up before you clean out that cabin. No reason to do it more than once if the wombat manages to get back inside."

Chris joined him at the ute, looking even younger and more vulnerable than usual wrapped up in a drizabone that looked two sizes too big for him.

"Oh, good, Caine found my old drizabone," Macklin said. "I knew it had to be there somewhere. We'll get one that fits you right when we go to Yass to get your cast removed. Jesse, you remember what I said out there. You're experienced enough to make the call about coming back or waiting it out."

Macklin strode off before Jesse could reply. The condom was burning a hole in his pocket as he contemplated the possibility of getting stuck in one of the huts with Chris for an indefinite period of time. God, he hoped Macklin didn't guess or he'd lose his job for sure. He had to think about something else or he'd give them away.

"You have to go back to Yass to get your cast removed?" Jesse asked as they climbed in the ute and started back to the highlands.

"Apparently. Boorowa doesn't have an X-ray facility, but Yass is only an hour farther away. It's not like we have to drive to Melbourne."

"That's not what I was worried about," Jesse said. "You were bashed in Yass."

"I know," Chris said, "but I don't have to go back alone. Caine and Macklin said they'd stay with me if I wanted them to."

"You don't sound enthusiastic."

"They already see me as a kid," Chris explained. "If I can't even handle getting my cast off by myself, how am I supposed to convince them I'm an adult?"

"It's not the cast, though," Jesse said. "It's the fact that you were beaten nearly to death. I can go with you if you'd prefer. I don't see you as a kid."

"I... I think I'd like that," Chris said. "It's still a couple weeks off. The doctor said six to eight weeks. I don't want to go twice so I'll wait the full eight weeks before I go back. That's only another month at this point. That way hopefully they'll just cut the plaster off and let me go home."

The light mist started as they crested the edge of the valley and drove north toward the huts they had not stocked the day before.

"Whenever you decide to go, just tell me and I'll be there, even if I have to take a day or two off to do it," Jesse insisted. "Remember what we said yesterday about being friends? Well, friends help each other out when they need it, and going back to Yass sounds like a time when you'd need it."

The surprised expression on Chris's face was too much for Jesse. He stopped the truck and tugged on Chris's arm, pulling him into a kiss. He kept it light, tender rather than arousing, because despite the condom in his pocket, the cab of the ute was not where he wanted to be when they used it. The first time he got inside Chris—or vice versa, he wasn't picky—he wanted to have the space and time to enjoy it. Chris wasn't some random fuck Jesse had picked up at a bar. They were friends, and he found he liked it that way. He liked going back to his bunk last night and knowing he'd see Chris again, that they'd laugh and joke and work together, and that eventually they'd get around to getting each other off again.

The way Chris kissed him back, licking and biting at his lips, tempted him to ignore that resolution, but they had barely left the valley that sheltered the station. In the ute or in a hut, they needed to get a little farther away before they got naked. Jesse would never survive the mortification if one of the other jackaroos, or worse, Caine or Macklin, caught them. This close to the station, that was not outside the realm of possibility.

"Hold that thought." Jesse's voice sounded rough to his own ears, testament to how deeply Chris's kisses, Chris's eagerness had affected him. "Let's get a little farther from home first, okay?"

Chris didn't look convinced, but he scooted back to his side of the ute and fastened his seatbelt again. Jesse put the ute back in gear and headed on to the first hut.

The light mist had turned into a definite drizzle by the time they reached the drover's hut, unpleasant, but not enough to keep them from doing their jobs. Jesse glanced at Chris to make sure his drizabone was buttoned up to keep him dry.

They did a quick inventory of the drover's hut, finding this one mostly stocked.

"I wonder why this one needs so much less than the others," Chris said as they changed the blankets and put fresh batteries in the flashlights. "Some of the others have been all but bare, and this one looks like we stocked it last week."

Jesse shrugged. "Could be it gets more use and so people bring supplies more often, or it could be it gets less use because it's relatively close to the station. If they're this close, they can just go home for the night."

"Yeah, that makes sense, I guess."

As they finished up, they heard the sound of the rain on the tin roof.

"How far to the next hut?" Jesse asked.

"It doesn't look all that far," Chris said, "but it's hard to tell sometimes. The map isn't exactly drawn to scale."

"Let's make a run for it," Jesse said. "We'll get wet a little, but I'd rather get more than one hut done before we have to call it quits because of the weather."

They dashed through the cold rain, not a downpour yet, but definitely stronger than just a drizzle. The gravel on the road kept it from turning into a quagmire even with the heavier rain, but Jesse wondered how long that would last. Long enough to get to the next hut, he hoped. The ute had four-wheel drive, but even that had limits.

Fortunately the second hut wasn't far. Jesse parked the ute as close to the door as he could manage and still have any hope of getting back on the road.

They dashed inside and began the inventory, but Jesse's mind focused far more on the ever-increasing pounding of the rain than on the task at hand. They had finished half the cabinets when a crack of thunder directly overhead startled them. Jesse opened the door and looked at the horizon appraisingly.

"I think we'll wait out the storm," he said. "I don't like the way those clouds look, and I'm not familiar enough with the area to gauge what kind of effects the weather will have on the roads. I don't think the boss would appreciate having to rescue another jackaroo from a storm."

"Fine with me," Chris said. "I have no desire to need rescuing, not when we're safe and dry here. Do you need anything from the ute?"

"No, do you?"

"Just our lunches if we're stuck here that long."

"I hope we aren't, but I'll grab them now before the weather gets worse." He turned up his collar and pulled his hat as low as he could on his head to protect his neck and dashed to the ute. The rain soaked his lower legs, but his back and neck stayed dry as he rummaged through the sacks for their lunches. Finding them, he ran back inside, shaking water from his drizabone as he stood just inside the doorway.

"Maybe we should get a fire going?" Chris asked. "I put some logs in the fireplace, but I don't really know much beyond that."

As wet as his feet were, Jesse thought a fire sounded heavenly. "I'll do it. Why don't you finish the inventory so we can get everything from the truck when the rain slows down?"

Chris nodded and went back to checking cabinets while Jesse started the fire. Once it was going, he pulled off his boots and propped his sock-covered feet in front of the flames to dry out and warm up.

"Your jeans are soaked too," Chris said. "I promise not to jump you if you take them off to dry. You can wrap up in a blanket if you're cold."

Jesse stripped off his pants, sitting back down in only his underwear. "Let it warm up in here and you can jump me all you want."

Chris grinned. "I like the sound of that."

Jesse grabbed his jeans and pulled out the condom he had hidden there before he left his room that morning. "You'll like this even better, then."

"I thought you didn't carry condoms when you were working," Chris said, swallowing around the lump of desire clogging his throat. Jesse's cock started to fill at the sound.

"I got tired of waiting."

Chris launched himself at Jesse, straddling him and kissing him wildly. Jesse ignored the rasp of denim on his bare skin as Chris devoured his mouth. The sense of being desired so powerfully fired his blood. He ran his hands down Chris's back and pulled the hem of his shirt free so he could reach skin. As easy as it would be to lift Chris up a little, push aside their remaining clothes, and let Chris ride him into oblivion, they had the time and privacy to linger, and Jesse intended to take advantage of it.

He broke the kiss, already breathing hard. "There's a perfectly good cot over there. We could actually get undressed and lie down."

Chris grunted, not moving as he worked a hand between them to stroke Jesse through his briefs.

Jesse caught his hand and pulled it away. "What's the rush?"

"The chance to have you fuck me?" Chris retorted.

"I will if that's what you want," Jesse promised, "but listen to that storm. We aren't going anywhere anytime soon, and I only have one condom, so there's no rush. We can take our time getting there."

Chris stood up and shrugged out of his drizabone, the sleeve catching awkwardly on his cast. Jesse followed him, freeing his arm and pulling him into an embrace, his back against Jesse's chest. "Not rushing, remember?"

He ran his hands over Chris's cloth-covered chest, enjoying the play of strong, sleek muscles. Chris might not have a jackaroo's wiry build yet, but Jesse would put money on him filling out by the end of the summer.

Chris leaned back against Jesse so trustingly Jesse nearly called off their sex. Chris needed someone so much better than Jesse, someone with a stable life and the ability to make promises and keep them. Jesse didn't know where he'd be after April when the seasonal work at Lang Downs ended.

Jesse rolled his eyes at himself. Chris would kick his arse for that kind of condescension. He'd proved his ability to take care of himself and his brother. He didn't need Jesse hovering over him and taking his decisions out of his hands. Furthermore, Chris had made his hopes for the next few minutes very clear. Jesse had no reason not to give it to him.

Especially not when Chris rubbed his tight, sweet arse against Jesse's erection. Oh, yeah, Jesse was going to enjoy this. It had been a while since he'd had the time to really linger over sex rather than feeling obliged to rush for release. He worked open the buttons on Chris's shirt, finding the dusting of chest hair he'd seen but not had time to explore when he helped Chris shave the last time. Lifting one hand to Chris's cheek, he nuzzled the nape of Chris's neck. "I'll have to help you shave again tonight. You're getting scruffy."

Chris tipped his head into Jesse's hand, the gesture so vulnerable Jesse felt his heart melt. He urged Chris to turn his head until their lips met in a tender kiss. Jesse shifted so they stood facing one another as the kiss continued. He pushed the shirt off Chris's shoulders, taking care to keep it from getting caught on Chris's cast, and tossed it aside.

Chris returned the favor one-handed, leaving them skin to skin for the first time. Jesse shivered at the contact and slid his hands around Chris's waist, simply holding him for the moment.

"I thought we were going to use that cot," Chris said.

"In a minute," Jesse replied.

Chris didn't seem inclined to wait, though, moving his good hand down Jesse's back and inside the waistband of his briefs. His fingers dug into the muscle of Jesse's arse, pushing him toward Chris.

Jesse took a step back. "Get naked."

"As long as you do the same," Chris replied.

Jesse raised an eyebrow at him, stepped out of his briefs, and toed off his socks. "Your turn."

Jesse resisted the urge to help as Chris fumbled with his boots and jeans, but while he would have enjoyed helping Chris undress, he'd already crossed far too many lines. They weren't lovers, not really, and he couldn't let himself think that way. Instead he stretched out on the cot, stroking himself leisurely as he watched the rest of Chris's hot, tight body come into view.

CHRIS looked up from getting undressed to see Jesse spread out on the bed, hard and ready, hand moving up and down his cock. He waited only a moment, drinking in the compelling sight before pouncing, never doubting for a second that Jesse would catch him.

Jesse's arms wrapped around him, pulling Chris down on top of him, and Chris burrowed close, wanting every inch of his body touching some part of Jesse's. Jesse obliged, wrapping his arms and legs around Chris, holding him close and tight on the narrow cot. Chris sighed into the kiss even as the need to drive Jesse wild increased. The cast on his arm kept him from what he wanted to do, but he'd been around the block often enough to have plenty of other ideas... if Jesse was willing. Jesse kept insisting they could take the time to enjoy each other instead of rushing for completion. Chris decided to take him at his word. He pushed back up on his good elbow and both knees. "Turn over."

Jesse's surprise showed on his face, but Chris didn't let that deter him. The moment Jesse was settled on his stomach, Chris slid down the cot, intent on his goal. Finding the right angle with his broken arm was awkward, but eventually he managed to bury his face in Jesse's arse and find the entrance with his tongue. Jesse grunted into the pillow, bringing a smile to Chris's face as he lavished attention on the square inch of flesh that would, he hoped, bring Jesse enough pleasure to want to fuck Chris thoroughly later.

The scent of Jesse's desire filled Chris's senses, spurring him to greater efforts. He worked his way lower, sucking Jesse's balls into his mouth. Jesse moaned this time instead of just the grunts from earlier so Chris sucked harder, until Jesse pulled away.

"If you want me to fuck you, now's the time to stop," Jesse said, his eyes glittering with lust as he rolled onto his back.

"Or I could get you off and then fuck you," Chris said, testing the waters.

"You could," Jesse agreed, his voice never changing tone.

Chris decided right then he'd take Jesse up on that offer before long, but he'd been imagining what it would feel like to have Jesse inside him practically since they met, certainly since he discovered Jesse was gay. Fulfilling that fantasy took precedence. "Next time."

He grabbed the condom from where it had fallen when they hit the bed and rolled it onto Jesse's cock. It was pre-lubed, fortunately, because he was out of patience. He straddled Jesse's hips, sinking slowly onto Jesse's erection.

"You could've let me stretch you a bit," Jesse said with a groan.

"I couldn't wait," Chris said as he rocked back and forth, feeling his muscles stretch slowly as he grew accustomed to Jesse's girth inside him. It burned, but Chris knew it would pass soon, and when it did, it would feel incredible.

Jesse grunted again, the tendons in his neck standing out as he held himself still beneath Chris. Chris appreciated the effort, but he was past waiting now. He reached behind him with his good hand and massaged Jesse's sac. "Fuck me already."

Jesse chuckled as he thrust up into Chris. "If you want me to really fuck you, you're in the wrong position."

Chris leaned forward and kissed Jesse swiftly. "Deal with it."

Jesse tweaked one of Chris's nipples. "Dealing."

Chris smiled, enjoying the repartee almost as much as the caress. Okay, maybe not, but the idea of laughing, teasing during sex instead of rushing for climax as fast as possible was completely foreign. He'd never experienced this kind of easy camaraderie in the midst of fucking. Now that he had, though, he wasn't about to give it up.

His head fell back as he rode Jesse harder, all the pent-up lust from the day and the weeks since he arrived and the months since he'd been fucked and rimming Jesse and being here with a friend instead of a fuck rising up inside him and choking him until he felt like the only thing keeping his lungs working was Jesse's cock forcing air out of him as he thrust in and pulling air back in as he withdrew. His thighs burned as he posted faster, harder, desperate for the release that hovered just out of reach.

Then Jesse's hand closed around Chris's cock and he cried out, the touch sending him into orbit until he swore he saw stars dancing behind his eyes and nothing existed but this moment and this man and the joining of their bodies. Time and space and responsibilities ceased to matter. Only making Jesse feel as good as Chris felt right now, because he could still feel Jesse hard inside him, still thrusting, still wild-eyed and straining beneath him. He squeezed as hard as he could on the cock inside him, bracing himself so Jesse could move as he needed to. Then Jesse grunted and shook beneath him, and Chris imagined he could feel the cock inside him twitch as Jesse climaxed too.

Completely wrung out, he collapsed forward onto Jesse's chest. Jesse held him tight as they shifted around to get comfortable. Chris had the passing thought that he should clean up the mess he'd made, but exhaustion claimed him first and he fell asleep.

FOURTEEN

CHRIS resisted the urge to pace the exam room of the hospital in Yass as he waited for the doctor to arrive with the X-rays and pronounce his arm fit to come out of its cast. He told himself it was simply impatience to get back to Lang Downs, but he knew it was more than that. He'd practically had a panic attack when they reached the outskirts of Yass. Jesse had held him through that bout of nerves, but now Chris was alone, and the panic was clawing at his throat again.

He'd gone round and round in his head since he realized he'd have to return to Yass to get his cast removed. He'd tried pretending it didn't bother him. He'd bluffed his way through the expressions of concern, but when he'd seen the sign for the town limits, all the fear and pain of the bashing had come rushing back. His vision had grayed out, leaving him gasping for breath as blows rained down on him.

Jesse had grabbed him and held him tightly, murmuring reassurances that had finally penetrated Chris's mind, allowing him to calm down and deal with the rest of the drive into town. Caine and Macklin had left them at the hospital, although Chris wondered what Macklin had said to get Caine to agree to that. Chris had been sure Caine wouldn't leave him there for anything after his overreaction in the car. Caine had gone, though, with orders to call as soon as Chris was done. Chris hated to admit he'd been reassured by that as well. The hotel wasn't that far from the hospital, but the thought of walking through town, past the restaurant where he'd used to work and the alley where he was beaten nearly to death, filled him with dread.

"Mr. Simms?"

"Yes, that's me," Chris said as the doctor came in.

"Your arm seems to have healed nicely. We'll get that cast off and then go over the PT you need to do for it."

"PT?" Chris asked.

"Your muscles and ligaments have atrophied after eight weeks of non-use," the doctor explained. "You have to work on stretching and strengthening them again or you could seriously injure your elbow. Do you have a job?"

"I work on a sheep station," Chris said. "I've been helping in the kitchen because of my arm, but I'm supposed to work with the sheep once the cast is off."

"Let's get rid of it then and see what shape you're in," the doctor replied. "You'll recover full use of your arm with proper exercise and care. You'll just have to give it a little time."

Chris didn't like the sound of that. He'd been waiting eight weeks already to really start learning to be a jackaroo. He didn't want to wait any longer.

Looking down at his arm once the cast was gone, though, he realized the doctor was right. His right arm looked about half the size of his left arm and it hurt to bend his elbow. "Let me show you the exercises you need to do."

"Would it be all right if my friend came back to listen as well?" Chris interrupted before the doctor could begin. "He'll be the one helping me follow through on everything, and I'd feel better if he heard from you what we're supposed to do."

"I suppose that would be all right," the doctor said.

Chris nearly sagged in relief when the man returned a few minutes later with Jesse in tow. He resisted the urge to reach out and grab Jesse's hand for comfort. Jesse seemed to sense his need, though, crossing the room and hopping up on the exam bed next to him. "How's the arm, mate?"

Chris held up his arm so Jesse could see. "Aw, nothing to it. We'll get you sorted in no time, right, doc?"

"I wouldn't say 'no time'," the doctor replied, "but with care and proper exercise, you should be back to regular use in about a month."

Chris wasn't willing to wait another month, but he kept his mouth shut and listened as the doctor explained the exercises he needed to do now and those he needed to add as he regained strength and flexibility in his elbow and arm. He hoped Jesse was listening carefully because it quickly became more than he could remember, and he didn't relish another drive to Yass for a refresher course.

When the doctor finally finished his speech and left them alone with a pamphlet that detailed everything he'd just said, Chris slumped back on the exam table. "I knew I'd have some recovery time once the cast came off, but this is crazy."

"He's giving you the same exercises he'd give someone who worked in town sitting at a desk job," Jesse reminded him. "Your normal routine at Lang Downs, or what will become your normal routine, will take care of the recovering your strength part. The trick will be not overdoing it until you've got enough flexibility back to support the rest. You don't have to spend time lifting weights. You're going to be lifting hay bales and shoveling manure, remember? That'll take care of the strength issues."

"Yeah, I noticed Macklin didn't release the pregnant ewes to the higher pastures."

"Let's go," Jesse said. "We can discuss your physical therapy over dinner. I don't know about you, but I'm starved."

Chris's nerves had his stomach still so tied in knots that he wasn't sure he could eat, but he'd be sick to his stomach the next day if he didn't, so he'd have to force something down. "As long as we don't go to the Eatery."

"Is that where you worked before?" Jesse asked.

Chris nodded.

"We'll find somewhere else to eat," Jesse said immediately. "No reason to bring back bad memories."

The memories had come back even without returning to the restaurant, but Chris didn't mention that. Jesse was being supportive, and Chris appreciated it. "I guess we should call Caine."

They left the exam room and headed for the hospital exit. Jesse called Caine as soon as they were outside. Chris let the conversation float past him, concentrating on breathing. Yass wasn't a large town, only about five thousand people, but after being on Lang Downs for eight weeks, it was a veritable metropolis. The noise of cars driving by, of children playing in a park across the street, of a garbage truck rattling down the street grated on his nerves. He'd always lived in a city, but having experienced the peace and solitude of the outback, he didn't think he could go back.

"Do we have to stay here tonight? Can we drive back to Boorowa at least?"

"I don't know," Jesse said. "That's up to Caine and Macklin. It's only an hour, so I suppose we could, but they may have already taken rooms in the hotel or made other plans. I have to pick up condoms too, and it might be more discreet to do that here than in Boorowa."

Chris's hands tingled, the unpleasant sensation moving up his arms as a group of teenage boys walked by, laughing and jostling each other. "I don't think I can stay here," Chris said, his pulsing pounding and his throat constricting until he felt like every breath was a struggle. Those boys hadn't had anything to do with the attack on Chris, but that did nothing to lessen his reaction to them.

"I really don't think I can stay here," Chris repeated, his voice sounding frantic to his own ears.

"Chris," Jesse said sharply. "Look at me."

Chris tried to focus on Jesse's face, but his vision went in and out of focus as the panic welled up inside him.

"Look at me," Jesse repeated, moving so he blocked Chris's view of the street. "There's no one here but me. You're safe. I'm not going to let anyone hurt you, and if they try, all we have to do is step back into the hospital. You're safe with me."

Chris wanted to nod, to acknowledge Jesse's words, to give some indication that they were helping, but even that little movement required more effort than he could spare. It took everything he had simply to breathe and to keep his eyes on Jesse's face.

The honk of a horn behind them sent Chris cowering against the hospital wall.

"It's just Caine and Macklin," Jesse said, taking Chris's arm and leading him toward the car. "Come on. You'll feel better once you're in the car and less exposed."

Chris followed Jesse to the car, climbing in.

"What did the doctor say?" Caine asked as soon as the door closed.

"In a minute," Jesse replied, wrapping his arms around Chris. "He's having another panic attack."

"Another one?" Caine said. "Do we need to talk to the doctor about those before we get back out to the station?"

No! Chris wanted to shout, but he couldn't force the words past the constriction in his throat.

"No," Jesse said for him. "He hasn't had a single one at the station, at least not that I'm aware of. It's being back in Yass that's causing it. Is there any way we can go back to Boorowa tonight instead of staying here? It won't be the station, but it won't be Yass either."

"I guess we could," Macklin said. "We haven't checked into the hotel here yet. It would mean having a late dinner, but we're well enough known around town that I don't think it would be a problem."

"If we could stop at Woolworths before we leave town, I have a couple of things I need to grab," Jesse added. "It'll only take a few minutes."

The normality of the conversation, not to mention the possibility of leaving Yass, helped ease some of Chris's panic. He still wanted to pull a blanket over his head so no one could see him, but at least he could breathe again.

"We'd already planned a stop there anyway," Macklin said. "Caine can stay in the car with Chris while you and I go inside to get what we need, unless you want me to pick something up for you."

A fresh jolt of panic hit Chris at the thought of Jesse telling Macklin what he intended to buy. He didn't think Macklin would care, but he really didn't want to find out otherwise if he did, especially not right now.

"No, I'll go in with you," Jesse said. "I need to see what they have."

Chris breathed a sigh of relief and relaxed against the back of the seat until they reached the store and Macklin and Jesse went inside. The moment Jesse was out of his sight, Chris felt the panic clawing at his throat again.

"When will the ewes have their babies?" he asked, trying to focus on anything other than Jesse's absence.

"Soon," Caine said, "although you'll have to ask Macklin if you want more details than that. This is my first lambing season too."

"Why did you come to Lang Downs?" Chris asked. "I mean, I know it belonged to your uncle and all, but you're a long way from home."

"I n-needed to d-do something d-different," Caine said. The sudden return of the stutter surprised Chris. He'd noticed it occasionally when they were in Yass and Boorowa before, but it hadn't ever been this strong.

"Do you miss your family?"

"Of c-course," Caine said, "but we e-mail and t-talk on Skype, and they're coming to visit at Christmas. Mom said she's looking forward to a break from the c-cold and snow."

"Oh, that's right," Chris said. "It's cold around Christmas where you're from."

"We had a white Christmas more years than not when I was growing up," Caine replied. "And then I moved to Philadelphia and we got even more snow. It will be strange to have Christmas in the middle of the summer. Are you feeling better now?"

Chris paused to take stock and realized he was. "Yes, thanks."

"Good. I'm glad Jesse was there to help you at the hospital. I wouldn't have wanted you to have a panic attack without someone else around."

"Jesse's right. It's just being here in Yass that's doing it to me," Chris insisted. "I haven't had anything like this at the station."

"I'm glad you feel safe at the station," Caine said. "Uncle Michael wanted it to be a place where people could feel at home and be themselves."

"I've been thinking," Chris said. "Now that the cast is off my arm, I'd like to work with the jackaroos more. I don't mind helping Kami, but I'm really not a cook, not like he is. If I'm going to stay at Lang Downs, I need to find something I like to do, not just something to fill the time."

"We never intended the kitchen posting to be permanent," Caine assured him. "You'll need a little time for your elbow to recover before you can take on some of the heavier tasks, but there's no reason you can't start going out with the jackaroos to check on the sheep. Do you ride?"

"I've been on a horse before," Chris said, "but I'm not sure I'd call that riding."

Caine laughed. "I can sympathize. We'll see what Macklin thinks, but I think I've reached the point where you could have Titan and I could move to a different horse."

"I don't want to take your horse," Chris protested.

"He's not *my* horse," Caine said with a laugh. "He's the horse Macklin gave me when he didn't trust me to ride any of the others. He's a good horse. He helped me save Neil's life, so don't think I'm giving you some broken down old thing, but from the sound of it, you need his steadiness more than I do now. After six months of riding almost every day, I'm a lot more confident than I was when I started. And if you don't want to ride, you can drive one of the utes, but like Macklin told me the first time I went out with him, you can't be nearly as involved in a ute as you can be on horseback."

"It might be safer until I'm sure my arm isn't going to give out on me, but I like the sound of being outside that way."

"There's nothing like it," Caine said with a content smile. "I couldn't go back now if I wanted to."

Looking at the window of the car at the "bustling" town of Yass, Chris thought he could understand that. "Do you miss the city at all?"

Caine shrugged. "When I l-lived in Philadelphia, I went to the symphony or the ballet occasionally, but it wasn't something I did every weekend or even once a month. When I n-need that again, Macklin and I will go to Sydney for a few days."

Chris tried to imagine Macklin sitting through a symphony performance without any luck, but he'd been around the two men long enough to know Macklin would go if Caine asked. Macklin would go to hell and back if Caine asked.

JESSE lingered as long as he could on buying the rest of the things he needed (or the things he claimed to need so he'd have an excuse to go shopping) before going to look for condoms. He hoped he'd waited long enough that Macklin would already be checking out or even outside. He rounded the corner of that aisle and came face to face with Macklin. Jesse glanced at the items Macklin was carrying, turning beet red when he saw the bottle of lube in his hand.

"I just... that is...."

"Get your condoms and hurry up," Macklin said. "Chris and Caine are waiting, and I don't want Chris to have another panic attack."

Jesse groaned with embarrassment as Macklin walked off. After everything he'd done in an attempt to be discreet, Macklin had seen right through him. He grabbed a box of condoms and headed to checkout. At least by the time he got there, Macklin had already finished his purchases and was walking outside so Jesse didn't have to endure that knowing stare as he paid. He wasn't sure how he was going to carry his bag to his room in Boorowa, though, knowing Macklin knew what was inside. He'd be terribly self-conscious sneaking into Chris's room. Maybe it would be better to wait until they got back to Lang Downs, except that with Chris's panic attacks, Jesse wasn't sure it was a good idea to leave Chris alone.

Deciding he'd worry about it when they got to Boorowa, Jesse walked back out to the car and summoned a smile for Chris and Caine.

"Did you get everything you needed?" Caine asked.

Jesse flushed again. "Yeah," he mumbled. "No worries."

"What's wrong?" Chris asked sotto voce as Macklin started the car and headed out of town.

"I'll tell you later," Jesse whispered back. "Are you all right? No more panic attacks?"

"No," Chris said, "but I'll be glad to be back at the station where I know everyone. I don't feel safe here."

Jesse couldn't imagine what Chris had to be feeling, back in the town where he'd been beaten nearly to death. He squeezed Chris's thigh in encouragement. "You're safe with us," he promised.

"I know," Chris said, "but that doesn't seem to stop the butterflies in my stomach from choking me."

"We'll be in Boorowa in an hour," Jesse assured him. "You can lock yourself in your hotel room if you need to."

"I don't want it to come to that," Chris said. "I want to be able to enjoy dinner with you and with whoever else is still around. Now that the cast is gone and I can start helping more, I want to get to know everyone better. I want to be part of the team."

"You can hang out in the bunkhouse in the evenings," Jesse suggested. "Even if you go back to the station house to sleep, you can come join the rest of us until it's time for lights out."

"I could probably move into the bunkhouse at this point," Chris said. "I mean, I stayed in the station house at first because I was working in the kitchen and because of Seth, but I won't be working in the kitchen much longer, and Seth doesn't need me the way he did when we first got to the station. I haven't seen him as happy and relaxed as he is now since Mum married Tony."

"There's an extra bunk, I think," Jesse said, wishing he could suggest Chris share his bunk, but he doubted the other jackaroos would be willing to accept that. They might overlook Caine and Macklin, and they might even overlook Chris and Jesse if they were discreet, but he doubted they'd want to know what Chris and Jesse would get up to if they were sharing a room.

Not wanting to think about that right now, he changed the subject. "We should do some of those stretches the doctor told you about so you can get your flexibility back as soon as possible. You don't want to hurt your elbow trying to work before you're ready."

"MR. ARMSTRONG, we didn't expect you back tonight."

"We weren't expecting to be back tonight, Adelaide," Macklin replied with a smile for the receptionist at the hotel where they always stayed when they were in Boorowa, "but we'll need three rooms for the night."

"I only have two left. I'm sorry," she said. "If I'd known you were coming back, I could have saved them for you, but I didn't know."

"It's fine," Jesse interrupted. "Chris and I can bunk together. It's no big deal."

He hoped the tan on his cheeks hid the flush he could feel when Macklin turned and lifted an eyebrow, but fortunately the foreman didn't say anything. "We'll take the two rooms you have left, then."

Adelaide handed them the keys. Macklin gave one to Caine and the other to Jesse. As they headed up the stairs to the rooms on the second floor, Macklin looked back over his shoulder at Jesse. "Just remember that the walls aren't all that thick. Whoever has the room next to you will hear any loud noises."

At Jesse's side, Chris started coughing. Jesse let the other two go on ahead.

"What did you say to him in the store?" Chris asked when Caine and Macklin were out of earshot.

"Nothing," Jesse said, "but he saw me buy the condoms. He, um, he was buying a bottle of lube."

"So was he giving us permission or telling us not to mess around?"

"I don't know," Jesse said. "Come on. We shouldn't discuss this out here where anyone could overhear."

They found the room they'd been assigned for the night and let themselves inside. When the door shut behind them, Chris slumped down on the bed. "So what happened?"

Jesse came and sat beside him, pulling Chris into his arms. "I got everything else I needed, not that it was much, hoping Macklin would be done and at the checkout line before I went to get the condoms, but he was in that aisle when I got there. He just looked at me and told me to hurry up and get my condoms so you wouldn't have another panic attack in the car waiting for me."

"Did he sound upset?" Chris asked nervously.

"No, I don't think so," Jesse said, hugging Chris more tightly. "He was very matter of fact about it. I'm not sure that makes it better or worse."

"Better," Chris said. "Embarrassing, but still better than having him upset and feeling like we'd have to sneak around even more to be together."

"True," Jesse said. "I could do without him knowing at all, though." He wasn't ashamed of being with Chris, but they hadn't talked about anything beyond the moment, beyond enjoying a little release now and then. If Jesse wondered how much more it could become, that was his problem, and not one he intended to share with the station foreman or anyone else. Chris was tied to his brother, and that meant being tied to Lang Downs, at least for now, and Jesse's employment would end in March. That left them only a few months of fun. Jesse intended to enjoy it rather than ruin it worrying about what couldn't be. "I don't want them making assumptions about us."

"No," Chris agreed. "I guess we'll just have to not give them any more reason to do so."

Jesse grinned. "How quiet can you be?"

Chris grinned back. "Maybe it's your turn to be quiet."

Jesse cocked an eyebrow. "If your arm is up to holding your weight."

FIFTEEN

CAINE bit his tongue all the way to the room he and Macklin would share for the night. He had no idea what had passed between Jesse and Macklin in the store in Yass, but something clearly had for Macklin to be as blunt in his comments now. Caine could only hope that also meant Macklin was coming around. He felt bad about using this to press the issue, and he couldn't even say why it seemed so important to him, but he knew it was. As long as Macklin held back that one piece of himself, Caine wouldn't be able to set aside the lingering fear that Macklin was somehow less committed to their relationship than Caine was.

It was a ridiculous notion, and he knew that too, but it didn't change the niggling doubt. He'd given Macklin everything he had. He needed Macklin to do the same.

"Now who's meddling?" he teased as soon as the door closed behind them.

"I wasn't meddling," Macklin insisted. "I saw Jesse buying condoms at Woolworths. I figured a little caution was in order."

"Careful there," Caine joked, "or I'll think you want me to win our bet."

Macklin frowned and pulled away, much to Caine's surprise.

"Don't push, pup," Macklin said, his voice as serious as Caine had ever heard it. "I know what you want, but some stupid bet isn't the way to get it. I'm just not ready."

Questions sprang to Caine's lips, demands for an explanation, a reason why, of what Caine could do that he hadn't already done to prove to Macklin that he was here to stay, that Macklin could trust him with this as he trusted Caine with his heart and his home. Then he looked at Macklin, took in the stiff, almost defensive set to his shoulders, the way he seemed tensed for an argument or a blow or both, and he relented. No matter how much Macklin's continued refusal baffled and hurt Caine, fighting over it would only make it worse. "I guess you'll have to use that new bottle of lube on me then."

Macklin summoned a smile and opened his arm. Caine stepped into the embrace.

"I'm sorry, pup. I'm trying."

"And I'll keep trying to be patient."

LYING in bed later, listening to Caine's light snuffling, Macklin stifled a sigh. He wanted to give Caine what he wanted. He hated the hurt Caine couldn't quite hide each time Macklin drew back from letting him top. He knew it wasn't rational, but he couldn't get past the fear of giving up control. Part of it was his father, but the rest, the larger part, was the jackaroos who looked to him for orders. He'd heard the occasional comment when the men didn't know he was nearby, speculating on him and Caine. "No way a man like Armstrong lets anyone fuck him."

They could deal with him being gay and living with Caine, but they still expected him to be the foreman, the one forever and always in charge. They'd lost some men they couldn't really afford to lose after he and Caine had settled their differences and committed to a future together. Not as many as Macklin had feared, but still too many. They'd replaced them in Yass, but not all of them were of Jesse's caliber, much less the caliber of the men who had left. He'd managed to make it work and to keep Caine in the dark about how much extra work Macklin and the year-rounders who remained were doing to keep things running smoothly. He intended to see that it stayed that way. Caine had such plans for the station, good plans that Macklin believed in, if they could just train and keep the men they needed. They couldn't take another hit, not now. A year from now, two years, when they'd worked off the bad winter that had preceded Michael's death, it wouldn't matter as much, but they needed every cent from every strand of wool and every lamb they could sell. Caine didn't seem worried that they'd run a bit in the red last quarter, but then he'd gone and announced that his parents—his *mother,* who owned the station, no matter that Caine was her representative—were coming for Christmas. They'd be at the station in six weeks, and Macklin intended to prove to Mrs. Neiheisel that she'd made the right choice in keeping the station and sending Caine to run it. He knew from talking to Caine that Caine had convinced his parents to keep the station and to let Caine take charge of it, and he had no doubt Caine stood by that choice, but he couldn't help feeling that he was about to stand inspection having been caught with his pants down, and not just down, but down from fucking the boss's son.

Caine was thriving on the station. He barely stuttered anymore. He'd won the respect and affection of the year-rounders and even many of the new jackaroos. Even Kami liked him, a feat unto itself since Macklin was pretty sure Kami didn't like anyone just on principle. They might never be rich—the biggest value at the station was the land itself—but they'd never go hungry either, and with all Caine's plans, in a year or two, they stood to profit from the growing interest in organic meat. They just had to stay the course. Caine's mother had to let them stay the course, and that meant convincing her he was the right man to stand at Caine's side, something he'd never do if he lost the respect of the men who worked for them.

"Go to sleep," Caine murmured at his side. "Whatever the problem is, it's not as bad as you think. We'll deal with it tomorrow."

Macklin flushed at being caught brooding. He rolled onto his side, spooning up behind Caine, determined to put all the negative thoughts out of his head for now. He could borrow trouble another time.

"FUCK, that hurts," Chris said as he tried to do the stretches the doctor had said were necessary to regain the flexibility in the ligaments of his elbow. "I can't do this."

"Yes, you can," Jesse insisted. The sun had nearly reached the horizon to the west, but it would be some hours still before it was dark. The breeze had cooled down finally from the heat of the day, allowing them to sit outside on the veranda of the bunkhouse to do Chris's exercises. "You already have more range of motion than you did when the cast first came off. That night in Boorowa, you could barely move your elbow at all. Now you've got at least fifty percent of your range of motion back. You're getting stronger too. You couldn't have lifted that full pitchfork when your cast first came off either."

"One full pitchfork before my arm gave out," Chris muttered. "Whole bloody lot of help that is."

"Stop it," Jesse said, smacking Chris lightly on the back of the head. "You're feeling sorry for yourself, and it's *not* attractive."

"Yeah, well, neither is being helpless."

Jesse sighed. They'd had this discussion every day for the past two weeks since Chris first got his cast off. Jesse could see the progress Chris was making. He didn't know why Chris couldn't see it. Most of the time he thought of Chris as his contemporary, but every once in a while, Chris did something that reminded Jesse of the difference in their ages. Eight years wasn't insurmountable, and indeed most of the time it was negligible, but right at the moment, it seemed like an impossible divide between them.

"You aren't helpless," he said, his words sharper than he intended them to be. "You're regaining strength and flexibility every day. Everyone sees that but you, and everyone but you is getting tired of the pity party. Get over yourself already."

The shock on Chris's face nearly made Jesse apologize, but he had to stick to his guns or nothing would change. He wanted his Chris back, the one who flirted and laughed and made the best of even a bad situation, not this sulky kid who couldn't be arsed to do anything but whine about how much his exercises hurt. Jesse was sure they hurt, but they were a necessary evil if Chris wanted to recover fully.

"I'm sorry to be such a bother," Chris said stiffly, rising from his seat and starting to leave the veranda. "I won't disturb you again."

"Bloody hell. Chris, wait. That isn't what I meant." He grabbed Chris's good arm to stop him from leaving. "Helping you isn't a bother. Having you around isn't a bother. It's just frustrating that you're in such a bad mood all the time. I miss laughing and joking with you. Getting your cast off was supposed to make things better, not worse. Look, I'm supposed to go up in the highlands tomorrow with Neil and Ian. Why don't you come along? It'll be a day of working with the dogs and watching the mob, nothing challenging for your arm, but nothing you won't be able to do either. You can see a different side of being a jackaroo. It's not all sheep dags and feeding the lambs."

"I'd have to check with Macklin," Chris said. "I don't know what he has planned for tomorrow, but if he says yes, maybe that would be a good thing. Caine's been helping me with my riding, and Titan is pretty docile. I should be able to ride out with you for the day."

CHRIS wasn't so sure going with Jesse, Neil, and Ian was such a good idea when his elbow twinged as soon as he tried to mount Titan the next morning, but he gritted his teeth and tried again, managing to pull himself into the saddle. No one seemed to notice the gracelessness of the motion, or if they did, they were too tactful to say anything. Chris could live with either option.

They rode out a moment later, Neil and his dog Max in the lead. Fortunately no one seemed in any hurry, both man and animal lethargic in the predawn gloom. Chris let Titan follow the other horses with a minimum of guidance, trusting his mount not to lead him astray. Fortunately Caine's assessment of the animal seemed accurate because Titan plodded willingly along behind the others, leaving Chris to stretch his elbow surreptitiously. He had to get his range of motion back.

As dawn approached and the sky lightened more, Chris switched his attention from his injury to the men in front of him. Neil and Ian lived on the station year-round, full-time jackaroos. Jesse might only work on stations in the summer, but Chris could detect no difference in the way the men sat their horses. Jesse's body language proclaimed his ease on horseback, riding out to tend the mob.

The sun had just peeked above the horizon, less of a feat now that they were out of the valley, when Neil led them to one of the drover's huts Chris and Jesse had stocked at the beginning of the season.

"Morning," Kyle called, stepping out of the hut.

"Morning," Neil replied. "How was the night?"

"Quiet," Kyle said, "but I noticed tracks on the edge of the paddock yesterday when we got up here. A dingo from the looks of it, and they weren't old."

"Not with the rain from a few days ago," Neil agreed. "You didn't see it last night?"

"No, the mob was quiet, and we didn't see or hear any sign of the dingo either."

"We'll hope he was just passing through," Ian said, "but thanks for the warning."

"Max will let us know if the dingo comes back," Neil said. "We can take a minute and have some coffee." He held up the thermos he carried.

Chris wasn't much of a coffee drinker, but it was still cool this early in the morning and something hot sounded wonderful.

"I have tea if you'd prefer that," Jesse added.

Chris brightened immediately. "I'll have some if you don't mind sharing."

"I brought it to share," Jesse assured him. "Next time, though, think about grabbing another thermos. It never hurts to have more."

Chris flushed, but Neil clapped him on the shoulder. "No worries, mate. You'll learn all the tricks if you stick with us."

"I like the sound of that."

"We'll make a jackaroo out of you," Ian agreed. "You're not any worse than some of the other blow-ins we got stuck with this season, and you've got a smile to go along with your inexperience. I hope Macklin gets rid of some of those drongos at the end of the summer. I don't have a problem with him and the boss—don't give me that look, Neil. You were the one with the bad attitude, not me—but it's cost us this summer."

"How?" Chris asked.

"We lost some people, more than usual, blokes who didn't come back after they found out about Caine, and not everyone we hired to replace them is as good as the people we lost," Neil said. "But we're making it work."

"And we'll keep making it work," Ian agreed. "I didn't mean otherwise. We're just keeping even longer hours than usual this summer."

"I won't be a drag on the station much longer," Chris promised. "My arm's getting better every day."

"Now you're putting words in my mouth," Ian protested. "You worked with Kami the whole time you had the cast on and now that it's off, you're doing what you can. I had a friend in school who busted up his elbow and didn't take care of it when he got the cast off. He never did recover from that completely. Nobody's asking you to get better faster. The difference is your attitude. You're worried about being a drain on the station. You volunteered to ride out with us today so you could learn more about the operation. That's a whole different kettle of fish from what some of these drongos are doing. They're trying to do as little as possible without getting Macklin's boot in the arse."

"So you really don't mind having me tag along?" Chris asked.

"Not at all," Neil said, finishing his coffee. A bark from Max drew his attention. "Let's go see what Max has found."

They trooped back outside to the open paddock where a small mob of about thirty sheep grazed peacefully. Max stood at the top of the nearby ridge, body on full alert.

"Whatever it is, Max doesn't like it," Ian said.

"Which means I don't either," Neil added, mounting his horse. "Chris, you may want to stay down here."

"No, I'll come," Chris insisted, finding it easier to mount Titan this time. The ride had loosened up his elbow. "I'll stay out of the way, but I need to see so I can learn."

Max yipped again as they headed up to the ridge to where he stood watch. "What did you find, Max?" Neil asked as they neared the dog.

Max yipped again. Neil dismounted. "Bloody snakes," he muttered. "Looks like it got trampled, but now we have to check the lambs. It's a tiger snake, not a brown snake, but if one got bit, we can't sell it for meat this season."

"The bite wouldn't kill it?" Chris asked.

"Not one of those, no," Neil said. "They'll make you sick as a dingo, a sheep, too, but the venom isn't deadly unless they get a newborn, which is why we keep them in the valley until they're a few months old." He picked up a stick and used it to carry the corpse to the edge of the paddock and toss it over the fence into the bush on the other side. "There, not a problem anymore."

"Other than checking the sheep," Jesse said.

"Yeah, well, I was being optimistic."

Jesse and Ian laughed and all four of them rode back down to the mob. "Ian, why don't you and Chris check the sheep and Jesse and I will drive the stragglers back down to the mob?"

"Will do," Ian said. "Ready to wrestle some sheep, Chris?"

"I'm game," Chris said, refusing to worry about his arm and whether he could handle a full-grown sheep in his current condition.

Ian led the way to the largest group of sheep, dismounting easily. "Check their legs," he said. "That snake wasn't big enough to get to their bellies."

"What am I looking for? I mean, fang marks, but their wool has already started to grow back in. I'm not sure I can see the skin."

"Swelling, limping, anything to suggest they're injured," Ian explained, "because even if it isn't a snake bite, if they've got any of those problems, we need to take a closer look at it."

Chris nodded and started examining the sheep. Ian, he noticed, ran his hands over each animal's legs, so Chris imitated him, hoping he'd be able to feel the difference if one limb was swollen. If he felt anything suspicious, he'd get Ian to check it too.

"Bloody hell," Ian muttered a few minutes later.

"Did you find something?"

"Yeah," Ian said. "Come see what you think."

Chris thought he'd agree with whatever Ian said because he sure as hell didn't know what he was looking for, but he peered obediently at the lamb Ian held.

"See the joint swelling?"

"Yeah, here," Chris said, pointing. "On its ankle."

"Yeah, its pastern," Ian said. "The snake probably only got one, but we should still check the others just to be on the safe side."

"What do we do for that one?"

"Isolate it for now," Ian said. "Keep an eye on it and make sure it survives. If it does, we'll have to see what shape it's in come time for breeding, because we can't sell it for meat. Who knows how long the venom lingers in the muscles after the swelling goes down? I don't know if we need another ram, but maybe we can sell it to Taylor or one of the other graziers."

"Yeah," Chris said. "I can take it back to the drover's hut and put it in the lean-to for the time being."

"No worries. Neil and Max will drive it down there after we're done checking the rest of the mob. As stiffly as this chap's walking, we aren't likely to mistake him for another."

"So the male lambs usually get sold for meat?" Chris asked as he went back to checking the mob.

"That's the way it usually goes," Ian agreed. "We keep a few rams, of course, for breeding in the fall, but they're more trouble than they're worth almost, so we don't keep any extras, and we only keep enough female lambs to replace the aging breeding stock. We sell the rest for meat. The idea is sustainable organic methods, and that means a stable herd size."

"I guess I never realized it was so complicated."

Ian laughed. "Ask to see the breeding book sometime. That's complicated, but Macklin has it down to an art. I worked a couple of other stations before settling here. You won't find a better foreman than ours, and with Caine doing all the research on the organic farming methods, we really are on the edge of great things."

"Even short-handed?"

"Even short-handed. Here come Neil and Jesse with the stragglers. Let's check them while Neil and Max take care of our invalid."

Ian explained the situation to Neil while Chris started checking the sheep Jesse drove his way. Fortunately, none of the others seemed bitten.

"Nothing like a little excitement to start the day," Jesse said when they had finished.

Chris chuckled. "So it's not always this exciting?"

"No," Jesse said with a wide grin that made Chris's insides wobble. "Usually it's a lot of sitting or standing around and waiting for the shift to be over. And maybe checking fences and stuff. Speaking of, if you feel up to a little ride, we could check the fences while Neil and Ian finish with the injured lamb." He wiggled his eyebrows suggestively.

Chris laughed, but he could feel his body reacting. Even if they just got a few kisses in, it would be a nice break after the crazy week they'd had. Chris was about ready to suggest checking all the drover's huts again, just to have a few minutes alone with Jesse. Riding fences wouldn't exactly give them time for sex, but Chris would take what he could get.

"Let me just tell the others where we're going," Jesse said.

Chris nodded and climbed on Titan's back again. His arm was sore, but he ignored it. He refused to let his injury keep him from doing what needed to be done. He had a life to build here, and that couldn't happen if he couldn't work.

Jesse joined him a moment later, leading his horse. Seeing Chris already mounted, he swung into the saddle with an ease Chris envied, and that added to the desire clawing at his gut. Neil and Ian might despair of some of the new jackaroos, but Jesse was the real thing, a stockman just like Neil, Ian, or Macklin.

"Up for a little run?" Jesse asked.

"I don't know," Chris said. "I'm not much of a horseman, but go ahead. I'll meet you at the fence line."

"Are you sure?"

Oh yeah, Chris was sure. He wanted to see Jesse really ride, not just sit his horse.

"Okay, see you at the fences," Jesse said, urging his mount to run.

Chris followed along behind at a much slower pace, relishing the sight of man and beast moving together. One day maybe he'd ride like that. For now, though, he'd enjoy the show.

As promised, Jesse waited for him at the fence line.

"I thought Caine said he had people check the fences earlier in the season," Chris said as they rode along the barbed wire barrier.

"I'm sure he did," Jesse replied, "but things happen. Trees fall, posts get rotten. It's like the huts. It's easy to bring a set of batteries if you know you need them, but if no one pays attention, suddenly you've got an entire ute full of supplies. It's easy to fix a small section of fence, but if you don't catch it early, it ends up being a huge job instead."

"I suppose that makes sense," Chris said.

Jesse looked back the way they'd come, then pulled on Chris's good arm until Chris leaned in for a kiss.

"Mmm," Jesse said. "It's been too long since we've done that."

Chris smiled and kissed him again. "We should do something about that."

"We should," Jesse agreed, pulling back so he could swing down from his horse. "C'mere."

Chris slid down into Jesse's arms, ignoring Titan's huffed snort. The horse could just get over it. Chris wanted to kiss his lover. The word brought his thoughts to a grinding halt even as Jesse kissed him. Chris's body reacted, returning the kiss, but his mind remained stuck on that word. Lover. Were they lovers? They had sex. They spent time together even when they weren't having sex. They were friends. They supported each other. Well, Jesse supported Chris. Chris wasn't sure how much support he'd provided Jesse so far. All of those things seemed to imply an affirmative answer, but lovers were people like Caine and Macklin, solid, committed couples. He and Jesse were just screwing around and passing the time. Weren't they?

Then Jesse's tongue interrupted Chris's musings, playing across Chris's lips until he parted them and sucked the wet muscle inside. His worry over details faded as Jesse's hands gripped his arms and dragged him closer.

"Hang out at the bunkhouse tonight," Jesse said when he broke the kiss. "We'll wait for the others to go to bed and then you can sneak into my room. Please, Chris. I need to fuck you."

Chris groaned. "I don't suppose you've got a rubber in your pocket."

"I'm working."

"That didn't stop you when we were stocking the huts."

"Neil and Ian are just on the other side of the ridge. They could come looking for us at any second."

"Then I'll have to be quick," Chris said as he tugged on Jesse's belt. "You can't fuck me without a condom, but I can take the edge off."

"This is a bad idea," Jesse said.

Chris shrugged as he sank to his knees. "Are you saying no?"

Jesse shook his head, so Chris unbuttoned his jeans and slipped a hand inside, ignoring the twinge in his elbow. He wouldn't need his arm for long. Just long enough to get his mouth on his prize.

An extra frisson ran through Chris as he pulled Jesse free of his clothes and licked the mushroomed head, already damp with Jesse's excitement. He'd never gotten off on exhibitionism, but this wasn't that. No one was watching. It was the possibility of being discovered that added the extra thrill as he slid his lips down the length of Jesse's shaft, taking him all the way in. It was the need to hurry that added urgency to his movements. They could be interrupted any second, and Chris didn't intend to get caught with his pants down. Or with Jesse's down in this case.

When Chris glanced up at Jesse, he was arrested by the vision of Jesse's face, eyes wild with passion and yet gaze flitting along the horizon constantly on alert for Neil or Ian. That only heightened Chris's desire as he rolled Jesse's balls against his palm, urging Jesse to find release as quickly as possible.

Jesse must have been as desperate as Chris because in a gratifyingly short time, he stiffened beneath Chris's hands and mouth as he found his release.

Licking his lips, Chris drew back. "That should hold you until tonight."

"What about you?" Jesse asked. "Damn it. There's Max." He fixed his clothes quickly. "I wasn't going to do anything but kiss you."

"Max can't tell tales."

"No, but if Max is coming this way, Neil isn't far behind."

Chris let Jesse pull him to his feet.

"Did you find something?" Neil called, cresting the rise that had hidden Chris and Jesse from the drover's hut.

"No," Jesse called back. "Just some brush tangled in the fence, but we wanted to make sure the wire was intact."

"Good man!" Neil said.

"How's the lamb?"

"He's going to be stiff and swollen for a while, but there's nothing to suggest it's worse than that. We'll keep him in the lean-to where it's warm and dry for a few days to make sure the swelling goes down. Any sign of more dingo tracks?"

"Not that we've seen," Jesse said, "but we just got started when we stopped to check the fence. We'll finish the perimeter and meet you back at the hut?"

Neil nodded his agreement and headed back toward the lean-to.

"That was close," Jesse said when Neil was out of earshot. "Let's get this finished."

"Don't be like that," Chris said, though he climbed back onto Titan immediately. "He didn't catch us, and he's Caine's biggest supporter."

"Because Caine saved his life," Jesse reminded Chris. "From what I heard, Neil was pretty nasty to Caine before that."

"He knows I'm gay."

"There's a difference between knowing and catching you with my dick in your mouth while we were supposed to be working. This can't happen again. A kiss is one thing, but nothing more."

Chris still thought Jesse was overreacting, but he let it go for now.

They finished checking the fence and rode back to the drover's hut. "What now?"

"Now we sit here and stare at the sheep until it's time for lunch," Jesse said. "As long as they don't need us, we can relax a bit."

"Sounds good," Chris said, dismounting and reaching for the saddle on Titan's back.

"Loosen the girth, but leave him tacked up," Ian said. "If we need to mount up in a hurry, you wouldn't want to have to tack him up again."

"Why would we need to do that?" Chris asked, even as he followed Ian's advice.

"Kyle saw dingo tracks. If one came around, we'd have a much better chance of scaring him off on horseback than on foot. We humans aren't very scary or fast, but a big horse is. One well-placed kick from old Titan there and that dingo's dead."

"Can you do that? I thought they were protected."

"We can't train Titan to do it," Neil said, "but if he does it out of self-defense, that's the dingo's problem, not ours. They're pests, nothing more."

THEY were cleaning up the remains of their lunch when Max's wild barking interrupted. The three experienced jackaroos dropped everything immediately, heading for the door without hesitation. Chris followed more slowly, not knowing if he'd be able to help and not wanting to be in the way.

At the far end of the paddock, Max raced toward a group of dingoes at the crest of the ridge.

"Bloody hell," Neil shouted. "They only hunt in packs when they're starving." He tightened the cinch on his horse before swinging onto its back and spurring it across the field. Ian was only seconds behind him.

"Stay here," Jesse told Chris as he mounted in turn. "You don't ride that well yet, and this could get messy."

"Do I need to call for help?" Chris yelled as Jesse started away.

"It'll be over before they could get here," Jesse yelled back as he sent his horse at an angle to the path Neil and Ian had taken, intercepting a dingo that had come from a different direction, intending to drive the mob into the trap of the rest of the pack.

Chris watched, his chest tight, as the three men did their best to run off the dingoes, Max racing into the fray as well. A particularly nasty snarl of canine flesh made Chris wince, but when Ian arrived on horseback to break up the chaos, Max emerged victorious, the dingo he had tangled with limping away as fast as it could move on three legs.

As quickly as it had started, the melee was over, and Jesse, Ian, and Neil were riding back toward where Chris stood, Max trotting proudly beside them.

"Bloody stupid dingoes," Neil muttered as he swung down from his horse. Chris grabbed the reins Neil dropped without care as he knelt to check on Max.

"Is Max all right?" Chris asked.

"He seems to be," Neil said, running his hands over the dog's sides and legs to check for bite marks. "The dingo took the worst of their fight."

"I didn't think dingoes would be that bold," Chris added. "I'd always heard they were pretty timid creatures."

Jesse nudged Chris's arm and shook his head. Chris took the hint and let the subject drop, especially when Neil glared at him. Deciding discretion was the better part of valor, Chris retreated to the lean-to with Neil's horse in tow. He took care to only loosen the girth a little in case they needed the horses again.

"Dingoes are a sore spot with a lot of jackaroos," Jesse said a moment later from the entrance to the lean-to. "I don't know Neil's reasons, but it wouldn't surprise me if he lost a dog to them in the past. Max is awfully young for a jackaroo with as much experience as Neil has."

Chris shuddered. "Yeah, I could see that souring him on dingoes."

"Even those of us who don't have that kind of reason still don't like them," Jesse added. "They're a threat to our sheep. A single dingo couldn't bring down a full-grown ewe, but a pack like the one we had today? They could have made off with several. I don't know how Caine runs things, but I've been on stations where the cost of those animals would have come out of our pay."

"Really?"

"Not all of them, and like I said, I don't know how they do things here on Lang Downs, but yeah, the argument is that if a dingo made off with a sheep on your watch, you were negligent and owed the station owner the cost of the animal. And believe me, they aren't cheap."

"Wow, that's kind of... mercenary."

"It's that kind of industry for the most part," Jesse said with a shrug. "Most stations are making ends meet, nothing more, unless they're huge and industrialized. It's going to be interesting to see what happens with Caine's organic certification plan. It's the exact opposite of the route most places seem to be taking."

"You don't think it'll work?"

"I don't know," Jesse said. "And at the end of the day, as long as he pays my salary, it's not my problem. This is my job, not my life."

The words made Chris realize how clear a picture he'd started painting for himself of the future, and how at odds that picture was with Jesse's apparent vision of his own path in life. He should have known better than to read any more into Jesse's support than the friendship he'd offered first. He'd never suggested it was anything more than that, but Chris had started to hope. He'd obviously been wrong.

SIXTEEN

CHRIS sat with Seth and Jason at the canteen that night, not wanting his brother to feel neglected after Chris had spent all day with the jackaroos. By the time Jesse made it to the canteen, all the seats at their table were full. Chris smiled apologetically at Jesse, but he made no move to clear a space or pull a chair over to squeeze Jesse in.

Jesse hadn't led him on, not really anyway, but Chris still felt the need to reestablish some independence. He'd fallen into the trap of thinking of them as a couple, of including Jesse in his thoughts of family things, and that was a mistake. Jesse was a fuck buddy he could pass the time with until the summer ended.

They had nearly finished eating when Neil stood up and clinked his glass with his fork. The rumble of conversation in the canteen dwindled to silence.

"Sorry to disturb everyone's dinner," Neil said, clearing his throat. Chris almost chuckled at how ill at ease the usually confident jackaroo appeared, but Neil wouldn't be standing there if whatever he intended to say wasn't important.

"I wanted to tell everyone that Molly has done me the great honor of agreeing to marry me at the end of the summer."

The men broke into cheers and applause as the woman in question rose as well. Neil slid his arm around her waist, keeping her by his side as the other jackaroos crowded around to shake Neil's hand or slap his shoulder and call him a lucky dog.

Chris joined the throng, holding back only to let those who knew Neil better approach first. "Congratulations," he said when he reached the couple. "I hope you'll both be very happy."

"I'm sure we will be," Molly said with a smile.

Chris stepped aside to let someone else speak to them, only to bump into Jesse.

"Hi," he said, not wanting to be rude.

"Hi," Jesse said. "I missed having dinner with you. Sorry I was late getting here."

As simple as the words were, they relaxed something in Chris's chest. He'd taken Jesse's words at lunchtime as a dismissal, but they weren't, at least not completely. Jesse might not be thinking in terms of forever—and he had no reason to; they hadn't talked about anything beyond the present moment—but he did enjoy Chris's company both in bed and out. They were friends, and Chris couldn't discount that. He had few enough friends at the moment to dismiss one simply because he'd jumped ahead in the playbook.

"I'm sorry I didn't save you a seat," Chris said. "By the time I realized you weren't right there, the table was already full."

"We'll just have to have a beer together instead," Jesse said with a grin. "Paul picked some up for me when he made the supply run into Boorowa today. It's in the bunkhouse if you want one."

"Sure," Chris said. He'd been trying to spend more time in the bunkhouse anyway, figuring Caine and Macklin would eventually like their house back. This gave him yet another excuse to spend the evening there. "Let me just make sure Seth doesn't need me."

"Chris," Jesse said, catching Chris's arm before he could turn away, "he's sixteen. He won't appreciate you hovering. There's not a lot of trouble he can get into out here anyway, not without someone stopping him before he does something stupid."

Chris hesitated a moment more, but Seth was still sitting with Jason talking, and Jason's father stood nearby with Neil, Molly, and a few other of the year-rounders.

"He'll be fine," Jesse repeated. His hand on Chris's arm turned from a grip to a caress, and Chris gave in.

"I could use a beer."

"SO... MARRIED, huh?" Macklin said, coming up to Neil and Molly when most of the others had drifted away. "Are you going to both fit in that little house of yours?"

"We'll make it work," Neil said. "Maybe we'll add an extra room over the winter when things are quieter around here."

"You could do that," Macklin said slowly. "You wouldn't be the first, but it occurs to me that there's this big house sitting empty now that I'm not using it anymore. Seems kind of a waste to add on when you could just move across the road and have all the space you need."

"But that's the foreman's house," Neil protested.

"It was the foreman's house," Macklin reminded him. "Unless you think Caine's planning on firing me any time soon."

"He wasn't that stupid when he was a blow-in," Neil retorted. "He's certainly not that stupid now that you're his partner."

"And if I did step down," Macklin went on, "I'd tell him to hire you in my place, so the house would be yours anyway. Unless you don't want it?"

"We would love to have it," Molly interrupted. "It's very generous."

"Consider it an early wedding present," Macklin said. "I'm pretty sure all my things are already out of the house, but I'll check this evening and you can start moving in on your next day off. Once you're settled, I'll see if Chris and Seth want some space of their own instead of having to bunk in the big house."

"They'll appreciate that," Neil said, "Chris especially."

"Oh?" Macklin asked, though he thought he knew what Neil was implying.

"Neil, that isn't any of your business," Molly scolded.

"I'm not trying to get anyone in trouble," Neil said. "I just… well, I think Chris and Jesse might have a thing going on."

"Are you okay with that?" Macklin asked, remembering all too clearly how badly Neil had reacted to finding out Caine was gay.

Neil shrugged. "They aren't bothering me. Jesse's a good jackaroo, and Chris is a hard worker and eager to learn. I didn't expect to end up surrounded by poofters, but then I've never known poofters like the ones here."

"Neil!" Molly scolded, slapping the back of his head. "That's a good way to get yourself fired."

"I knew what he meant," Macklin said despite the shiver of dread that went through him at hearing the slur, however innocently intended, on Neil's lips.

"It's still not appropriate," Molly insisted. "We will be working on that."

Neil looked appropriately henpecked so Macklin chuckled and left them to enjoy the evening. He looked around for Chris but didn't see the younger jackaroo on the veranda of the bunkhouse. He considered searching longer, but he'd see Chris in the morning or at some point the next day. Chris and Seth would have to wait for Neil to finish moving out anyway. Instead, he went back to the house he'd lived in for fifteen years before Caine came along and upended his entire world. He didn't think he had anything left there, but he'd check and make sure.

"WHAT'S in the bag?" Caine asked when Macklin came into the house.

"Stuff," Macklin said, setting the bag down on the table. "I couldn't very well expect Neil and Molly to deal with all the junk I hadn't bothered to move over here because I never use it anymore."

"What are you talking about?" Caine asked, closing the laptop so he could give Macklin his undivided attention.

"Neil and Molly are getting married."

"I heard," Caine said. "What's that have to do with your old junk?"

"Neil's house is fine for a bachelor, but not really for a family," Macklin explained. "I thought they could move into the foreman's house since I'm not using it anymore. That way they'd have plenty of space now, and if they decide to start a family, they wouldn't have to worry about adding on or anything like that."

"So what was left to move?"

"Mostly clothes that don't fit anymore, stuff like that," Macklin said. "Nothing important, but nothing Neil and Molly needed to deal with either."

"Shall we just toss them all then?" Caine asked, reaching for the bag. Macklin snatched it back so fast Caine blinked. Whatever was in the bag, it wasn't just junk, but Caine didn't press. He'd wait until tomorrow when Macklin was out in the paddock and then sneak a peek.

"I... well, I found an old picture I'd forgotten I had," Macklin said slowly. "I'll just put it away and then we can get rid of the clothes."

"May I see it?" Caine asked.

Macklin reached in the bag slowly and pulled out a plain plastic frame. Caine took it and examined the photo within. A teenaged boy stood next to a tired-looking middle aged woman. Caine extrapolated he could see the boy growing into the man in front of him. "Your mother is beautiful."

"She's beat down."

"She's beautiful," Caine insisted, "and she obviously loves you very much."

Macklin nodded curtly, which Caine took as a sign to drop it. He set the picture aside for now and pulled Macklin into his arms.

"So how soon will Neil and Molly move in?"

"That's up to them," Macklin said, "but I thought Chris and Seth could have Neil's house when he moves out. It's a little small for two people, but it'll be better than sharing with us."

"Ready to have the house to ourselves again?" Caine teased.

"Well, it's hard to fuck you in the living room if I'm worried about someone walking in on us all the time."

Caine laughed. "There is that." He was tempted to joke about changing places, but that had backfired in Boorowa. Macklin giving up his house, not just temporarily but in a way so that he couldn't move back in, would have to do for proof of his commitment. Maybe he'd push again after his parents left, but for now, he'd take what he could get and make sure Macklin knew how much Caine appreciated it.

Maybe tomorrow he'd start searching for Macklin's mother. Even if Macklin had no intention of seeing her again, it might help him to know what happened to her.

SEVENTEEN

Six weeks later

"I DIDN'T expect you to have anything in the way of Christmas decorations," Jesse said as he came into the little house Chris and Seth had moved into after Neil and Molly moved into the foreman's house. "Did you go into Boorowa?"

"No, Caine gave it to me. He said he knew I didn't have anything of my own and he had more than enough to share and to consider it a welcome to the station gift," Chris said. "I think I've been here long enough not to qualify for welcome gifts anymore, but it was still a nice gesture on his part."

"He's one hell of a man," Jesse agreed. "Even after three months, it still surprises me how much he treats all the men like family, even the ones who are probably just passing through."

"Maybe some of the ones passing through will change their minds because of his kindness," Chris said.

"It's possible," Jesse replied. "You never know what a little kindness will do."

It wasn't quite the answer Chris had hoped for, but he wasn't ready to come out and ask Jesse point blank if he would consider staying. Jesse's company had been a lifesaver for Chris when he first arrived and knew no one, but while he still enjoyed the time they spent together, both as friends and as fuck buddies, Chris had made other friends on the station. He had learned his way around the various chores that made up the daily routine. He might not ride as well as Ian or have Neil's way with the dogs yet, but he was learning. He no longer *needed* Jesse the way he had at first. If Jesse left in March, Chris would miss him, but he wouldn't be lost without him. He just wished he had a better idea of how Jesse felt beyond their obvious friendship and mutual lust.

"You're awfully quiet," Jesse said, breaking into Chris's thoughts. "You missing your mum?"

"A little," Chris said, clinging to that excuse. "She couldn't afford to make a huge fuss over Christmas when we were little, and Tony was such a tightwad that it didn't get a lot better even after they got married, but we had our traditions."

"You and Seth can still follow those traditions if you want," Jesse said.

"That's just it," Chris said. "I'm not sure I want to follow them anymore. That's a different life than the one we're living now. It wasn't all bad—don't think that—but it wasn't all good either. Other than missing Mum, I'm much happier here than I ever was living under Tony's roof, and money was so tight before him that I never knew whether there'd be enough dinner for all three of us. A stable job, a stable home, regular meals… friends. I'm better off than I've ever been, and Seth is, too, even if he bitches about not having cable or being able to go to the movies."

"Tell him that's what winter is for," Jesse said. "What do you think I do in Melbourne for ten weeks?"

"Fuck everything that moves since you don't know what the next station will be like?" Chris joked, but his heart pinched at the thought.

"Hey, now, I'm not that big of an alley cat," Jesse protested. "I mean, I'm not going to turn down a good offer, but I don't go out cruising every night when I'm in town."

That didn't reassure Chris. "Have any of the others talked about how or if the station celebrates Christmas?"

Jesse shook his head. "Most of the talk has been about Caine's parents arriving. Apparently his mother is the one who actually owns the station, so everyone is worried about impressing her."

"You're not?"

"From everything I've heard about Caine, he didn't know anything about sheep when he arrived, so I can't imagine his mother knows more than he did. I think she's coming to see her son, not to see the station. That's not to say we should be rude or lazy or anything like that, but I don't think this is the inspection everyone else seems to think it is."

"And if you're wrong?" Chris asked.

"Then she'll see me doing my job just like I always do," Jesse replied. "Macklin seems satisfied with my work. I can't imagine her being any more demanding than he is even if she is here to check on the station."

"That's true."

"Stop worrying." Jesse nudged Chris with his shoulder. "Where's Seth?"

"He's staying late at Jason's to finish a project for school. Patrick said he'd probably just have Seth stay over there."

"So we have the house to ourselves?"

Chris grinned. "Did you have something in mind?"

"Making out on the couch," Jesse replied. "We don't get to do that when Seth is around."

Jesse was a regular enough visitor that Seth had stopped commenting on Jesse's presence in their house, but by silent accord, Chris and Jesse kept their interactions on a friendly plane while Seth was around. If they'd been serious, in a solid committed relationship, Chris wouldn't have minded Seth knowing about them and seeing whatever signs of affection passed between them, but Seth had been disappointed often enough. Chris didn't want to add to it by creating an illusion with Jesse that would be shattered when fall came.

"What are we waiting for?" Chris said with a grin as he leaned into the curve of Jesse's shoulder. Jesse pulled him close but didn't kiss him right away. Chris didn't even mind. Sitting there, smelling the fresh scent of Jesse's skin from his shower, feeling the warmth of

Jesse's body at his back, Chris thought he could sit like that all night and it would be more than enough for him.

Then Jesse's lips slid over the sensitive skin along Chris's hairline behind his ear, and Chris decided more would be lovely indeed.

He tilted his head to the side, reveling in the luxury of being held. He'd always had to be the strong one. Chris's earliest memories were of his mother telling him to be strong for his brother, to show him everything was okay even when it wasn't by being in charge, in control of himself even if he couldn't control anything else. He didn't have to be strong with Jesse. He didn't have to be in control. He could lean on Jesse's friendship and know it would be there to support him. He sighed and tilted his head to the side, inviting more of the tender caress.

This was what had been missing from all his furtive, fumbling encounters as a teenager with his schoolmates and in the bars and clubs he'd gone to looking for release. This connection, this tenderness... even if Jesse had made no more promises than any of Chris's past fucks, Chris knew this meant something. It might not be love, but it was companionship, friendship, support. It was something real and good, and it made Chris realize how much he'd been missing out on.

He hummed softly, then gasped when Jesse's nuzzling turned to a soft nip along the tendon on the side of his neck.

"No marks," Chris said automatically.

"Why not?" Jesse asked. "Who do you think would notice or care?"

"Seth would notice."

"But would he care?" Jesse pressed.

Chris shook his head.

Jesse nipped at the now tanned skin again before returning to a softer caress. Chris breathed out a sigh, of relief or disappointment, he couldn't have said. Then Jesse pushed aside the collar of Chris's shirt and latched onto the upper curve of his shoulder, biting and sucking hard enough to make Chris cry out as lust hit him hard, pooling in his groin until he ached with it.

"Bloody hell," he gasped when Jesse released his hold on Chris's shoulder.

Jesse leaned around so he could see Chris's face. "You liked it. Don't pretend you didn't."

"Not pretending anything," Chris said as he pressed down hard on his needy cock. "I just need a minute so I don't shoot in my jeans."

"Can't have that." Jesse pulled Chris's hand away and pushed him down on the couch. He slid up Chris's body until they lay face to face and hip to hip. "I'll just lie here and kiss you until you're in control again."

Jesse rubbing against him and kissing him was not designed to help Chris regain control, but he didn't complain, not when it felt this good. To Chris's surprise, once Jesse found a comfortable position, he stopped his frottage, keeping Chris pinned to the couch but otherwise doing nothing to arouse him but kiss him.

Long, slow, deep kisses. Soul-stealing kisses.

The kind of kisses that made Chris hungry for more than just sex.

He took a deep breath and gave up thinking, falling heart first into those addictive kisses.

Jesse wasn't a big man, not like Macklin or Kami, but he was taller and broader than Chris, fully filled out, while Chris still had some of the thinness of youth, and the difference in their sizes made Chris feel surrounded by Jesse's body. Chris draped his arms around Jesse's neck, not that Jesse was trying to pull away. It was more a matter of indulging his need to touch. He ran his hands down Jesse's back, reveling in his strength. Chris might have developed some muscle since he started working with the other jackaroos, but not so much that he had stopped finding Jesse's build hot as hell. He worked one hand beneath Jesse's shirt, the other tangling in brown hair that had gotten long and shaggy while they'd been at Lang Downs. Chris hoped Jesse wouldn't cut it for the rest of the summer.

"I love your hair longer," Chris said, his lips moving against Jesse's as he spoke.

"It gets messy," Jesse protested.

"That's why I like it," Chris replied, silencing any additional protests by deepening the kiss. He twined their tongues together, not rushing, but determined to engage Jesse as fully in the moment as Chris himself was engaged. The way Jesse shifted against Chris suggested he was succeeding.

When Jesse lifted his head again, his breath rushing over Chris's face, Chris smiled up at him and gave up deluding himself. This might not be anything more for Jesse than a way to unwind at the end of the day, a better option than a weekend trip to Melbourne, but for Chris, it had become more. He had fallen for Jesse.

He had no delusions Jesse felt the same way, but he could live with that. He wasn't pretending Jesse would stay, even if he knew. He couldn't control Jesse's feelings or his actions, but as Jesse bent and kissed him again, Chris realized he didn't care. His heart was his to give as he chose. Jesse might not keep it, but if the other option was breaking things off now, Chris realized he'd rather have a broken heart later, having loved now for all he was worth, than never have that experience at all.

MACKLIN drove in silence as Caine leaned over the back of his seat so he could talk to his father, sitting in the front next to Macklin. Macklin hadn't been sure about that, but Caine explained his father got carsick in the backseat. Macklin didn't want to spend the trip from Sydney worrying about Caine's father, especially once they got off the paved roads and onto Taylor Peak.

Caine's parents had been nothing but gracious since their arrival the day before, insisting Macklin call them by their first names, but Macklin hadn't relaxed since he and Caine had left Lang Downs. He couldn't get past the fact that the woman sitting beside Caine could sell Lang Downs out from beneath them if she chose. He'd struggled with this when Caine arrived almost a year ago. Caine had won him over, but Mrs. Neiheisel was an unknown quantity, and Macklin hated not feeling like he was in control.

She had been nothing but cordial, embracing Macklin and saying how glad she was to finally meet him. She had asked about him, his family, his history, but nothing directly about the station itself. Of course Macklin could hardly talk about himself without talking about the station, since he wasn't about to tell her about his life before coming to Lang Downs. It had been all he could do to tell Caine.

"How much longer until we get home?" Caine's mother asked, her American drawl so like Caine's that Macklin couldn't help smiling when he heard her speak.

"About half an hour until we reach Taylor Peak," Macklin said. "Then we have to cross it and a chunk of Lang Downs. It's about five hours from Boorowa because we can't drive very fast on the dirt roads."

"I had no idea it was so remote."

"Mom, I told you all of this," Caine said.

"Yes, I know, dear, but five hours is a drive to Chicago across three states."

"On the interstate at seventy miles an hour, not on farm roads at ten, twenty at the most," Caine reminded her. Macklin's stomach sank at the reminder of the disconnect between Caine's mother's experiences and life in the outback. She'd take one look at the rustic station and wash her hands of it completely.

"I know, I know. It's just a lot to take in. I'll get used to it, I'm sure. It can't be as odd as Christmas in the middle of summer. I'm used to thirty degrees Fahrenheit, not thirty degrees Celsius at Christmas."

"We can agree on that," Caine said with a laugh. "I've never worn shorts on Christmas before."

He reached forward and squeezed Macklin's shoulder, the easy gesture of affection helping to settle Macklin's nerves. Caine might laugh about Christmas in the summer, even if a cold Christmas was what seemed odd to Macklin. He might joke with his mother about distances, but he loved Macklin, and that made all the difference. Macklin took one hand off the wheel long enough to squeeze back.

"MY PARENTS like you," Caine said that night as they were getting ready for bed. Caine's parents had retired immediately after dinner, still suffering from jet lag, leaving Caine and Macklin to attend to everything that had built up while they were gone. Neil had taken his responsibilities seriously, and Macklin had been impressed at how little had been left undone.

"Are you sure?"

The vulnerability in Macklin's voice tore at Caine. He had heard many tones from his lover in the nine months they had known each other. Doubt was rarely one of them.

"Yes, I'm sure," Caine said. "My mother hugged you before they went up to bed. She wouldn't have done that if she didn't. And my father made a point of shaking your hand. He didn't have to come over to you that way. He could simply have said good night. I know it's subtle, but they're my parents, remember. I know the way they do things. I know the way they were with John, and they were never as warm to him as they were to you tonight."

"The Galah?" Macklin scoffed. "He didn't have enough sense to keep you. Why would they like him?"

"My point exactly," Caine replied, kissing Macklin tenderly. "They've only just met you and they already see the difference between you and him. Imagine how they'll feel after they've been here a couple of weeks."

Silence was Macklin's only reply, but he returned Caine's kiss and pulled him down into bed, which was answer enough for now.

CAINE spent most of the next day with his mother. His father had decided to go out with Macklin and see the barns, but Caine's mother had no real interest in the sheep. "You're happy here."

"I am," Caine said, though it hadn't been a question.

"I can tell. You haven't stuttered once since you met us at the airport."

"It's... different here," Caine said, struggling to put into words the reality of his new life and all the changes it had wrought in him. "This isn't what I imagined when I dreamed of my life in high school or college. I always pictured myself in a city like Philadelphia or New York, working in a big accounting or advertising firm, doing something important, but that couldn't have happened. I might have had the education, but I didn't have the confidence to make that life a reality. As much as I thought it was what I wanted, I didn't have the drive to make it happen. This isn't what I ever expected, but it's what I want. I have such plans, Mom. We've started the process of going organic. In another six to twelve months, we'll have the first stage of the certification complete and can start marketing our wool and meat as Stage 1 organic. It'll be another two years before it can be labeled Grade A organic, but even in the interim, we'll be able to start charging more for it. We'll take Uncle Michael's dream and make it a sustainable one for the future."

"I have no doubt you will," Caine's mother said, hugging him tightly. "You've always been capable of so much more than your life let you do. I'm glad you've finally found a place that pushes you ahead instead of holding you back."

"You know it's not the place as much as it is the man," Caine said, honesty compelling him to point out Macklin's role in his transformation.

"Sweetheart, you wouldn't have ever caught the eye of a man like that if you hadn't had it within you to begin with. I may be old, but I remember men like your Macklin. He wouldn't have given you the time of day if you hadn't had all this success and confidence in you just waiting to come out."

"So you don't mind that I'm staying in Australia?"

"Of course I mind," she scolded. "You're much too far away for me to come visit you regularly, but I also approve, and I know Uncle Michael would have felt the same way. I'm glad you talked me out of selling the station. You belong here."

"I do," Caine agreed.

"When your father and Macklin come back, we should discuss business for a few minutes."

"I didn't prepare any reports," Caine joked. "You didn't tell me you wanted an accounting."

"I don't," his mother said. "I'll explain when they get here."

Caine wasn't entirely sure he liked the sound of that, but his mother didn't seem tense or upset, so whatever she wanted to discuss, it wasn't bad news, or she didn't perceive it that way.

"Macklin doesn't really like surprises."

"Everyone likes surprises," Caine's mother insisted. "Especially this kind."

"THIS is an impressive spread you have here," Mr. Neiheisel—*Len,* Macklin corrected himself silently—said as Macklin showed him around the shearing barns, empty now that all the lambs had grown large enough to move to the upper paddocks with their dams. "I won't pretend to know anything about raising sheep, but even I can see you run a tight ship."

"Caine does a good job," Macklin said.

"Let's be honest, Macklin. I love my son, but I know him too. He's a good man, but he isn't a cowboy. If he's making something of the station, it's because you've taught him what he needs to know to do so."

"That's not true," Macklin insisted. "The idea for the organic certification was his. He's done all the research, made all the arrangements, and filled out all the documentation for it. All I did was explain to him what we were already doing so he knew where we had to start. The improvements have all been his idea."

Len shook his head. "Then you've done an even better job than you realized. Caine's stutter has been the millstone around his neck his entire life. I haven't heard him stutter once since we got here."

Macklin had, but he wasn't about to tell Caine's father that Caine stuttered when Macklin was making love to him, especially when it was long and slow and… Macklin cleared his throat to dispel the image of Caine writhing beneath him. He didn't want to explain his reaction to *that* to Caine's father either.

"He rarely stutters anymore. Only when something has really upset him, and the men here like him well enough to avoid that when they can, but that's his confidence in himself and his place here, not anything I did."

Len looked at Macklin piercingly, reminding the foreman that his lover's father wasn't just a portly, jovial old man. He had been a sharp businessman before he retired, used to seeing into people with a quick glance. "You loved him. That's all it took."

Macklin almost demurred again. He knew Caine's transformation had been an internal one, but Macklin had grown tired of the years of hiding who he was. The past six months with Caine had shown him how good life could be, and owning up to his emotions was part of that. "Then I'm glad it worked."

Len nodded once, then turned back to the station. "So show me the rest of the valley. I'm not riding out on horseback, but Caine said we could see most of the production without going out into the mountains."

"SO YOU said something about talking business?" Caine said to his mother after they had finished eating lunch. Next to him, Macklin tensed, but Caine ignored it. His mother had been in far too jovial a mood when she brought it up for it to be bad news, whatever it was.

"We've talked with our accountant, and having the station's value and earnings on our taxes is disadvantageous for us at the age and stage of our lives that we're at," Len explained. "It makes our total net high enough to devalue our planned retirement income and outflow with taxes."

"What does that mean?" Macklin asked tersely.

"It means we have a Christmas present for Caine," Mrs. Neiheisel said with a warm smile. "As soon as we can get Caine's signature on the files notarized, or whatever the equivalent is here in Australia, the station is his, free and clear. It would have been his anyway when I died. This way you can both stop feeling like you have to answer to me for anything. Not that you ever did. This has been Caine's project from the beginning."

"Now it's his in every sense of the word," Len finished. "Everything I've seen today assures me this is the right choice for everyone involved."

"Thank you, Mom," Caine said, rising to embrace her tightly. "For giving me this chance a year ago and now for giving it to me forever. I won't let you down."

"You couldn't let me down, honey," she said, cradling his cheeks in her hands. "I look at you here, and I see it's where you're meant to be. Even more importantly, I see you know it too. You'll fight harder for this place than I ever could. It was already yours in reality. Now it's yours legally as well, and I can rest easy knowing you're happy and settled in your life."

She hugged Caine tightly one more time before reaching for her husband's hand. "Let's go for a walk, Len. I suspect our sons have a lot to talk about."

Silence reigned until Caine's parents had left the house. Caine turned to look at Macklin, still sitting on the couch. He didn't look like he'd moved a muscle since Caine's mother had made her announcement.

"You okay?" Caine asked, coming back to sit next to his lover.

"She said sons."

"She did," Caine said. "Is that a problem?"

"No! Of course not," Macklin replied. "But she said sons. She just met me a few days ago."

"That's all the time she needed to see that I'm happy and that we love each other. Mom and I talked a long time ago when I first came out about getting married or not getting married and what that would look like, since there wouldn't ever be a church wedding and a bride in a white dress. I remember feeling bad because she wouldn't get that chance. You know what she told me?"

"What?" Macklin asked so softly Caine could barely hear him.

"She told me she didn't need all that pomp to make someone a part of our family and that when I found the right person, all she'd have to do was look at him and she'd know. And when she did, he'd be her son as completely as I was, and nothing would change that, not even if something happened to me and she was left with just my partner to call her own," Caine said. "She l-looked at you and she kn-n-new."

"You're stuttering."

Caine shrugged. "K-kind of hard n-not to when I'm holding b-back t-tears."

"Good ones?"

Caine nodded.

"Me too."

The admission shattered what little control Caine had left and the tears welled up, tumbling down his face as he laughed and pulled Macklin into his arms. The kiss was wet and sloppy, sweet with joy and salty with tears, but neither of them cared. They kept kissing and laughing and kissing some more until the tears had passed and only the joy remained.

Finally Caine turned so he could snuggle up under Macklin's arm. "So where do we have to go to get the deed notarized?"

"To Boorowa," Macklin said. "There isn't anyone closer unless Taylor's hired someone I don't know about."

"We can do that in a few days," Caine said. "Or even as we're taking my parents back to Sydney. We'll have to get them to make one more change before we sign it, though."

"What's that?" Macklin asked.

"It needs your name on it too."

"Caine," Macklin protested.

"Macklin," Caine mimicked. "Don't say it. Don't tell me you're just the foreman or whatever other idiotic thing you're thinking. You are the backbone of this station, and I know it. Everyone knows it, except you apparently. You loved Uncle Michael like a father. You've lived here more than half your life. If anyone deserved to inherit the station when Uncle Michael died, it was you. I would never have asked my mother for the deed, but she gave it to us."

"She gave it to you."

Caine snorted. "Were we listening to the same conversation? She specified that you needed to be here when she told me she wanted to talk business. She explained her decision to you. She called you her son. The deed might only have my name on it right now, but that's because she didn't know you yet when she had the paperwork drawn up. If she'd gotten here and you hadn't been, well, you, she could have given it just to me, but she got here and you are you and they both see it. More than that, though, you're my lover, my *partner*. If Australia allowed it, I'd marry you and then we wouldn't even be having this conversation. As it is, consider this your marriage proposal."

"Just… just let me think for a minute," Macklin said. "You get going and you're so bloody persuasive and I forget all the reasons I had why whatever you're saying is a bad idea."

"This isn't a bad idea," Caine said.

Macklin glared at him so Caine shut his mouth, waiting in silence while Macklin gathered his thoughts.

"Did you mean it?" Macklin said finally. "That you'd want to get married if we could?"

Caine didn't know whether to shake Macklin for zeroing in on the one piece of the conversation that should never have been in question or kiss him to assure him how deeply and truly Caine meant it. He settled for a simple "Yes."

Macklin went silent again.

"I expected to spend the rest of my life alone. When Michael died, I expected to have the station if the new owner didn't fire me and nothing else. I gave up my family when I ran away. My adopted father had died. Nobody would ever accept a gay stockman. I figured that was it. I'd have the respect of the jackaroos, hopefully the faith of my employer, and a week in Sydney in the winter, and that would have to be enough."

"And now?" Caine asked softly, heart breaking at the thought of all the despair in those words.

"And now I don't know what to think," Macklin admitted. "I can't think, because every time I do, I have to think about losing everything I have the same way I've always lost everything. You're it for me. You know that. I... I can't seem to go beyond that thought, though."

"You're it for me too," Caine said, taking Macklin's hand in his. "The rest, it's all just a way to live that. Your name on the deed makes sense because there's no one else I would want making decisions for the station if I couldn't. If something happened to me, I'd want you to have the station. The fastest way to make sure that happens is to make you a partner in it, not just in reality, because we would have gone under without you—and don't argue with me, I know that's the truth—but legally as well so that no one can come in and take that away from us. Maybe we'll lose a few more jackaroos if we do it. Maybe we'll have to work a little harder to take up the slack as we train the new people who are willing to come work for us."

Macklin's expression suggested he'd hoped Caine had missed that little detail.

"Yes, I noticed," Caine continued, "but that just proves my point. You're already invested in the success of the station. Nothing changes except the legal side of things. Please say yes."

Macklin swallowed visibly a couple of times, fighting some internal demon, but Caine let him wrestle with it on his own. He'd said everything he could say. The rest was up to Macklin. And if he said no, Caine would ask again in a year, and a year after that, and a year after that until Macklin finally relented.

"Yes."

MACKLIN had never allowed himself to imagine a moment like this, so he had no preconceived notion of how it would play out, only the sense of rightness as Caine tackled him to the couch, kissing him hard and fast with whispered "I love yous" interspersed. Macklin didn't manage an answer because Caine never gave him time, but internally he answered every declaration as fears he'd thought laid to rest died a sudden and final death. Caine's mother wouldn't sell the station out from under them. Caine wouldn't get bored and walk away. Caine knew about the worst of the issues with the station Macklin thought he'd hidden and wanted this anyway. Caine's parents wanted him. Caine wanted him.

Caine *wanted* him.

"Maybe we should go upstairs," Macklin said, finally breaking the kiss. "We wouldn't want them to come back and find us on the couch. They might not care that we're gay, but they don't need to see it either."

Caine chuckled and rose, holding out his hand. Macklin took it. He planned to spend the rest of his life taking it.

They walked upstairs to their bedroom, hand in hand, pausing to kiss occasionally, but mostly walking together like it was the simplest thing in the world. Macklin wasn't sure if it was the simplest or the most complicated, but he knew one thing to the depths of his soul: it was the most important.

Inside the bedroom, Caine turned into Macklin's arms, renewing the drugging kisses from the couch. Macklin leaned into them, drawing the courage he needed for what came next.

Caine wanted him.

They undressed slowly, arriving at a silent accord of tenderness rather than lust. The lust would come, Macklin knew, but only when they had loved so thoroughly that lust was an afterthought. Macklin lingered over every bit of Caine's skin as it came into sight, kissing, caressing, licking, or stroking, cherishing his lover as dictated by his heart and the new commitment between them. When Caine was naked, he returned the favor until Macklin knew himself loved beyond the slightest doubt. His legs trembled by the time Caine was done undressing him, and he had to hold onto the bedpost to stay upright, but he didn't ask Caine to hurry. The moment could not be rushed.

Finally Caine rose to his feet again, their bodies touching from toes to lips. Macklin kissed Caine deeply, languidly, lingering over this thorough possession of Caine's mouth. His lover tasted sweet, which made no sense since they had eaten curry for lunch, but Macklin didn't try to chase down the explanation. It was enough to taste, to explore Caine's mouth again with all the ease of familiarity and all the determination of the first time. Caine leaned into him, asking for more, so Macklin obliged, running his hands over Caine's back and down to his arse, pulling him close to rock their hips together. Caine groaned into the kiss and rubbed against Macklin more urgently.

"Don't come yet," Macklin warned, pulling back just enough to allow air to pass between them. "You can't make love to me if you come first."

"What?" Caine said. "But you didn't want...."

"And now I do," Macklin said. The thought still made him nervous, but the time had come to let that go. Caine wanted him. Nothing else mattered.

"You won't regret it," Caine promised. "I'll make it so good for you."

"I know you will," Macklin said. That had never been the problem. The problem had been his own hang-ups and issues, but they all seemed insignificant in the face of Caine's proposal. If they lost more men because of it, they'd hire new ones. If they had to work twice as many hours to get everything done, they'd do it.

Caine wanted him.

Everything else paled in comparison.

"Lie down," Caine said, giving Macklin a little shove toward the bed.

Macklin reclined on the pillows, eyes fixed on Caine as Caine pulled the lube from the drawer and knelt next to Macklin. He really was the most beautiful thing Macklin had ever seen. Macklin lifted a hand to Caine's cheek as Caine stroked Macklin's erection with a slick hand. "I thought you were fucking me."

"I will," Caine said, "but I thought I'd make you feel good first."

"You make me feel good just by being in the same room with me, pup."

"Then this will feel even better."

Macklin grinned as Caine nipped at his skin, lingering on his nipples until they were hard little buds, desperate for more attention. All the while, Caine moved his hand slowly on Macklin's cock, keeping the stimulation constant. Macklin shifted on the bed, spreading his legs as he planted his feet so he could thrust into Caine's hand. Caine chuckled and shifted his attention from Macklin's nipples to his balls, licking and sucking at them without speeding the damnable slow rhythm of his hand. When he felt the fingers of Caine's other hand slip into his crease and begin their explorations, he didn't even tense. He'd grown accustomed to their touch. Not immune, not by any means, but he no longer tensed up in rejection as they slipped through his guardian muscle and probed inside, stretching and opening him.

"Don't wait too long, pup."

"Why?"

"Because I'll come."

"Can't get it up twice anymore?" Caine teased.

"I'm not twenty anymore."

"I bet I could persuade you," Caine said, fingering Macklin's prostate and licking at the head of his cock. "I know all your hot spots."

Macklin couldn't argue with that. "I don't want to wait any longer. I want you, Caine."

Caine's answer was to kiss Macklin until Macklin dug his fingers into Caine's back. Then he felt Caine's weight settle against him, covering him as he slotted his cock against Macklin's entrance and pushed until the head popped through. They both froze, breaths coming in pants, bathing each other's faces.

"I love you."

The instinctive need to tense fled and Macklin relaxed completely, allowing Caine to slide deeper inside him. "You're inside me."

"Some," Caine said, pushing a little more. "You okay?"

"Never been better," Macklin said, and he meant it too. All the reasons for refusing suddenly seemed ridiculous in the face of the overwhelming sense of rightness. He belonged to Caine and Caine to him and the station—and the future—to them both. The need that had been building slowly demanded more attention now. He wrapped his legs around Caine's hips, urging him to move. He felt each thrust from beginning to end as Caine drove into him, still careful but less hesitant as Macklin urged him on.

The scent of musk and desire surrounded them, so that Macklin breathed it in with each inhale. His eyes closed without his volition, hiding the sight of Caine's beloved face, but Macklin didn't need to see to know every nuance of desire and love as Caine pushed them toward release.

"Please, pup," Macklin begged, needing to come.

Caine's hand returned to Macklin's cock, providing the final stimulation Macklin needed. He clenched and cried out as his orgasm escaped him. Seconds later, Caine joined him. Macklin could feel the stickiness between his thighs and the sensation made him quiver with renewed need. He wouldn't be ready for round two anytime soon, but he'd carry the memory with him all day, and that would have him ready again come tonight.

"Thank you," he said softly.

"For what?" Caine asked.

"For loving me enough to stay."

Caine's only reply was another long kiss.

EIGHTEEN

EVERYONE on the station had come out for Christmas dinner as far as Chris could tell, even the families who probably had or would later have smaller celebrations just for them. Chris was glad for the huge dinner. It lessened the feeling of missing his mum and of not being able to make it a real holiday for Seth. Their little house might not have much more in the way of decorations than the wreath Caine gave them, but Seth was still getting as much Christmas cheer as any teenager could ask for.

"How's the ham?" Jesse asked, sitting down next to Chris with a plate piled high with ham, lamb, spuds, and all the fixings for a perfect Christmas feast.

"Delicious," Chris said, skewering another piece with his fork, "but everything Kami makes is delicious."

"One of the great joys of working at Lang Downs," Jesse agreed.

Chris pouted. "You mean I'm not?"

"I didn't say that," Jesse said, tapping Chris's protruding lower lip with his fork. "I said *one* of the great joys, not the only or even the greatest."

Chris knew he should leave it at that, but he couldn't stop the words. "And what is the greatest?"

"If I say it's not having to hide being gay, I'm going to be sleeping in the bunkhouse tonight, aren't I?" Jesse teased.

"Maybe not," Chris said after a moment's internal debate. "After all, not hiding means being able to be with me more."

Jesse chuckled and shook his head. "The best part of this summer has been you without a doubt, Chris. I was just teasing."

Chris wanted to say he'd known that and reply in turn, but the words meant too much now that he'd admitted to himself how he felt about Jesse. Jesse's comment might not be a declaration of love, but it was one of regard, and that made Chris's heart beat just a little bit faster.

He wanted to say more, but some conversations needed privacy, and the canteen in the middle of Christmas dinner did not provide anything resembling privacy, so Chris changed the subject. "Seth's birthday is coming up in a couple of weeks. Mum always made a big deal out of it so he wouldn't feel like it got lost in Christmas, but I have no idea what to do for him here."

"We'll have a surprise party," Jesse said immediately. "Jason will help us keep Seth away from your house while everyone comes over. We don't have to invite the whole station if you don't want to, but I bet if you really wanted to do it up big, Caine and Macklin would let you use the canteen and have it here. It could be almost as big as Christmas."

"That *would* make Seth feel good," Chris said. "They've done so much for us already, though. I'd feel bad about asking for more."

"But that's just it," Jesse said. "Kami's already cooking, so it's not like he'd be cooking anything extra except maybe a cake. We'd have to get decorations from Boorowa, but we can pay for those. The only thing you'd be asking is permission to use this space instead of doing it at your house, and that doesn't cost them anything."

"Yeah, I guess," Chris said, turning the idea over in his head. "I'm still not sure how I feel about it, but it's for Seth. It's been such a hard year. He deserves to have something special."

"Exactly," Jesse said. "We'll talk to Caine after dinner and see what he says. If he says no, then we'll plan it at your place instead."

Chris still wasn't completely comfortable with the idea of asking Caine and Macklin for more special favors, but it was for Seth, and he'd do for Seth things he wouldn't consider doing for himself.

"What's his favorite meal?" Jesse went on. "We can ask Kami if he'd be willing to make it that night. With a couple of weeks' notice, it shouldn't be a problem to rearrange his menu even if he's already planned that far ahead."

"He plans meals at least a month in advance so he can be sure to have supplies on hand," Chris said, thinking back to his tenure in the kitchen, "but if it's something he makes regularly, he could probably swap days without too much trouble."

"So what would you have him make for Seth?" Jesse asked.

"I don't know," Chris said, squirming internally at the thought of being so out of touch with his brother despite all the time they'd spent together. "Before we came here, we ate whatever we could afford or I could bring home from the restaurant, and once we got here, it's been whatever Kami served. There hasn't been a lot of time to think about what we'd have if we actually had a choice."

"And asking him would ruin the surprise," Jesse said. "There's Caine. Let's ask him about using the canteen. We can figure the rest out if he says yes."

Chris checked to make sure Seth was still occupied with Jason and the other kids. When he saw that Seth wasn't paying attention, Chris nodded and waved Caine over.

"Merry Christmas," Caine said. "Are you having fun?"

"Yes, very much," Jesse said. "Chris wanted to ask a favor."

Chris glared at Jesse. "Happy Christmas," he said first. "It's Seth's birthday in a couple of weeks, and my mum always had a big party for him so he wouldn't feel like it got lost in Christmas. I know it's a lot to ask, but could we use the canteen and have his party here?"

"Of course," Caine said immediately. "We'll get Kami to bake a cake and everyone will celebrate."

"We want it to be a surprise," Chris said. "We thought Jason could help distract him."

"Jason will love that," Caine said. "He loves a good surprise. We'll give Seth a party he'll never forget."

"It'll be enough to decorate the canteen and have everyone here."

Caine frowned. "When's his birthday?"

Chris gave him the date.

"My parents will still be here. Let us give Seth a party he'll remember. We can tell him it's for my parents, since they're leaving soon after and I don't know when I'll get to see them again. That way he won't be suspicious of any preparations he might see or overhear."

"But then your parents won't have a going-away party," Chris protested.

"No, they'll have Seth's birthday party, and they'll enjoy that far more. Trust me. My father hates people fussing over him. This will let me do it without upsetting him and while making Seth happy at the same time. You and Jesse figure out what you want to do and let Kami know. I'll tell him to make it happen. If it means an extra trip to town, well, there's always a list of things to buy so it won't be wasted."

Emotion welled up in Chris's throat, making it hard to talk. Kami had told him months ago that he only had to stretch out his hand and take what Lang Downs had to offer, but Chris hadn't really believed him then. Even the offer of moving into Neil's house hadn't convinced him completely, because it served Macklin and Caine to have Chris and Seth elsewhere. This, though, this was different. Caine didn't have any reason to do this other than to be kind to Seth. Sometime over the past three months, Chris had become a part of Lang Downs, and now he was benefiting from it, just as Kami had promised.

"Thank you," Chris said, too touched to say anything else.

"I TOLD you he'd say yes," Jesse said later when they were back at Chris's house. Seth had begged to go over to Jason's house for the evening, and Patrick had repeated the invitation when Chris checked with him, so Chris and Jesse had the house to themselves. Jesse wasn't complaining. He'd gotten to spend more time alone with Chris after Chris and Seth moved out of the big house, but it was never enough.

"It's not so much that I thought he'd say no as that I worried about imposing on him," Chris explained. "I'm still not convinced I'm not imposing, but we're committed now, so we'll do what he said."

Jesse supposed he could see Chris's concern, but Chris had no frame of reference. "Lang Downs is the only station you've ever worked on," he said. "You don't see it because you don't have anything to compare it to, but even a party like the one we had today for Christmas wouldn't have happened on any other station I've worked on. The grazier might have given us the day off and let us have a barbie at the bunkhouse or something, but it would have been up to us to organize it, to do the shopping, everything. The idea of having the party at the canteen with the grazier and his family in attendance, the idea of the seasonal jackaroos being treated like part of that family, would never have occurred to me until I got here. Now it's the most logical thing in the world because Caine makes it that way, and nobody who's been around seemed surprised, so Caine's uncle must have made it that way, but it's still special. Lang Downs is special. It's a place to keep coming back to, summer after summer, no matter what you do in the winter."

"So I guess I'm worrying over nothing?"

"Something like that," Jesse agreed, "but I promise not to rub it in. What should we have Kami make for dinner?"

"A good old-fashioned barbie," Chris said after a moment. "Steaks and lamb and snags, all the good stuff, and all the barbie fixings. We'll eat in the canteen, but that way it feels like a party with the grill going outside and everyone hanging around celebrating."

"Seth will love that," Jesse agreed. "We'll have to make a trip into town to get him something for his birthday. Even if everyone else just gives him the party, you'll want a present for him, and I'd like to get one for him too."

Jesse had seen Seth grow up so much since they arrived on the station. To Jesse's knowledge, Seth hadn't played a prank on anyone since he'd messed up Patrick's toolbox. Instead, at Jason's side, Seth had blossomed, learning about the station and sheepherding. From what Chris had said, Seth had almost completely caught up in his schoolwork and would be able to finish high school on time during the next school year. "Has Seth talked at all about what he wants to do once he gets his HSC?"

"He loves machines," Chris said. "I imagine he'll look for a job as a mechanic somewhere."

"Do you think he'll stay here on the station?"

"I don't know," Chris replied. "I'll support him, whatever he decides."

That was one of the things that made Chris so remarkable as far as Jesse was concerned. He'd learned the lessons of intolerance the hard way and so did everything in his power to keep his brother from the same experience. Seth might not appreciate it now, but Jesse hoped he would see it eventually.

NINETEEN

"HAPPY birthday, Seth!"

The chorus of cheers rang out in the canteen as Seth and Jason came in. Seth looked so startled Chris nearly laughed out loud. Then understanding sank in and gratitude replaced startlement. Seth searched him out of the crowd and ran to him, throwing his arms around Chris and hugging him so tightly Chris couldn't breathe. Breathing didn't matter, he decided, as he held tight to his little brother. "Happy birthday," Chris repeated.

"You did this for me?"

"With a little help from Jesse, Caine, and Kami," Chris said. "We wanted your first birthday here to be a special one."

Seth looked around the room at all the smiling faces, the decorations, the platters of food, and the pile of gifts. "You did it. This is off the hook."

"Go on," Chris said, nudging Seth toward the food. "Everyone was waiting for you to get here so we could eat."

AS PEOPLE began finishing their dinner, someone, Jesse never saw who, turned on a radio. He pitched in to help push the tables to the sides, opening the center of the canteen for anyone who wanted to dance.

To Jesse's surprise, Caine's mother grabbed Seth's hand to pull him out to dance. Seth laughed and tried to demur, but Caine had seemingly come by his tenaciousness naturally, and Seth eventually gave in. The dance was more comical than graceful, but it got everyone else out on the floor with them. When the song ended, Molly took Mrs. Neiheisel's place as Seth's partner, much to Seth's embarrassed delight, if the look on his face was anything to go by. Jesse had no interest in women from a romantic perspective, but he could see why Neil—or Seth—would find Molly attractive.

Caine's mother moved on to Macklin, who danced much better than Jesse had expected. He saw Macklin as more of a loner, not someone who'd spent a lot of time dancing or anything like that, but Macklin acquitted himself quite well.

"Your turn, Caine," Mrs. Neiheisel called when the song finished. Caine came out to take her hand, but she shook her head and pushed Caine toward Macklin.

Jesse held his breath, not sure how anyone would react to that: Macklin, Caine, or the other jackaroos. Caine laughed and shook his head, but his mother insisted and Neil quickly echoed it. In a matter of seconds, everyone in the room was cheering for Caine to agree and dance with Macklin.

"Fine, you win," Caine said, laughing as he took Macklin's hand.

The music started again, and Jesse could tell they'd never danced together before as they tried to figure out who would lead, but it didn't take them long to find their rhythm.

"You should dance with Chris," Seth said, appearing at Jesse's side.

"What?" Jesse said, so surprised that Seth would suggest it that he couldn't think of anything else to say.

"Everybody wanted Caine and Macklin to dance," Seth said. "Nobody will care if you and Chris dance."

"Chris and I aren't...." Jesse waved a hand helplessly in Caine and Macklin's direction. Panic clawed at him at the very thought. He hadn't even realized Seth knew about him and Chris, much less that anyone else might. They were friends, sure, fucking around when they had time and energy, but they weren't together. They weren't a couple.

They didn't have the kind of relationship that would let them dance together for everyone to see.

"Tell me another one," Seth said with a disbelieving snort. "Chris's totally gone over you, and don't try to tell me otherwise. I know my brother better than that."

Jesse swallowed hard, looking over to where Chris danced with Molly, carefree and beautiful and so desirable. Jesse didn't have any trouble admitting his desire for Chris, not that he'd say that aloud. Some things Seth didn't need to hear. But more than that?

Jesse had never thought in those terms. He was a drifter, and he liked it that way. Eight or nine months of work, then a few months off, no stress, no responsibilities, nothing to hold him down when the next good thing caught his eye. Chris wasn't that way, though. He was tied to Seth if nothing else, but Jesse had seen the longing in Chris's eyes for a place to belong. Lang Downs could provide that, not just for Seth but for Chris, giving them both a home and a future they'd thought lost. Chris deserved that. He deserved better than someone who didn't want to commit past the current season. Sure, Jesse liked Lang Downs. He'd pretty much decided to come back next summer, but that was as far as he'd gotten.

He'd thought Chris was okay with the way things stood in their relationship. Chris had never said anything to suggest he wanted anything more from Jesse than exactly what they had. Seth's words, though, implied differently.

They implied Chris wanted a relationship, a family, the white picket fence and all the trimmings. The thought clawed at Jesse's brain, making him crazy with panic. That wasn't his life, his future. He couldn't have that. He didn't want that. He never had.

"So what are we going to do for Chris's birthday?" Seth asked, interrupting Jesse's thoughts. "If you won't dance with him now, we may as well start planning the next party."

"When is his birthday?" Jesse asked, ashamed to admit he didn't know.

"End of May," Seth replied.

"I won't still be here then," Jesse said automatically. "The season ends before that."

"You mean you aren't staying?" Seth asked. "But I thought...."

He ran away before Jesse could say anything else.

"Bloody hell," Jesse muttered, going after him, but Seth had disappeared outside before Jesse could see where he went. "Fuck."

"Is there a problem?" Macklin asked from the doorway.

"No... yes... I don't know... I...." The crazy roil of his thoughts intensified as he struggled with his need to find Seth and make things right and the warring need to run away while he still could. He could feel responsibilities closing in around him like a net, ready to hold him prisoner until they sucked all the life out of him. He took a deep breath and pulled himself together. "I need a week off. I can't think here. Everything's all messed up in my head, and I can't get it straightened out."

"Running away never solved anything," Macklin said.

"I'm not running away. I just need to figure things out, and if I stay here, I'll end up making things worse. I can't do that to Chris and Seth."

"And leaving will be better?"

"They deserve better than me, Macklin. I'm a no-account drifter with no plans beyond the end of the season. They're a family. They need someone they can depend on to be a part of that."

"So be that person."

"I don't know if I can," Jesse said honestly. "It's not as easy as just making that decision."

"Actually, I think it is," Macklin said. "It wasn't that long ago I was standing right where you are, feeling just as lost and confused. You just have to decide what you want."

"I only signed on for the season."

"Contracts can be renegotiated."

Jesse shook his head. "I just need to think."

"Be back in a week," Macklin said, "or you won't have a job to come back to."

"Thank you," Jesse said, bolting for the bunkhouse. He grabbed a bag, dumping things into it haphazardly, and dug out his keys. He hadn't driven his car since he got to the station, preferring to use the station's utes out on the rough roads and in the paddocks, but he couldn't drive off in one of those. Tossing his bag in the boot, he headed toward Taylor Peak and Boorowa.

"HAVE you seen Jesse?"

Chris's words interrupted Macklin's dour thoughts. He'd wanted to shake the younger jackaroo and tell him he was making a mistake, running away like this, but some lessons had to be learned the hard way.

"Yes," Macklin said, staring at the taillights disappearing out of the valley. "He left."

"What? Where is he going?"

"He didn't say," Macklin replied, wishing he had a better answer for Chris. He should have told Jesse to suck it up and be a man, but it was too late for that now.

"Is he coming back?"

"We'll see in a week," Macklin said. "I don't know what happened tonight to set him off, but from what little he said, I think he suddenly saw a future he never knew he wanted staring him in the face and got scared. If you'll take a little advice from someone who's been where he is, give him some time to figure things out, but not too much time. Sometimes a swift kick in the pants is a good thing too."

"Kind of hard to do when I don't know where he's going."

"Then we'll have to hope he comes back," Macklin said, "or that you can figure out where he'd run to if he needed to get lost in a crowd for a while."

"I... I ought to say fuck him and forget about him," Chris said, his voice breaking on the words.

"You can do that," Macklin agreed. "Nobody would blame you if you did, least of all Jesse, since he already thinks he's a 'no-account drifter' to use his words. You can write him off as exactly that, chalk up whatever happened between you to experience, and move on. Relationships end, people learn from them, and life goes on."

"He's not no-account," Chris protested.

"I didn't say he was," Macklin replied, smiling a little at Chris's defense of Jesse even in the face of Jesse's desertion. "I said he thinks he is, and that's why he wouldn't try to stop you if you decided to forget about him."

"Is that what you think I should do?"

Bloody hell, Chris was so young. Macklin wanted to pat him on the head and send him to bed, but Chris was asking for his help.

"I don't know what you should do," Macklin said honestly. "I don't know what's happened between you, what promises you made or didn't make to each other. I don't know what you want. I can guess what Jesse thinks he wants, but I don't think he really knows what he wants either right this second. He said he needed to think. My advice is for you to do the same. While he's gone, figure out what you want from him if he comes back. Ideally, but also what you can live with if you can't have your ideal. And if he does come back, you have to talk to him about what you figured out or all your thinking won't do either of you any good."

Chris nodded slowly.

"Chris," Macklin said as Chris started to walk away, "whatever you decide, whatever happens with Jesse, you and Seth have a home here for as long as you want it. If that includes Jesse, that's fine, but you've earned your place on the station and so has Seth."

The muffled sound that reached Macklin's ears might have been a sob, but Chris bolted before Macklin could figure out how to determine if it was and what to do about it.

"Are you all right?"

Macklin sighed as he turned to pull Caine against his side. "It's a good thing we called off that stupid bet or you'd never get to top."

Caine frowned. "Trouble in paradise?"

"Jesse left, and I'm pretty sure Chris is hiding in his house crying, and I don't know what to do about either of those things."

"I guess we take your advice all along and let them find their own way, unless they ask for help, of course."

CHRIS stumbled into his room, blinded by the tears he was fighting not to shed. He took one look at the rumpled sheets of his bed and lost the battle.

Jesse had *slept* with him last night. Not fucked him and then snuck back to the bunkhouse like usual. Just held him through the night like he didn't ever mean to let Chris go. They hadn't had sex, so mercifully his sheets didn't smell of it, but he'd let himself start dreaming when he woke up this morning with Jesse's arms around him.

Everything had seemed fine between them all day. They hadn't spent a lot of time together. Jesse had ridden out to the north paddock with Ian and Kyle while Chris worked with Neil and a couple of others closer to home, but Jesse had been all smiles at breakfast and again at dinner as they laughed and joked with Seth. Nothing in any of those interactions had implied Jesse was at all concerned about anything between them.

Had it been seeing Caine and Macklin dance? Chris had cheered along with everyone else when Caine's mother pushed them together. If Caine and Macklin chose to be more open, it could only make things easier for Jesse and Chris if they decided to stay on the station. He hadn't noticed Jesse's reaction at all, though, so he had no idea if it had bothered Jesse for some unknown reason.

It didn't really matter what had set Jesse off. He had left without an explanation.

"Fuck him," Chris said, righteous anger welling up inside him. "If that's the way he's going to be, I don't need him anyway. I've got better things to do than waste my time on someone who runs away at the slightest sign of a problem."

"Chris?"

The sound of Seth's voice, nearly as distraught as Chris imagined his own must be, derailed the train of Chris's thoughts. "Just a minute," he called to Seth as he slipped into the bathroom to wash his face and recover his composure. He didn't expect it to keep Seth from noticing, but it might give him a little more self-control when his brother asked him what was wrong.

"Hey," Chris said when he came into the living room a few minutes later. He took another deep breath, determined to keep his voice level and his emotions under control while he talked to Seth. "What's up?"

"I fucked up," Seth said, looking at Chris with such contrition that Chris knew he'd never manage to be angry at Seth.

"What did you do?"

"I thought you and Jesse were a thing," Seth said. "I asked him about helping me plan your birthday, and he said he wouldn't still be here then because the season would be over. I, um, kind of told him you loved him."

That explained the running away. Chris closed his eyes as he fought the urge to scream at the unfairness of the situation.

"You probably should've let me tell him that first," he said when he thought he could speak evenly.

"How was I supposed to know you hadn't?" Seth asked. "He's over here all the time. You're always kissing and stuff when you think nobody else is around. He slept here last night. That looked like a couple to me."

"I know," Chris said with a sigh, "but Jesse didn't see it the same way, apparently. He left tonight. Macklin gave him a week of vacation."

"Is he coming back?"

That was the million dollar question.

"I don't know," Chris said because he wasn't about to lie to his brother. "We'll have to wait and see."

"What will happen if he doesn't?" Seth asked.

"We'll stay on here and keep working," Chris replied, determined to accept that possibility so he'd be prepared if it happened. "You still have to get your HSC if you want to go train to be a mechanic somewhere, and I have a job to do. Jesse's decisions don't change any of that."

"What if he comes back?" Seth said, his voice small.

"Then it'll depend on what he has to say," Chris answered. "I won't be with someone I can't depend on."

"I'm sorry I scared him off."

Chris pulled his brother into a tight hug. "If he was going to be scared by us, it would have happened eventually. Better we know so we can get over it instead of planning a future with him in it. I'm sorry we messed up your party with our drama."

TWENTY

JESSE stared at the neck of the bottle of beer he held, the only alcohol he'd been able to find in Boorowa at the time of night he'd arrived. He was lucky anything was still open, even the hotel, but he'd gotten a six-pack and a room, so he was set for the night. Now, three beers in, he'd lapsed into self-pitying misery. He hadn't signed on for this. He'd signed on for a summer of work and a bit of fun with another jackaroo. He'd gotten both, but apparently he'd gotten more than he realized.

He took another gulp of his beer.

He *liked* his life as it was. He liked being able to leave a place at the end of the summer and not have to go back if it wasn't somewhere he felt like returning. He liked the freedom of knowing no one was depending on him beyond his work as a jackaroo. He could handle sheep; he didn't have a good track record with people.

If he accepted what Seth said, he'd be taking on not just Chris, but Seth as well. He might think about it if only Chris was involved. Chris was an adult, responsible for his own choices the same way Jesse was, but Seth was still a kid, and he'd be affected by both Chris's and Jesse's choices.

The devil on his shoulder pointed out he'd already affected Seth by leaving, but he rationalized the choice by arguing that this way he'd only hurt Seth once instead of every time he made a bad choice, as he was sure to do if he stayed.

Of course he'd told Macklin he'd be back in a week, so he'd have to face Chris and Seth eventually, unless he just didn't come back. He'd lose half his pay that way and the possibility of returning to Lang

Downs in the future, not to mention the lack of references when he tried to get a job elsewhere next summer, but it would almost be worth it not to have to see the hurt in their eyes at his desertion.

He could get a job waiting tables or something in Melbourne to make up for the lost income, and he still had his references from other summers. It wouldn't be ideal, but it would be better than nothing.

Better than hurting Chris even worse than he'd already done.

When had Chris fallen in love with him? When had Seth started seeing them as a family?

Jesse had no idea, and drunk as he was getting as he opened the fourth bottle, he doubted he could figure it out, but the guilt remained even through the haze of alcohol. Had he done something to lead Chris on? Said something to make the other man think Jesse was offering more than they'd originally agreed on?

They'd been very clear early on, talking about how they weren't Caine and Macklin, how they were just friends with benefits. Chris had repeated that more than once himself, and Jesse hadn't noticed any doubt or hesitation in his voice as he'd spoken.

Sure, he'd helped Chris out in Yass, but he'd have done that for any friend in need. Granted, he didn't have any other friends who needed that kind of support, but he wouldn't have hesitated. Had Chris misread his presence at the hospital? Had he taken it as more of a commitment than Jesse had intended?

Jesse supposed it was possible. Chris had used the word friend when talking with the doctor, but that could have been as much self-preservation as anything else. After all, he'd been bashed in Yass once. Opening up to a stranger about being gay a second time would have seemed incredibly risky, especially since just a group of teens walking down the street was enough to trigger a panic attack for Chris.

They'd shared a hotel room in Boorowa that night, but they hadn't had a choice. There hadn't been a third room available, so it was either share or sleep in the car. Jesse had done that a few times. It wasn't an experience he'd care to repeat if he had a choice. But again, he'd have shared with any of the Lang Downs jackaroos rather than sleep in the car, so surely that wasn't what had made Chris's feelings change.

They spent a lot of time working together on the station, but that was Caine or Macklin's doing, not Jesse's own. He and Chris made a good team, and he didn't mind showing Chris the ropes, so assigning them to work together was a logical choice, and Jesse hadn't complained since it meant they could sneak in the occasional kiss (or blow job if Chris had his way), but Jesse hadn't taken that to be anything more than Chris having the typical horniness of a guy in his early twenties. Had Chris seen it as more? As a sign of a commitment Jesse hadn't intended to make?

God, he hoped not.

He could deal with a lot of things, but leading Chris on, however unintentionally, would eat at him. He had always prided himself on being upfront about his intentions. If he'd somehow said something or done something to suggest he wanted more, he'd hate himself even more than he already did.

He gulped down his beer. He wanted to stop thinking so he could sleep, but his mind wouldn't shut down. He took another deep gulp, hoping he could lose himself in the oblivion of drunkenness if he couldn't lose himself in sleep.

"YOU should know something about Aussie stockmen."

The words startled Chris so much he nearly dropped the pitchfork he'd been pretending to use to muck stalls while he turned Jesse's desertion over and over in his head.

"I'm sorry?"

"I said there's something you should know about Aussie stockmen," Caine repeated. "Come walk with me. The stable is not the most conducive place for a heart-to-heart conversation."

"Is that what we're going to have?" Chris asked warily. He wasn't sure how he felt about the idea. He didn't doubt Caine could give him good advice, but it would mean telling the grazier about him and Jesse, and Chris had never had anyone he could really confide in about anything concerning his sexuality.

"I think it's time we did," Caine replied, leading Chris out of the barn and toward the veranda on the big house. "Macklin convinced me not to say anything earlier in the season, but you obviously need a friend right now, and the man who filled that role since you got here is the reason why. I love Macklin, but he isn't the talking type, so that leaves me to fill the role."

"You say that so easily," Chris said with more than a little envy.

"I didn't grow up here. You have to remember that. Like you could forget it listening to me talk, but it's more than just an accent or a choice of words now and then," Caine said. "I came out to my parents when I was in high school, and it was a complete non-issue. I was out in college, and other than one guy in my dorm who was a little weirded out by it, nobody cared. I moved to Philadelphia, met a guy I thought I'd be with forever, got an apartment in the Gayborhood—yes, that's exactly what it sounds like. Sure, I ran into the occasional asshole, but I lived a pretty uneventful life as an openly gay man."

"So why did you come here?" Chris asked. "I mean, not that I think you shouldn't have, but why would you leave all that behind for Australia?"

"Because I was in a d-dead-end job, the g-guy I thought I'd be with d-dumped me, I couldn't afford the apartment by myself, and I'd always wanted to visit my uncle's sheep station," Caine said. "My mother was g-going to sell it. She didn't have any need for a sheep station and no way to run it either. It was about to be my last chance, and even if I b-blew it, it couldn't be any w-worse than what I was leaving b-behind."

"You're stuttering. You never stutter."

Caine laughed. "You didn't know me a year ago. I don't stutter very often anymore, but strong emotion still brings it out. My point, though, is that being gay wasn't ever something I needed to hide, so of course it's easy for me to talk about being with Macklin. I don't think of it any differently than Neil would think about telling people he and Molly are getting married, but I've been here long enough to realize I'm the only one in the outback who feels that way. Honestly, it didn't take twenty-four hours to realize I was the only one who felt that way. So yes, I say it easily, and the people around me have reached a point where I can even live it fairly easily, but that doesn't mean reaching this point was easy. You've met Macklin. You can't believe for a second that he was out before I came."

"No," Chris said. "You're right. I couldn't believe he danced with you last night."

"He couldn't believe it either," Caine said. "He's a stockman through and through. Hard as nails and strong as the mountains we're standing on, and anything that might imply weakness is stomped out before it can take root. It's one of the many reasons I love him. He will always be there for me to lean on, offering his strength, but it sometimes makes me want to beat his head against the wall because he's as stubborn and set in his ways as he is strong, and that's the thing you need to know about Aussie stockmen. They respect strength and determination. They're strong enough, or maybe repressed enough, to turn off their emotions and walk away from everything they really want if they think it's not right or good or whatever stupid ideas they get in their heads. Macklin tried to do it to me, and I'd venture a guess Jesse's trying to do the same thing to you."

"So what do I do about it?" Chris asked.

"Well, that depends," Caine replied. "Just like water wears down rock, it's possible to break them down and get inside their heads and their hearts, but it's a hell of a lot of work, and it's not something that happens overnight. I was lucky, in a sense. I almost drowned, and that scared Macklin right out of his stoic shell. If that hadn't happened, I'd probably still be working on him because it hasn't been a year yet since I got here, much less since I realized Macklin was what I wanted. So the first question isn't what to do about it. The first question is what do you want from Jesse?"

"Nothing at the moment," Chris muttered.

"I don't blame you," Caine said, giving Chris's shoulder a sympathetic squeeze. "And if that's really your answer, then you don't need to worry about anything else. You can forget everything I told you except for future reference if you meet another stubborn stockman you want to try your luck with."

"No," Chris admitted, "it's not really my answer. I'm angry and hurt that he left without a word, but Macklin seemed to think he was pretty upset, so maybe Seth letting the cat out of the bag about me falling in love with him really bothered him."

"I take it you hadn't talked about it?"

Chris shook his head. "It never seemed like the right time, and besides, we were just messing around, you know? It wasn't supposed to be anything serious, just two guys letting off a little steam now and then. There's no harm in that."

"No, there isn't," Caine agreed. "So Jesse's problem is he thinks you changed the rules on him mid-game, and he doesn't know how to deal with that."

"That's why I didn't tell him," Chris said. "My emotions are my problem, not his. I mean, I hoped he'd eventually feel the same way, but I wasn't going to make a big deal out of it or ask him for anything or expect him to do anything differently."

"Even to the point of letting him go at the end of the season?"

"I hadn't gotten that far," Chris said, "but I knew he planned on going. He'd made comments about spending the winter in Melbourne and stuff, so I knew he wasn't planning on settling down yet, but he also made comments about maybe coming back next summer, so I figured we'd pick up where we left off, and maybe next summer would be different."

"It sounds to me like you already know the answer to my first question, then," Caine said. "You want him, whatever that ends up looking like."

"Yeah, but will he still want me now that he knows how I feel?"

"I can't answer that question for you," Caine said, "but I'll repeat what I said about those stubborn stockmen. If Macklin thought for a second that the station and I would be better served without him here, he would leave and never look back. Fortunately I disabused him of that notion before he could actually do it, but I have no doubt it could have happened. If Jesse's got it in his head that he's bad for you, he's perfectly capable of leaving, no matter what he really wants, just because he's got a stubborn streak a mile wide and core of steel that he's built up from hiding who he is and being strong enough to protect himself if someone does find out. Granted, Macklin's had a few more years to build that up than Jesse has, but Macklin's been on Lang Downs since he was sixteen, and until a year ago, he had Uncle Michael to back him up if necessary. Jesse's moved from station to station, so he's had to start over each time with convincing the people around him he's as hard and tough as they are."

"So what do I do?"

"You fight for him."

THE bar in Melbourne where Jesse spent most of his winter evenings was just as crowded and just as dingy in the summer, but the drinks were still as cheap and the men just as available. Jesse figured it was the best he could ask for. Now he just had to find oblivion in hard liquor and some twink's tight ass. An anonymous fuck to help him get Chris out of his system. Just what the doctor ordered.

If only he could find one.

He ruled out all the blonds because he'd end up picturing a pair of deep, dark eyes to go with the light hair. The brunets all rubbed him the wrong way too. They were too tall, too short, too buff, or too skinny. He'd had enough seductive looks cast his way to take his pick, but he obviously wasn't drunk enough yet since none of them sparked more than a passing flicker of interest.

"You're back early," the bartender said as he brought Jesse another drink. "We don't usually see you until the end of April."

"I took a week off," Jesse said, refusing to think about why he had the time. "Where else would I go?"

"I can think of a couple regulars who'll be happy to see you, early or not," the bartender said with a leer.

"Point me their way," Jesse said with a joviality he didn't feel. "Better yet, send one of them a drink from me."

"You don't want to know who it is first?"

"It doesn't matter," Jesse said. "I'm just looking for some action, not romance."

The bartender looked skeptical, but he indicated a guy at the end of the bar—not a blond, thankfully—and Jesse nodded. A few minutes later, the man came down to lean on the bar next to Jesse. "Welcome back."

"It's just for a few days," Jesse said, not wanting to give the man any false hope. He'd done enough of that with Chris apparently.

"I could deal with a few days," the guy said. "I'm Matt."

"Jesse."

"You wanna dance, Jesse?"

Dancing was the last thing Jesse wanted, not when he'd been too afraid to dance with Chris, but he had to have some prelude to dragging the guy into the bathroom or back room to fuck him. "Why not?"

Matt grinned and pulled Jesse onto the dance floor, grinding against him more than actually dancing as he felt up Jesse's chest through his shirt.

Jesse's body reacted to the stimulation, his nipples tightening and his cock waking up in his pants. Matt grinned and turned in Jesse's loose embrace so he could press his arse against Jesse's groin. Jesse groaned and used the new position to run his hands over Matt's chest in turn. The man was hot and obviously eager, and the combination of lust and drunkenness made it easy to forget the desperation that had brought him Melbourne at the height of summer. He closed his eyes and let the music add to the pounding in his blood. He couldn't have danced like this with Chris, even if he'd given in to Seth's urging. He would have had to keep it clean, not this raw, needy build-up to mindless release. Matt didn't care who was watching, and no one in the bar cared how lewdly they rubbed against each other. Hell, half the bar would probably cheer if Jesse got Matt's shirt off and started giving them a real show.

If the way Matt egged him on, bucking against him and moaning loud enough to be heard over the music every time Jesse squeezed his nipples was any indication, Matt wouldn't mind either.

"Let's go somewhere a little more private," Jesse said as he slid one hand from Matt's chest to his dick. "I want to get a taste of this."

Matt flashed him a seductive grin and pulled him toward the shadowy restroom corridor. Jesse ignored his conscience screaming that this was wrong, that he'd regret it in the morning, that Matt deserved better than to be used as a path to forgetfulness even if he didn't mind being a casual fuck.

The fluorescent lights of the restroom were glaring after the relative darkness of the bar itself, making Jesse wince as his head pounded and his gut churned from everything he'd drunk before dancing with Matt. Matt wasn't paying attention to Jesse's discomfort, though, pulling Jesse toward one of the open stalls and locking them inside.

Chris would have noticed, Jesse's conscience said. *Chris would have cared.*

Jesse silenced the annoying internal voice by pushing Matt against the wall and shoving his hand down the other man's pants. "You're in a hurry," Matt purred. "I like that in a man."

There wasn't any choice, Jesse thought cynically. They were in the bathroom of a bar, likely to be interrupted at any moment. This wasn't the time for slow and sweet.

Matt undid Jesse's jeans, pulling him free and pumping him roughly. His grip was tight, almost too tight, but his palm was smooth, a city dweller's hand.

Not Chris's hand.

Jesse got Matt's shirt open to reveal a startlingly smooth chest. Jesse ran his hand over it in surprise, only to feel the slightest hint of stubble.

Waxed.

Fake.

Reminding himself he didn't have to approve of Matt's choices to fuck him, he turned his attention to Matt's pants instead, but when he pushed them down around his hips and saw the nearly shaved pubes, he groaned and turned away.

"I'm sorry," he said. "I can't do this."

"What do you mean you can't do this?" Matt demanded behind him. "You didn't have any trouble all but screwing me on the dance floor."

Jesse's stomach roiled, bile rising in his throat.

"I said I can't do this," Jesse repeated, straightening his clothes and turning back to face Matt. He opened the stall door and gestured for Matt to leave. "Get out."

"Fucker!" Matt shouted. "Tease."

The invectives continued as Jesse closed the door again in the other man's face, but the words carried over the thin partitions. Jesse couldn't even hear them after a moment. Nothing Matt could say was worse than what Jesse was saying to himself.

He didn't want a mindless fuck. He didn't want some polished, pretty body who'd fuck anything that moved.

He wanted Chris.

His stomach heaved and he collapsed to his knees, everything he'd drunk coming back up in one foul rush. He puked hard, gagging as the bile nearly choked him.

He'd had Chris. He'd had not just the fucking but the friendship and even the love, and he'd thrown it back in Chris's face like it was as meaningless as every other encounter he'd ever had.

Sweat poured down his face as another wave of nausea shook him and he vomited again. He didn't think he had anything left in his stomach, but his body disagreed, spasm after spasm leaving him weak and shaking.

He'd blown it. Despite Jesse's inability to see what was in front of him, Chris had fallen in love with him, warts and all. Jesse hadn't tried to impress Chris, hadn't approached him as he would have if he'd been thinking about romance, and Chris loved him anyway.

The vomiting turned to dry heaves, his body still trying to purge all the alcohol he'd consumed even though his stomach was empty, and Jesse's ragged breathing turned to sobs.

Fuck, he'd sunk low, on his knees in a grungy bar loo that probably hadn't been cleaned in months, stinking of alcohol and bile.

It served him right.

TWENTY-ONE

CHRIS sat outside on the tiny veranda of his little house, staring up at the stars. They made him think of Jesse, of all the nights they'd sat together looking up at them with Jesse pointing out constellations or simply watching them wheel overhead, not that Chris could think about much else since he and Caine had talked two days before.

Fight for him.

Such simple words, but Chris had no idea how to begin. If Jesse were asleep in the bunkhouse where he belonged, it would be easy. He'd keep talking, keep seducing, keep loving until Jesse had no choice but to see how good things were between them, but Jesse wasn't there, and Chris didn't know if he was coming back.

He'd resisted the urge to snoop in Jesse's room to see if Jesse had left anything behind. Clothes and things could be replaced, of course, but if Jesse had left stuff behind, it meant he'd planned to come back when he left, even if he'd changed his mind since then. If the room was completely empty….

That didn't even bear thinking about.

He could wait and see if Jesse came back, see what the man's mood was when he arrived, but that hardly counted as fighting for him. Maybe it wouldn't matter. Maybe Jesse would work out whatever demons had sent him running and things would be back to normal, but the cat was out of the bag now. Chris wasn't sure they could go back to "normal." Jesse knew how he felt now, even if Chris hadn't said it to him yet. Even if Chris said he could accept their old arrangement, his feelings would be there, hanging between them, and he'd always wonder what would make Jesse run the next time. And that assumed Jesse would be willing to have any kind of arrangement with Chris, knowing how Chris felt.

"Are you still out there?" Seth asked, sticking his head through the open doorway.

"Yes," Chris said. "Just thinking."

"About Jesse?"

"Yeah," Chris said.

"Do you want to talk about it?"

"Do you want to hear about it?" Chris said with a laugh.

"Maybe not the details," Seth said, "but you're my brother. You've been taking care of me for months, and this is kind of my fault. If you need to talk, I'll listen."

"I have to figure out what I want with Jesse," Chris said slowly. "I may or may not get what I want, of course, but if I don't know what I want, what I can live with, and what I can't, how can I figure out where to go if he comes back?"

"So what do you want?" Seth asked, taking the other seat.

"What Caine and Macklin have," Chris said. He almost laughed with the relief of saying it aloud for the first time. "God, I never thought I'd say that. I never thought I'd be *able* to say that. Are you okay with that?"

"I've never had a problem with you being gay," Seth reminded him. "I like Jesse, and I like it here on the station. If you want to shack up with Jesse and spend the rest of your life here, I'm good with that."

"Then I guess I'd better figure out how to make it work, huh?"

"Do you know where he went?"

"Not for sure," Chris said. "He mentioned Melbourne more than once, saying he spent the winters with friends there, but Melbourne's not exactly Boorowa or Yass. Just showing up there isn't going to be enough to find him."

"You could try calling him," Seth suggested. "I'm sure Caine has his contact information somewhere."

Chris blinked a couple of times. "God, you're brilliant. Okay, first thing in the morning, I'll get the number from Caine and then I'm going after him. Will you be okay alone here for a few days?"

"Alone?" Seth said with a laugh. "How many people live on this station? I'll be lucky to spend a second of the time you're gone alone with everyone coming to check on me."

"You okay with that?" Chris asked.

Seth grinned. "Oh yeah."

JESSE woke up the next day, well past noon, still feeling hung over and shaky. His friend had already left for work, but Jesse knew the apartment well enough to stumble into the kitchen and start a pot of tea. He hoped the caffeine would help clear his head. The bottles of water he drank after he got back to the apartment last night hadn't made a difference, but his stomach wasn't threatening to empty again like it had been last night.

He prepared the first cup of tea on autopilot, letting the force of habit move him through the motions. By the time he poured the second cup, he could feel his brain starting to kick in and with it, the sense of loss that had driven him to his knees the night before.

He'd blown it with Chris. He knew that, but maybe everything wasn't as hopeless as it had seemed the night before when he was drunk off his arse. If Seth was right and Chris really did love him, maybe Chris could be convinced to forgive him. Not that Jesse thought it would be that easy. Jesse hadn't just freaked out at the thought that Chris might love him; he'd run. And now that things had gone down the way they did, he didn't expect they could go back to the way things had been before. Ignorance had allowed Jesse to imagine they were comfortable with the status quo, but those blinders had been stripped away. If he went back, if he asked Chris to forgive him and give him another chance, he had to be willing to accept Chris's feelings and all that entailed. He had to be willing to commit to something.

The thought made him twitchy after years of avoiding anything that would tie him down, but he ignored the feeling. That had landed him in this mess already. He had to get past the inclination to run at the first sign of commitment and decide what he could offer Chris, because if he went back unprepared, Chris would be perfectly justified in telling him to take a hike.

Could he go back and offer to stay? Could he commit to Chris, to a family with Seth, to a life on Lang Downs?

He'd pretty much decided to return to Lang Downs next summer, so the thought of staying on the station was the least unnerving of the three questions. He *could* make a life there, and a good one if the experiences of the other year-rounders was any indication.

He'd enjoyed being footloose for the past ten years, but he couldn't live that way indefinitely. He'd always known it, but he'd always figured when he got tired of the wandering life, he'd get a job working as a mechanic in a shop in Melbourne or Sydney, where he wouldn't be immediately shunned for being gay and where he had at least the possibility of congenial company from time to time. He hadn't been to Lang Downs, though, when he'd formulated that approximation of a plan. He hadn't imagined he could find a sheep station that wouldn't run him off, much less one where he could envision living comfortably with a partner.

Lang Downs could be home if he chose to let it be.

That left Chris and Seth.

He enjoyed Chris's company. They were friends. They worked well together. They were comfortable together whether they were herding sheep, hanging out in the bunkhouse, or fucking like madmen. None of that necessarily equaled love.

Last night had shown him that it was more than fucking around, though, because last night he'd tried to go back to empty fucking, and it had felt nothing like what he shared with Chris. Maybe he hadn't labeled it for what it was, but he'd felt the difference almost from the beginning, chalking it up to having sex with someone he knew and cared about rather than with a stranger.

He might not have been ready to call it love, but he'd known Chris was more than another random fuck, so it wouldn't be so much a matter of changing things between them as it would be admitting what was between them. The risk inherent in that proposition unnerved him, setting his stomach churning again, but he reminded himself he wasn't taking that leap with no safety net. He knew Chris loved him, or, to be precise, he knew Seth thought Chris loved him, but that was close enough.

That brought him back to Seth, because Chris wasn't a one-man deal. Starting a relationship with Chris meant taking on some responsibility for Seth as well, for the next year and possibly beyond that. Seth wasn't a baby to need constant supervision, but he would be there, part of Chris's life, desiring (and deserving) attention and love from Chris and from anyone who wanted to be more than a passing part of Chris's life. It wouldn't quite make Jesse a father, but it would make him a whole lot closer to older brother or uncle than he'd ever expected to be.

He lifted his tea to his mouth only to realize he'd emptied it. Staring down into the dregs, he considered his two options. Life at Lang Downs with Chris openly as his lover, Seth at their side for the next year or two until he went off to uni and then visiting as he had breaks from school, or an endless series of nights like the preceding one. Suddenly the choice seemed obvious.

He dumped the cup in the sink and looked around for paper to leave a note for his friend. He had to get back to Lang Downs.

He had some groveling to do.

CHRIS parked the car in the car park outside the Boorowa Hotel. He'd hoped to get away first thing after breakfast so he could make it to Melbourne before the end of the day and hopefully find Jesse before that night, but circumstances had conspired against him and he hadn't gotten away until well after lunch. If he'd left on time, the twelve-hour drive to Melbourne might have been possible in one day, but as it was, he wouldn't get much farther than Yass if he tried to continue, and the thought of spending the night alone in a hotel room in Yass was enough to convince him to stay in Boorowa instead. The hour's extra drive the next day would be worth not having panic attacks every time someone walked past his hotel room door.

He would eat dinner, get a good night's sleep, leave early the next morning, and be in Melbourne in time for lunch. He could call Jesse once he got to Melbourne and figure out how to meet up with him. And if he was wrong and Jesse had gone somewhere else, he'd decide what to do then. For tonight, he'd settle for a place to sleep.

The hotel had rooms available so he took the cheapest one, tossed his bag on the bed, and went back down for dinner. As he was finishing up, he heard an all-too-familiar voice asking for a table.

"You don't need a table," he interrupted Jesse and the hotel waiter. "You're welcome to join me."

The smile that lit up Jesse's face made Chris's heart beat faster with hope, love, and desire. "Chris! What are you doing here?"

Chris shook his head, not wanting to have this conversation where others could hear them, but he pushed the chair opposite him back with his foot. Jesse took the seat, ordered something to drink, and turned back to Chris expectantly as the waiter walked off.

"I was coming to find you," Chris said, keeping his voice soft. "I wasn't taking the chance that you weren't coming back."

"I'm coming back," Jesse replied. "I'll always come back."

Chris liked the sound of that except for one little thing…. "Does that mean you plan on leaving again?"

The waiter interrupted with Jesse's drink. Jesse ordered bangers and mash without even looking at the menu.

"Maybe this isn't the best place to talk," Jesse said after the waiter had left again. "I got a room. We can talk after we eat."

"I have a room too," Chris said. He and Jesse had shared a room here the last time they'd come through town at the same time, but that had been a combination of availability and Chris's panic attacks. Now, though, they didn't have either of those excuses, and until Chris knew what Jesse intended, he didn't think falling back into bed would be a good idea. They'd made that mistake once. He didn't want to make it again. They could talk in Jesse's room, but Chris would return to his own room to sleep unless Jesse said all the right things.

"Where did you go?" Chris asked while they waited for Jesse's meal to arrive.

"To Melbourne," Jesse replied. "I crashed with a friend for a day or two."

"Why did you leave?"

"We'd better save that for later too."

Chris nodded and let silence fall between them. They had spent many a silent hour together riding fences or keeping watch on the sheep during the night, but the silence between them had never been as tense as it was now. Chris twitched on his seat, racking his brain for something to say to break the silence, but he drew a blank. He could wait to discuss the issues between Jesse and himself, but he couldn't fill the intervening time with meaningless chatter.

"How's Seth?" Jesse asked when the waiter had brought his food and the silence had truly reached the uncomfortable stage.

"He's fine," Chris said. "He's feeling guilty for messing things up."

"He didn't mess anything up," Jesse replied. "He just made me see some things I hadn't realized before. Or would you have let me leave in April without saying anything?"

"It would have depended on what happened between now and then," Chris answered honestly. "You'd never given any indication of wanting to stay."

"I'd never had any reason to think about staying," Jesse reminded him.

"Oh, and sleeping with—" Jesse's hiss drew Chris up short. He leaned forward and lowered his voice to a whisper. "And sleeping with me even when we weren't fucking wasn't a reason to think maybe something had changed?"

"I was a blind, stupid drongo," Jesse said with a sigh. He pushed the food around his plate, looking so forlorn Chris almost took pity on him. "I owe everyone an apology, and I'll give yours to you as soon as we're somewhere private to talk."

"Fine," Chris said, trying to keep the hurt and anger out of his voice. Somehow he didn't think blowing up was what Caine had in mind when he told Chris to fight for Jesse.

Jesse ate a few more bites of his dinner before pushing the plate back. "Let's go."

They paid and walked up to the rooms they had rented for the night. They reached Chris's room first so he unlocked the door and gestured for Jesse to go inside. If nothing else, he could kick the other man out if he got fed up with the course of their conversation.

Fight for him, not with him, Chris admonished silently.

"Why did you leave?"

"Does it really matter?" Jesse asked. "Isn't it more important that I came back?"

"I don't know," Chris said. "Why did you come back?"

"Because I realized something when I ended up drunk and puking in a bar in Melbourne," Jesse said. "I didn't know how good I had it until I nearly threw it all away. As soon as I could drive, I started back to Lang Downs."

Chris arched an eyebrow.

"Back to you."

That was more like it.

Chris wanted to throw himself into Jesse's arms and kiss him, but they hadn't actually resolved anything.

"So what happens now?"

"What do you want to happen?" Jesse asked in reply.

"I'm not the one who freaked out and ran off," Chris reminded him. "I'm not the one who has to explain myself."

"But that's just it," Jesse said. "I can't tell you what's going to happen unless I know what you want to happen, because what I want is to give you what you want."

That sounded a little too good to be true. "Stop it, damn it. You're talking in riddles. Just answer the question. Why did you leave and why did you come back?"

Jesse reached for Chris's hand, drawing him closer. "Seth told me you'd fallen in love with me," he said. "He was talking about your birthday and making plans about me being a part of your family like it was a given, and I hadn't thought about any of that and I freaked. I didn't start the season expecting to settle down somewhere and stay. I didn't even kiss you the first time with that thought. It was supposed to be exactly what we said it would be. It was supposed to be a nice way to pass the summer. I didn't plan on falling in love with you, even if it took running away to realize it."

"That's why you left," Chris said, although the words appeased some of the hurt and anger he'd been feeling since watching Jesse's taillights disappear into the night. "Why did you come back?"

"Because I'm not quite stupid enough to throw away the best shot at a future I'll ever get," Jesse replied. "I've been around enough to know there aren't many stations like Lang Downs." Chris frowned, opening his mouth to protest, but Jesse held up his hand, forestalling the words. "It's more than that, but that's part of it too, because you're tied there already. I don't know if you've seen it, but you've already made the station part of your future. You've put down roots there with Seth, whether you were looking to do that or not. So if I want to be with you, I have to want to be at Lang Downs too, and that's what I figured out while I was gone. I want it all. I want you and Seth and Lang Downs and a future I'd never imagined could be possible. Maybe I'll make a mess of it, but I want to try. Will you give me another chance?"

"I was coming to find you," Chris said slowly. "I'd come to the conclusion that you didn't just get to walk away and pretend like nothing had changed since the beginning of the season. I was going to fight for us if I had to."

"You don't have to," Jesse said, "but I kind of like knowing you would have. It's probably a good thing you didn't find me last night, though. You wouldn't have wanted me if you had."

"You said you went out," Chris remembered, suddenly leery again. "Did you pick up some guy and fuck him?"

"No," Jesse said. "I thought I would, but I didn't do it. I couldn't do it. I ended up comparing every guy I looked at to you, and I didn't want any of them because they weren't you. When I was sober enough to drive this morning, I started back north. I'm glad I stopped for the night instead of trying to get all the way back tonight, or I would've missed you entirely."

"I was going to call you when I got to Melbourne so I could come wherever you were," Chris said with a chuckle. "That would've been bad, if you'd been back on Lang Downs and I'd gotten all the way to Melbourne."

"So am I forgiven?" Jesse asked, leaning his forehead against Chris's.

"I don't know," Chris teased. "You haven't kissed me yet. Are you sure you're in love with me?"

Jesse growled, the sound sending both amusement and desire through Chris. "Yes, Chris, I love you."

Chris ran his fingers through Jesse's hair. "Then kiss me and I'll forgive you."

RELIEF surged through Jesse as Chris stroked his scalp. He bent the little bit to close the gap between them, keeping the kiss gentle and loving for the moment. He didn't expect it to stay that way for long, but he lingered for now, brushing their lips together, back and forth in sweet, tender contact to feed the heart. Chris made no move to speed things up, his fingers stroking through Jesse's longer hair but otherwise resting trustingly in Jesse's embrace.

The emotion of the moment overwhelmed Jesse, and he pulled Chris tightly against him, burying his face in the crook of Chris's neck. "I'm sorry I fucked up," he said, his voice muffled by Chris's skin.

"Hey," Chris said, pulling back and tipping Jesse's chin up so their eyes met, "that's life sometimes. We're back where we need to be, well, mostly, and back on track. Nothing's fucked up."

Jesse nodded. "I think it'll take me some time to really realize that. Last night was, well, bad."

"You love me. I love you. We have a place we can be together. The rest is just a question of working out the details," Chris said. "We can spend the rest of our lives doing that if we need to."

Jesse sucked in a breath at hearing the words from Chris directly. Not that he'd doubted Seth, but he hadn't realized how badly he needed the reassurance of hearing it from Chris.

"I don't suppose you brought condoms with you," Jesse said hopefully.

"I was coming to fight for you, remember?" Chris replied. "Of course I brought condoms because I couldn't be sure what you'd taken with you and I wasn't going to search your room. I might have given up before I ever left the station if it'd been empty."

"It wasn't empty," Jesse said. "I was coming back. Well, no, last night when I realized what I'd done and how badly I'd messed up, I thought about not coming back, but I came to my senses this morning."

"Good," Chris said. He kissed Jesse quickly and opened his bag to pull out condoms and lube. "Caine warned me I might have to make you see reason, and I would have done my best, but this is so much better."

"Straight to the make-up sex?" Jesse teased.

"Do you have a better suggestion?"

"No."

Jesse kissed Chris again with more passion this time, licking the seam of Chris's lips. They parted for him, inviting him inside the way he hoped he'd soon be inside Chris's arse. He took advantage of Chris's willingness, twining their tongues together as he slid his thigh between Chris's legs. Chris moved against him, rubbing provocatively against Jesse. It felt so good, so right, after the gut-churning nothingness of the night before. Jesse slid his hands down to cup

Chris's arse, urging him to move faster, harder, anything but stopping. Chris moaned and followed his head.

Jesse attacked Chris's mouth, hard, nearly brutal kisses born of desperation and near loss. Chris met him kiss for kiss, bite for bite until they were clawing at each other's clothes. Jesse finally pulled back.

"Naked. Now."

Chris groaned and practically tore his clothes off, his lightly furred, perfectly *real* body coming into view. Jesse advanced on him, pushing him backward onto the bed. He followed Chris down, biting at his nipples before soothing them with his tongue, doing everything he could think of to drive Chris wild.

It worked if the way Chris bucked up against him was any indication.

He followed a meandering path over the line of Chris's ribs down to the treasure trail that bisected Chris's stomach. He lingered for a moment at Chris's navel, fucking it with his tongue, but the seductive scent of desire beckoned him on.

Chris tasted so fucking good when Jesse finally licked his way to the head of Chris's cock. Chris's wordless shout made Jesse smile and want to wring more delicious sounds from his lover.

God, just thinking the word made him tremble. He wanted to cover Chris with his body and fuck him into oblivion, and then hold him all night long. And tomorrow night. And the night after.

He sucked Chris deeper and reminded himself he could do all of that. Tonight, tomorrow night, forever.

"I'm not... gonna last," Chris groaned.

Jesse thought for an instant about pushing Chris now and getting him all worked up again for a second round. Chris was only twenty. His recovery time wasn't in question, but Jesse didn't want to wait. He pulled back and stripped quickly before returning to the bed to cover Chris as he had imagined doing. The sheen of sweat on Chris's skin eased the slide of skin against skin as Jesse pressed Chris into the mattress.

"Enough foreplay," Chris groaned. "Fuck me already."

Jesse grabbed the lube and made quick work of preparing Chris, urged on by the constant stream of admonishments, obscenities, and groans coming from his lover. Another time, he'd draw this out, fucking Chris with his fingers until Chris couldn't stand it anymore, but Jesse's own patience had waned, and the need to seal their promises in the most carnal of ways spurred him to hurry.

When he replaced his fingers with his cock in Chris's arse, he leaned up to find Chris's lips again, echoing the driving of his hips with the movement of his tongue, claiming Chris, giving himself to Chris in every way he knew how.

Chris returned his devotions kiss for kiss, caress for caress, until Jesse thought he'd come apart at the seams, simply explode because his feeble skin couldn't possibly contain this much joy, this much need, this much love.

Then Chris came apart beneath him, writhing on the bed as his body shook with release. Jesse bit his lip, trying to prolong Chris's pleasure, but his own need had grown unbearable, and he gave in trying to stave off his climax.

He collapsed on top of Chris, all the upheaval and alcohol of the past few days catching up with him and leaving him feeling hollowed out and created anew.

Chris's arms wrapped around his shoulders, keeping him in place when he would have rolled to the side. "Don't leave."

"I wasn't leaving," Jesse promised. "I was just going to stop squashing you."

Chris draped his legs over the backs of Jesse's thighs. "Squash away."

JESSE took a deep breath as he stepped out of his car shortly after lunch the next day. He and Chris had each driven their own car back to Lang Downs, but he'd kept Chris in sight through his rearview mirror the entire way.

"You're back sooner than I expected," Macklin said as he came out of the barn.

"I figured things out faster than I expected," Jesse replied.

Macklin nodded. "There's stalls that need mucking out."

Jesse figured that was as close to a "welcome back" as he was likely to get given the way he'd run out, but he wasn't just back for the season. He wanted to stay.

"I'll get started as soon as I change my clothes, but first...." He took a deep breath and reminded himself this was what he wanted. Chris came up behind him and put his arm around Jesse's waist. The simple gesture sent all the doubts scattering. "Do you have room for one more around here permanently?"

Macklin didn't answer immediately, studying Jesse's face, looking rather pointedly at Chris's stance, and then at Chris's face. "You'll have to stay in the bunkhouse or move in with Chris and Seth. We gave the only empty house to Neil and Molly."

"Is that a yes?"

"Store your kit and get to work. I expect my year-rounders to set a good example for the others. Chris, that goes for you too."

He strode off before Jesse could stop him.

"That's a yes," Chris said, as if Jesse could really doubt it, but it made him smile.

"So where should I toss my kit?" Jesse asked Chris, not wanting to presume.

"In our house, of course."

Jesse leaned over and kissed Chris quickly.

It was good to be home.

ARIEL TACHNA lives outside of Houston with her husband, her daughter and son, and their cat. Before moving there, she traveled all over the world, having fallen in love with both France, where she found her husband, and India, where she dreams of retiring someday. She's bilingual with snippets of four other languages to her credit and is as in love with languages as she is with writing.

Visit Ariel's website at http://www.arieltachna.com/ and her blog at http://arieltachna.livejournal.com/.

Read Caine and Macklin's story in

ARIEL TACHNA

INHERIT THE SKY

Contemporary Romance by ARIEL TACHNA

Also by ARIEL TACHNA

ARIEL TACHNA

A Summer Place

Alliance in Blood

ARIEL TACHNA

ariel tachna
FALLOUT

ARIEL TACHNA

the Inventor's Companion

http://www.dreamspinnerpress.com

Also by ARIEL TACHNA

In Italian by ARIEL TACHNA

I Suoi Due Padri

ARIEL
TACHNA

http://www.dreamspinnerpress.com

Romance in Australia from DREAMSPINNER PRESS

www.ingramcontent.com/pod-product-compliance
Lightning Source LLC
Chambersburg PA
CBHW051637260626
47170CB00004B/1220